PRAISE FOR OLIVER PEPPER'S PICKLE

"Caitlin Doggart of Where the Sidewalk Ends Bookstore in Chatham recommends *Oliver Pepper's Pickle* by John C. Picardi (Camel): 'In this vibrant, funny, and heartfelt novel, a self-described 'boring' 36-year-old 'privileged white man' named Oliver Pepper endures a stretch of failures before he's hired as a substitute teacher in a violent New York City middle school. His new job begins as a way to catch the eye of the sexy principal but becomes an unexpected boost to Mr. Pepper as he influences his students in surprising ways."
—Pick of the Week, *Boston Sunday Globe*

"The book has a comfortable, compelling rhythm. It's an interesting one-man study of how parents and childhood experiences can have an enduring affect on later lives, and how it's possible for even the most distorted of human beings to find salvation in self-examination and hope for the future. An amusing read, *Oliver Pepper's Pickle* serves up both extremely light and extremely heavy moments until the very end."
—Leia Menlove, *ForeWord Magazine*

"*Oliver Pepper's Pickle* is the story of a man who bellies up to the bar of self-loathing self-destructiveness and is pulled, in spite of himself, into a brave new world—friends emerging from closets, fish-sauce-flavored Thanksgivings, special-needs ghetto kids at the Met, growing a new set of balls ... It's a touching love story that will make you spit out your food laughing when you least expect it. John C. Picardi is an original."

—Kate Christensen, author of *In the Drink*, *Jeremy Thrane*, *The Epicure's Lament*, *The Great Man*, *Trouble* and *The Astral*. Winner of the 2008 PEN/Faulkner Award for Fiction

"In this comic, compelling and provocative novel, John C. Picardi—and his hapless hero—dare to raise a 'forbidden shade' on modern-day manhood. Picardi's tale of Pepper's 'Pickle' is as crisp, tart and sneakily sweet as a classic dill. Picardi loves his wayward characters and he masterfully muscles us into loving them too."

—Elizabeth Searle, author of *Celebrities In Disgrace* and *Tonya & Nancy: The Rock Opera*

"Oliver Pepper is the teacher you always wanted: irreverent, kind, outrageous, smart, eager to wake you up to the world."

—Paul Lisicky, Author of *Lawnboy* and *The Burning House*

"Picardi has created a delicate yet emotional story that sneaks up on you like a lovely relationship, evolving slowly and gracefully, 'peppered' with hope and despair, and above all, humanity. Picardi reveals his characters so subtly, so artfully, that suddenly you realize they are a part of your family. I loved this book."

—Steven Cooper, Author of *Deadline* and *Saving Valencia*

"*Oliver Pepper's Pickle* is a ruefully humorous, fast-paced, and insightful read. Picardi's comic gifts are formidable, and he has plenty to tell us about failure, heartbreak, love, and, finally, recovery."

– John Fulton, author of *Retribution* and *More Than Enough*

"*Oliver Pepper's Pickle* is a poignant coming of age tale of an adult who begins to find his muse when he meets troubled children.... They help Oliver come to grips with the death years ago of his father and how to cope during a midlife crisis.... John C. Picardi provides a winning, upbeat character study."

—Harriet Klausner

"When it comes to getting your life back on track, sometimes you have to embrace the madness around you.... *Oliver Pepper's Pickle* is a humorous and fun read that will ring true with those facing their own midlife crises."

—The Midwest Book Review

PRAISE FOR JOHN C. PICARDI

"Often humorous, eventually gripping. Mr. Picardi renders his characters timeless."

—*The New York Times*

"You don't have to be Italian American to enjoy *The Sweepers*. An appreciation for good writing will do."

—*Daily Item*

"Skillfully written, solidly theatrical."

—*Patriot Ledger*

"Hauntingly dramatic."
—*American Theater Web*

"Picardi deftly moves his audience from tears to laughter and back again."
—*Metroland*

"Picardi's twists of tale are worthy of a Miller play."
—*Times Union*

"Invigorating, often galvanic."
—*Berkshire Eagle*

"A hit with audiences."
—*Schenectady Gazette*

"Picardi's comedy-drama has plenty of laughs along with a gut-wrenching emotional wallop."
—*The Los Angeles Times*

"An epic in the making."
—*The New York Times*

"Storytelling at its finest."
—*Curtain Up*

"If you like a good story well told, add this play to your 'must see' list!"
—*Chelsea News*

OLiVER PEPPER'S PiCKLE

OLiVER PEPPER'S PiCKLE

JOHN C. PICARDI

CAMEL PRESS
Seattle, WA

CAMEL
PRESS

Camel Press
PO Box 70515
Seattle, WA 98127

For more information go to: www.camelpress.com

Cover design by Sabrina Sun

Oliver Pepper's Pickle
Copyright © 2011 by John C. Picardi

ISBN: 978-1-60381-857-5 (Trade Paper)
ISBN: 978-1-60381-858-2 (eBook)

Printed in the United States of America

To my Auntie Florence (Picardi)
1926-2006
with love

ACKNOWLEDGMENTS

Thank you, Kathleen Picardi-Bandera, for reading the first chapters and pointing me in the right direction. Your wisdom and intelligence were invaluable. Many thanks to Hadley, Wes, Sam, Oscar and Edie Spiegel for allowing me to live in your cottage on Cape Cod while I wrote the first draft. Thank you also to the following people for your feedback and help: Kate Christensen, Diane Almeida, Lauri Folkins, Sarah Buff and Jesse Szewczyk-Buff, Jean and Glenn Gould, Cate and Elizabeth, Amy and Robbie Murray, Maryanne and Kevin Jago, Vincent Picardi, Tonia Coletti, Joy Tutela, Johnathan Wilbur, Luke Thomas, David Callahan, Sue Gormley, Cheryl Merlis, and Frances Hill-Barlow. To "the kids"—Courtney, Nina, Emily, Kevin, Robbie, Vincent and Miss Jackie—and the lovely Loretta Smith-Christopher, who many years ago encouraged me to write: thank you, all of you! I am grateful to Catherine Treadgold at Coffeetown Press for her patience and superior editing skills. And finally, a very special thanks to my wonderful parents, Vincent and Nina Picardi, and Suzanne Plavos for helping me find the way ...

ONE

A year ago I was teaching Art History at the Bolton School for Girls, where the most desirable students of Manhattan learn to present themselves and their ideas with grace, charm, power, confidence, and credibility. Bolton boasts an atmosphere that fosters self-confidence and high academic standards, all in a spirit of collaboration. I helped inspire some of the most privileged girls in the world, except that I hadn't been feeling particularly inspiring.

In fact, I had a strong desire to escape. Escape *what* I wasn't sure. My wife had been due to give birth, but she lost the baby at three months. One morning she told me I needed to come right home after work. She told me this while pulling a suitcase down from the closet. That morning my wife told me she was leaving me.

"Make sure you come right home from school. We need to talk. I mean it, Oliver. No stopping at the bar. I'm leaving today."

"You make it sound like I'm a drunk. Like I stop at the bar every day after school."

"You do stop at the bar every day. This is it, Oliver. Today is the day. You need to face it."

"What day is here?"

"I'm leaving you. I've been telling you for months I was leaving."

"I have to go. I'll be late for school. I'll see you tonight."

"Oliver. I mean it."

"Let's go out for Mexican tonight. We can talk."

"I don't want to be cruel, Oliver. I will wait thirty minutes for you so we can finally talk this out. No more avoiding the inevitable. I'm being as nice as I can."

"We can always go out for Ethiopian food," I said.

That is when Beth threw my *History of Art* book at my head. As I dodged the book, my hair was tousled. I left for school, stopping at the mirror in the downstairs hallway to fix my thick and wavy locks, which comes with an abundance of cowlicks. There are touches of gray at my temples, which Beth used to say gives me a refined, studious look. I have a Roman nose, blue eyes, and thick brows. I am of average height and broad shouldered. Not the type of man most wives would throw a book at.

I stood alone in my classroom, looking out the window at PS 189, the other school across the way. I had lifted the forbidden shade. When I first came to Bolton fifteen years ago, our headmistress, Miss Macey, would enter my classroom and promptly close the shade. She would smile and leave. After she had done this a number of times, I began to understand. I kept opening the shade, but Miss Macey kept coming in to close it.

One day, while having lunch with me in her office, she whispered, "Mr. Pepper the school across the way is for children who were dismissed from other public schools for behaving objectionably. You understand. It's not the best idea to expose the girls to that school. Don't you agree?" She had been eating Campbell's Vegetable Soup from her thermos. She placed a Tupperware container of sliced oranges in the center of her desk and offered me a slice. I took one.

"Yes. I understand. But I don't know how much I agree with … I mean, it's good exposure to see how other students live and, and … there are no minorities at the school, and I was—"

"Thank you Oliver, I knew you would understand. Shade

down for now on. And by the way, tell June that her sour cream coffee cake was marvelous! I will have to send her a note."

My sister June had made the teachers a coffee cake. It had been my Monday for coffee, tea, and pastry in the teachers' lounge. Little did they know that June had made four attempts before she was successful; she had burnt the first three cakes because she had been playing with the gas knobs. She did that when she became upset. That time, Beth and I had had a horrible argument; June hated it when we fought.

"I have a wonderful idea! Do you think June would make a Red Velvet Cake next month for Black History month? We're going to do an entire theme on New Orleans," Miss Macey said.

"What?" I asked. I was so stunned that I almost choked on my orange slice.

Despite the lack of light, I kept the shade closed for years and taped a small print of the Velazquez painting *An Old Woman Cooking Eggs* onto it. I'd found it downtown in an old print shop in the West Village. I was thinking of my mother. I thought it was a rather nice tribute to her. When I was a small boy, she would fry eggs in lots of butter for my father. My sister June and I would look over her shoulder and inhale the sweet smell of melting butter and delight in the crackling sound of eggs bouncing in the fry pan. My father loved my mother's eggs.

However, after my father's death, when the truth of who he was had been exposed, my mother burned eggs until they were black and crispy. Poor June made endless jaunts to William-Sonoma to replace ruined sauté pans. My mother liked to burn other things, too: Tupperware, rugs, sofas, rolls of toilet paper, her clipped toenails, and pictures of my father. She then passed her psychosis onto June like a flaming Olympic torch. But June was not like our mother; she only *feared* she would end up like her. There was no chance of that happening; June only played with the gas knobs when she became upset. I was working on helping her break the habit.

Although I was not usually a rule breaker, that week I had started to lift the shade after swigging from my flask between classes. That made two broken rules.

The Velazquez print was now over my desk.

Said window provided me both air to breathe and relief from boredom. Looking out, I saw the students of PS 189 fighting, writing obscenities on the blackboard, throwing desks across classrooms, and being accosted by police. I saw teachers throwing their hands up in disbelief and frustration and finally leaving, never to be seen again. What I saw frightened me, but at the same time excited me. Those students had such freedom. They did whatever they fancied. They wore oversized clothes, expensive sneakers, gold neck chains and slanted baseball caps.

Sometimes I fantasized about a nice Bolton girl writing something nasty on the blackboard, "Fuck this school!" or "Miss Macey is a lousy, racist bitch." Sometimes I imagined two girls pulling on each other's hair, swinging each other around and socking each other in the face like you see on those woman wrestler shows on cable that I watch late at night when I'm feeling naughty. But no such luck. Bolton girls are non-violent. Well, at least on campus they are non-violent. (However, there was one girl a few years ago who stabbed her mother in the kidney with a Waterman Hemisphere Gold Fountain Pen. That story was on the cover of the *New York Post*.)

Mostly though, when I stood by the window, I did a lot of meditating. Why didn't I get along with my wife anymore? Would I ever recover from the loss of the baby? Would the blissful dreams of fatherhood ever dwindle? Then I thought about what I'd observed while in the Indian restaurant on Twenty-Eighth and Lexington. I'd been eating Kashmiri Bhagari Shrimp while looking out the window. An Indian man standing on the sidewalk had held his baby up toward the sky, smiling widely, proudly. He looked like the happiest man on the planet earth. I couldn't finish my meal.

I would have been a good father—loving, caring, and sensible. I would have pushed our baby in a carriage in Central Park. I would have read books at bedtime and saved my baby from ugly trolls in the night. My child would be happy to see me when I came home. If our baby was a girl I wanted to call her Sophia, and if a boy, Christopher, and if my baby was born with three heads, four hands, six nipples, and fang teeth I would simply call the atrocity Edgar, or if a girl, Eldora. Boy, girl, or monster, I would have loved my child.

TWO

I continued to stare out the window at PS 189. I saw a boy sitting in a classroom. He was about twelve years old, tall and skinny. He glanced over at me. He ran his hand over his head. His hair was very close to his scalp, woven in tight cornrows. Other boys now entered the classroom and walked past the boy, slapped, punched, and humiliated him. His eyes were round, quizzical, and imploring. I scanned my own classroom. I took a piece of chalk in my hand and opened the window. I chucked the chalk across the way. It tapped the window of the other school with a startling crack-pop! This diverted the attention of the menacing boys and, for a moment, they stopped their torment. They opened the window, and I received a series of middle fingers and shouts: *motherfucker, cocksucker, cracker, freak, motherfucking asshole, honky asshole, and faggot.*

I gave them my middle finger. They laughed.

Beth was wrong about me. I am not a bore.

The unruly boys took off. The remaining boy looked over at me and turned up his lip as tears spilled down his face. I smiled at him. He shrugged and waved. I waved back, reassured. I imagined extending a wooden board across the sills.

The girls were now entering the classroom. I shut the shade promptly and walked to the front of the room. *Chicken shit!*

They took their places in my classroom, and they all

6

chatted quietly; a few spoke about a pop star, and others about the situation in the Middle East. Their voices sounded chirpy, some smooth and sweet as honey, others breathy and low, but all articulate and precise. They clutched their books close to their chests. Most of the girls had their hair tied back in a single pony tail with a blue ribbon keeping it in place. The blue of the ribbon perfectly matched their uniforms— blue plaid skirts and white blouses, black patent leather shoes—and they all seemed to smell soft and pure, like baby powder. I looked at their gleaming faces, clean and white as fine porcelain, their eyes eager and ready for knowledge. Most of the girls would live a safe life filled with hope. They were perfect in their posture and smiles as they sat and folded their hands on their desk.

I glanced at the shaded window to their backs. I walked to the back of the class. The girls turned toward me in near-unison, their eyes full of astonishment. The girls gasped when I opened the window shade.

"Now, girls, shades are meant to be open."

I could feel their eyes follow me to the head of the class. I began my lesson on *Mary Cassatt*. My young friend from the other school continued to stare in at my class.

Was I drawn to his uncommon eyes? Or was it the disappointment reflected there? Maybe he was like me when I was a boy: scared, lonely, wanting to understand the world, the changes taking place in his young life, wishing he could express how he really felt. Wanting someone to help him get the opportunity. Could I help this young boy who was now looking in on my class?

I took my usual route home; I would not stop at the bar. The September sun shone, and two small birds swooped overhead, landed in the gutter, and chirped. They fought over one lone piece of pastrami thrown into the street. I became warm, and I loosened my tie.

As I rounded the block and walked down Eighty-Sixth Street toward York, I saw next to me the young boy I saved from being bullied in his classroom. I glanced at him, nodded, and smiled.

"Hey Mister, why don't you teach at our school?"

"Because I teach at the other school. And why are you following me?"

"Shit. That school for rich white people. You rich?"

"No."

"I bet you are."

"I bet I'm not," I said.

"Why you open that window shade they always closed?"

"It was a nice day. I was warm. I like the sun. I was bored. Did it bother you? Did you mind looking over at my school?"

"Shit. Did I say I minded? I like looking at those girls."

"What's your name?"

"You got a dollar?"

"What's your name?"

"What do you want to know for?"

"If I give you a dollar I should know your name."

"Just like the white man—can't help the black man without taking something from him. Shit. My name is Franco."

"I'm Oliver Pepper."

"That's a fucked-up name." He started to laugh.

"What do you want the dollar for?"

"I want to buy a slice of pizza."

I handed him five dollars.

"Really? Thanks Mister." He took the money from my hand. His oversized shirt hung around his knees. His jeans' inseam hovered just above them, and the hem crumpled around the edge of his sneakers.

"When I was in the seventh grade, boys picked on me, too. I had pimples and a big nose. They also picked on my best friend Hank. He was portly and, well, they called him disgusting."

"What does portly mean?"

8

"It's a nice way to say 'fat disgusting pig.' "

He roared with laughter.

"You have a friend who is a fat mess? Shit. Buy the dude some carrots." He laughed.

"Hank hasn't had a vegetable since 1982."

"Damn. He must be real fat."

"Never mind. I know it's not easy being picked on. Don't worry. When your friends are catching rats in subway tunnels, you'll be CEO of some big corporation downtown."

"No one picks on my ass. What are you talking about—what's a CEO?"

"Then I guess I was mistaken when I saw those boys harassing you."

"You fucked up."

"You shouldn't speak that way. You're a young man," I said.

"You speak fucked-up."

"You think I'm boring?" I said. "Well, it's all a put-on. I'm a real person. So, uh, fuck off." I stopped.

We both laughed.

"I didn't say you were boring. Why? You boring or something?"

"I'm not. I said 'fuck' didn't I? It's *that* school. I walk in, and it makes me stuffy."

"You got to loosen up, dude; you look like you got some pole up your ass." He started to laugh. He held his hand to his belly, let out a howl of laughter, and pointed at me.

"That's it. That's it. You got some pole up your ass," he continued.

I couldn't help but grin and shake my head. Then I laughed, too. "You shouldn't speak that way."

"Look at the white guy telling the black boy what to do again. You one bossy mother. But you cool. You cool. Thanks for the money, whitey."

"You think I'm cool? Really?"

"Yeah, you all right."

"Enjoy your pizza. I have to get home. I have papers to correct."

He stopped in front of a small electronics store and put his hand on the window.

"Damn shit." He seemed distressed. I stepped closer to him. His eyes were fixed on something inside the store window.

"What's wrong?"

"Nothing wrong. Look at that." He pointed to an iPod in the window.

"That thing holds millions of songs. You like music, Pepper?"

"Of course I do."

"I want one of those things, man, more than anything. It's one of my dreams, man."

"I know what that's like," I said.

"You know what what's like?"

"To want something really bad," I said.

"Why, what does whitey Pepper want? You can have anything you want. You white."

"That's not true. Some people live their entire life wanting 'something,' but they don't know what they want. At least you know. Consider yourself lucky. You have dreams."

"Pepper, you a weird Dude. I'm getting my pizza. Later, bitch." He gave me a high five and went into the pizza joint on First and Eighty-Forth.

"Ugh. Later bitch to you." I smirked.

Skipping the bar just in case Beth was serious, I whispered to myself all the way home, L*ater bitch. Later bitch. Later bitch. Later bitch.* I decided I was going to open that shade again tomorrow. *Fuck Miss Macey. Later bitch.*

THREE

The chair I sat in was worn in the seat—an antique, ruby velvet number that my wife and I found together at the Chelsea flea market when we were first married and still loved the same kind of things.

Beth stood over me. I told her about Franco. She wasn't interested in Franco or me, and she certainly could have cared less what this day could have meant for us.

"This is for real. I'm leaving you," she said.

"Where are you going?" I asked and continued to make notes for the next day's lesson on *Bronzino*.

When my eyes met hers, my attention wandered. I thought how beautiful her auburn hair looked wet and combed back. She had stepped out of the shower moments ago. Her hair was so auburn, silky, straight, and magical that Botticelli might have painted it. I especially loved the way she spread her hair over our bed pillows at night. It was the only thing I liked about her as of late.

"I want to be as nice as possible about this," she started. Her skin had a ruddy, fiery quality to it.

"That's good," I said.

"Moonbeam says that you're boring and a drunk. That you have stunted my growth as a woman. She says I have stunted your growth as a man. We married too young."

"Moonbeam is not a good therapist. I am not a drunk."

Beth then marched triumphantly into the kitchen and returned holding a green plastic trash bag. She dumped the contents at my feet. The bag was full with nips and pint bottles.

"These aren't my bottles, and they're not June's. I guess they belong to that alcoholic troll who lives under the floor boards? Come on Oliver, stop the denial."

"Stop," I said. I finally closed my book and put my note pad on the side table.

My knees began to shake. I pulled on my thumb until I heard a sharp crack. Had I really drunk all that?

"I'm sick of living here! Oh, Oliver, I love June, she's like a sister to me, but I'm sick of living with her and you and now Ralph is always around and Hank, too! And he is just gross and ... and ... Oliver, I'm suffocating here in so, so, so many ways."

"My sister is not perfect. Is it her casseroles? The fire thing? She does that for attention; you know that."

"No! Don't you dare, Oliver. This is not about June! Frankly I stayed because of her, but I am not married to June! This is about you and me. It's about growing up and learning who we are in this world. Oliver, come on, you know this marriage has been over for a while now. We haven't slept together in months. We've grown apart. Once I leave, you'll realize that it's for best."

"Is this all about the baby?" I finally asked her. I could not look her in the eye, so I studied the floor.

She was silent for a long while. Then she spoke. "I don't want to talk about that, not now. But I'll only say the baby had nothing to do with me leaving."

"Can I speak?" I started to pace. I could feel my eyes fill up. I wanted to claw them out of my head.

"It's painful to talk about, but we need to. When we lost the baby, I didn't know what to say. I wanted a child more than anything. I wanted all of us to be together. A real family. I didn't want to make you feel bad. I was hurt for you and hurt for me. I'm lousy with that stuff. Just because I don't verbally express things doesn't mean I don't feel them inside. You know that about me. We can always try and have another child. We could, and who knows? Maybe June and Ralph will get married and she'll move out. You know that. I can't abandon her. I love you. But June and I, we didn't have it so easy as children."

"I don't care about your problems or your parents' disastrous lives or this weird bond you have with your sister, which is really so unhealthy, by the way. And I no longer give a damn what you promised your mother, either."

Beth took a long, deep sigh. I backed off a bit. I thought at any minute she was going to spit fire. But it was worse than fire. It was an atomic bomb.

"I have a real lover now, Oliver. I'm moving to Vancouver to be with him. He's teaching me what sex and love can really be like." Her face was changing now; she seemed excited and looked almost like a different person, a person who was having wild sex or was possibly in love.

"What? Beth? Beth!"

"Oliver, come on, don't act so surprised. Can you look at me and honestly say you want to spend the rest of your life with me? You don't care; it's your macho ego."

I looked at Beth for a very long time. She did not avoid my eyes; she was being straight with me. I knew she was right. It was time to say goodbye.

"I love you, Beth. I guess you're right."

"I want you to keep everything," she said. "I'm really doing you a favor, Oliver. One day you'll realize it. I want you to be happy. I bought this book for you. Moonbeam said you should read it." She handed me a pocket-size book: *Castration of the 20th Century Man: How to Grow a New Set for the 21st Century.*

"What is this for?" I asked.

"You need to be a man. You need to grow up. You need to look inside yourself and figure out who you are. All that crap with your Dad and Mom, it's heavy stuff—not to mention everything with June. Oliver, it's a new dawn for men. You need to be a man for the Twenty-First Century. I'll always love you, Oliver."

She kissed me on my forehead, lifted her suitcase, and left.

I reached under the sofa, grabbed the nearest bottle, and swigged from it. I thanked God it was the Bushmills. This wasn't a gin or vodka moment.

FOUR

After finishing the bottle, I didn't know what else to do, so I went to my bedroom and locked myself in. I heard June come home. She knocked on my bedroom door and asked if I was okay. I told her I was fine and was going to bed early. I told her Beth was sleeping. June whispered goodnight. I would wait until morning to tell her about Beth. From my bedroom, I could hear June watching re-runs of that 1960s show, *Fire Engine 814*. She would fall asleep soon on the sofa. Because June had a sharp nose for all things burning, I would not burn *The Castration of the 20th Century Man* yet—a good excuse to look through it.

I went to the kitchen, made myself a grilled cheese and tuna and poured myself a glass of whiskey. Moving to the living room, I covered the sleeping June with a blanket, gave her a kiss on the forehead, shut off the TV. I went back to my room. I opened the book. To summarize chapter one, here's what *The Castration of the 20th Century Man* had to say.

Men have become whining, petulant creatures because they can't control women and minorities anymore, and therefore the divorce rate has escalated. The book claims it's now a world of equality and women and minorities are sharing the wealth the American man has hoarded for centuries. Therefore the book calls for all men to reach deep into their inner beings, heal the hurt of not being *número uno* anymore, dip their balls into bowls of ice cold water and revel in the numbness, because the pressures of the world are shared pressures now. Take your balls out of the cold water and slowly feel your gonads grow into a glowing new set, warmed by a new world of hope and love where there are no more enemies—only compassion and regret for the wrong that has been perpetrated by men.

Well, thank you very much, but there was no way I was going to put my balls in a bowl of icy water; the idea made me wince. So instead I patted my balls ever so gently. I then took a look at the remaining chapter titles:

Chapter Two: Men and War
Chapter Three: Football, Baseball, Basketball, and that Pat on the Ass
Chapter four: Sexual Politics and Penis Size
Chapter Five: Showing Emotions through Farting and Burping
Chapter Six: Fear Of Male Homosexuality. The Ego Is Knocking

I was now thinking this book was for real losers. How could it be the number one bestseller in the country? Then, to make matters worse, there was a note in the beginning of the book addressing all male readers:

Dear Men: These are the facts. Men in today's world are oppressed. Men are falling under the pressures of the expectations put on them by our society! Reading this book is your first step to making a commitment to growing a new set. You're on your way!

Today's world is a busy place. Who has time to read books? So we have put an index in the back of the book for your convenience. Find your issue, find the page, read it, keep it in your pocket, use it, and grow a new ball set today!

I went to the back and looked up a few of the issues. The issues went on and on and on and on and on some more.

We men are completely sad and desperate. So much so that we seek hope in a book about testicles, currently the number one bestseller in the country. Go figure. But it made me wonder why Beth gave me the book. Did she think I was repressed? Did she think I was that narrow-minded and unsophisticated? Was I that out of touch with my feelings?

I slept fitfully and woke in the morning with a sadness deep inside of me. In my bed, I was encompassed by an eerie silence, broken only by the sound of the Saturday Morning garbage truck pick-up outside. Garbage men shouted to one another and unloaded and banged barrels against the truck's side. I wanted to leap from my window into the truck's bowels.

When I told June that Beth had dumped me, she closed her eyes, went to the stove, and turned the gas on and off repeatedly. I went to her, taking her hands off the knobs.

"June, stop. You're not like mother, so *stop*, and there is nothing I can do. *Stop*."

She turned to me. She was crying, and I hugged her tightly.

"I know you love Beth, too. It will be okay. I promise."

FIVE

I called my best friend Hank to tell him the news about Beth and me, and I knew he'd been drinking his *Chivas* since eleven o'clock that morning, alone. He'd be in his black socks with his naked, hairy belly hanging over his boxers, his skin all freckled and red from drinking, his pores enlarged and oily. He would be sitting on that old *Jennifer Convertible* we had forced up three flights of stairs almost fifteen years ago.

Saturday was Hank's day off from the Ethiopian Restaurant he managed and loathed. He worked there only because his parents owned the building and had made a deal with the restaurant owners to employ their son. Like me, Hank was thirty-six; he was also a loser and, for the longest time, hadn't been able to keep a job. Hank's desire to tell people the truth is often mistaken for rudeness. I explained to him that telling his former boss at Bloomingdale's that she smelled like the East River on a hot day in July and then suggesting a female deodorant spray was not being truthful or honest. It was being rude. He couldn't understand why he was fired and escorted out of Bloomingdale's by three security men or why later a restraining order was filed against him.

Over the phone I could hear that he was watching reruns of *Bewitched* on Nickelodeon. He had a spooky obsession with Elizabeth Montgomery. I also knew he was rubbing his bald head. He usually wore a toupee, but Saturday was his Scalp Breathing Day.

"She said horrible things about me," I told him.

"She should talk! God, the day you married her I cringed. I told you. Look, you knew she was going to leave anyway. We all did." His voice sounded peculiar.

"Have a heart, Hank. It still hurts."

"Come, Ollie, you don't care all that much."

"It still makes me feel like a loser."

"She's the loser! Is she officially gone? Is she? Be honest. I want to know the truth," Hank said.

Hank and the truth! When Hank and I were kids, we went to summer camp for a week in Maine, but when he came home, he found his bedroom completely painted and his dog Rascal, a long haired Chihuahua, gone. His parents said that Rascal had been hit by a car. But when Hank found Rascal's tail and ear under his bed, he was horrified at his parent's lie. His brother Barry had put a cherry bomb up Rascal's butt, and Rascal had exploded. Hank had a difficult time trusting people after that.

"Yes. Yes. Yes. SHE IS GONE! Please don't keep asking me. You need to trust me. Damn! Not now, Hank."

"You sure? I want to know the truth."

"I said she's gone. Now stop, Hank. She's gone. Fuck!"

"Then I'll tell you. Shit, Ollie ... for months, at lunch time, she closed her own shop long enough to get herself porked by your buddies at the bar in the back room of The Blarney Stone. She was like this wild insatiable porno star, man!"

"That is not funny, Hank."

"She also bragged about hooking up for sex on the Internet."

"On the Internet? Hank, this is not funny!"

"Everyone at The Blarney Stone feels bad for you, but look at it from their point of view. A hot babe like Beth comes in and flirts around, asks for some loving, if that's what you want to call it. I'm sorry, my friend, but the truth is, loyalty goes out the door when a hot lady like Beth is looking for some, you know, hot action."

"Fuck you, Hank! How can you say this to me? We're best friends. We were boys together. You didn't do anything with Beth, did you? My God!"

"No! Are you crazy? Oliver. I don't know what else to say. Perhaps you should look on her computer. The truth is on the screen."

"I'll call you later." I slammed down the phone, gulped down more Bushmills, and stared out my bedroom window, which faced south down York Avenue.

I looked out at the vast apartment buildings before me and at the water tanks on their rooftops, which made black silhouettes against the blue morning sky. I wished I were inside one of those water tanks, drowning.

I went over to the desk and moved the mouse on her computer and presto—Beth had left the site on, more than likely for me to see. The sex site's big red letters flashed out at me, *Do Me While My Husband is Out Working.* I clicked on her photo; she was smiling. Her profile read:

> *Hot Pepper Wants It Now!* 5'6", 112, completely waxed (need I say more?), juicy and sweet. Insatiable appetite for hung men with hot, international meat! Any French, Mexican, or Italian guys out there? Fill me with your meat, and make me your Taco. Spread me with Foie Gras, and let me be your delicacy. Fill me with your sweet cream, I'll be your Cannoli. Love to get titty f---ked and on occasion like it up my burrito basket or, for you Italian guys, the Espresso expressway and, for you French men, my Arc de Triomphe! What's it going to be, men? Fish Taco? Steak Tartar? Italian Sausage? You tell me. Eight inches or more ONLY.

I clicked on a tab that said *Enter This Profile*.

Wham! More photos of my wife.

I knew yoga would change her, but who would think her legs could go over her head like that? I was overcome by a complete array of frightful emotions and bodily reactions. The room was spinning, and my heart was pounding with jealously. My wife had never told me she liked it up her damn burrito basket. If I had known *that,* perhaps we could have worked things out. Is that why she was eating guacamole and corn chips in bed the last months of our marriage?

She had written many e-mails to strange hairy men with huge salami-like peckers that would put *Oscar Meyer* to shame. She wrote that our marriage was loveless.

Bitch. Yoga enthusiast. Sex Foodie! *Later Bitch.*

I was starting to really hate her.

Then I read a series of e-mails from a guy called *MooseDick*. My body started to shake. I was getting warm now, both figuratively and literally. Beads of perspiration formed on my forehead. For most of the last year, she had been writing once or twice a day to her *Mr. Canada,* from Vancouver, British Columbia. In one of her first e-mails to *Mr. Canada,* AKA *MooseDick,* she wrote:

> My husband is insufferably boring. When he comes home from work or from drinking all night with his loser friend, all he wants to do is talk about his work or art history. I want to pull my hair right out of my scalp. I hate being in this loveless marriage. He doesn't even know how I screw all the guys in the bar he hangs out in. I only want sex and lots of it. How about you? Love, *Hot Pepper*

My wife Beth. Charmer. Picture Framer. Store Owner. Neighborhood Nymphomaniac. Internet Slut. *Hot Pepper.*

In one of her latest e-mails to *Mr. Canada* I learned how

adventurous my *Hot Pepper* wife could be. She wrote:

> O Canada, I love when you make me come and I
> can't wait to suck you off again. I never thought I
> could do it in a public place, never mind on a
> downtown subway. I love your huge cock. Oliver is
> still so boring. I can't wait to get back to Vancouver
> and do it again. All I can think of is being outdoors
> with you, doing what you told me you would do to
> me next time. Oliver couldn't come up with that in
> his wildest dreams, if he ever has any. He couldn't
> even do it with an instruction sheet and a map. I want
> you so much it hurts to think about it. Cover me in
> maple syrup and lick me all over! Love, *Your Hot Hot
> Pepper*.

Again! If I had known she liked to give head in public
places I would gladly have done my part to satisfy her fetish. I
never knew Beth had this other side; the kinkiest we ever got
was doggie style. That package of gourmet maple syrups she
got in the mail a few months ago—it all made sense. She said
it was from her mother.

Beth must have saved and hid every cent she made that
last year at her store, *Frames By Beth*. After all, there would be
legal fees, in addition to even more frequent visits to her pricy
Upper East Side "shrink," Moonbeam. The name alone
should be enough for you to imagine her personal profile: a
dedicated raw food vegan who looked like a walking skeleton.
I always found it difficult to resist the urge to throw a nitrate-
heavy hot dog at her.

Moonbeam must have introduced Beth to Internet sex.
Undoubtedly, she coached my wife through this entire affair.
And I know that Moonbeam gave Beth that "toy" she brought
to our bed last year. Moonbeam assured Beth that it was made
of organic plastic—whatever that is—and that it was

environmentally safe. I threw it away. And not in the recycle bin, either.

I then did what any man would do. I looked at more photos of sex-starved naked women on that sick and disgusting website, pulled on my pickle, made a mess on the keyboard, and drank my Saturday away. Drunk and stumbling, I searched for the box of gourmet maple syrup so I could pour it down the drain. The box was nowhere to be found. However, I found a can of expensive Foie Gras, which I devoured gladly, washed down with a new bottle of cognac.

SIX

Amy Cumberland was an ill-tempered senior who didn't have a chip on her shoulder but rather a whole damn forest. The previous year, I'd reported her smoking on the steps of the Met during a field trip.

On Monday, after being dumped, finishing my lecture on Corregio's Frescoes in Parma, and watching the last of the students leave, I reached for my briefcase and took what I believed was a quick, inconspicuous sip from my silver flask. Then I opened the forbidden shade and took a deep breath. The classrooms in PS 189 were empty. Must have been lunch time.

I heard a small, soft cough, and I turned. Amy Cumberland was standing behind me. She curled her lips at me and laughed in that *I-am-so-gonna-bury-your-ass* way. She turned and ran from the room, eager to spread the Good News.

I looked at the unruly students as they entered the classroom across the way, took another sip and said "fuck it" to myself. Then I saw Franco across from me. I concealed my flask. He saluted me, and I saluted back. I had begun to shut the shade, when three boys lifted a desk and threw it out the window. I watched the desk fly through the air into the alley. As impressed as I was, I gave the boys a disapproving look and shut the shade.

Alone in my classroom, I contemplated doing what the boys did. I smiled so hard it hurt my cheekbones. Would I dare? I walked down the rows of desks and touched each one. No. If caught, I'd be locked up.

On Tuesday morning, I was awakened early by a phone call from Miss Macey.

"Oliver, you need to see me in my office before classes begin this morning."

"Of course, Miss Macey, I'll be there by eight forty-five," I said, sitting bolt upright in my bed. I wouldn't dream of speaking to Miss Macey in a prone position.

I hung up the phone and began to wonder whether I'd be fired. A large part of me didn't care. I was worried about my cavalier attitude. June had always feared she was going crazy like our mother, but perhaps I was the crazy one.

I took an extra look in the bathroom mirror before I left the apartment that morning. I dabbed extra VO-5 in my thick hair, gingerly tugged on my red striped tie and smoothed it against my starched white shirt. I took my flask out of my briefcase and saw my blue eyes looking back at me from its hazy surface. *Stop. Stop, you fool. Don't even think about it.* But I filled the flask and put it in my briefcase nevertheless. I then looked over at the small table by my bed, and I saw, hidden under some papers, the book Beth had given me; it was calling out to me. *Oh hell*, I thought and put it in my back suit pocket; I could read it between classes.

I walked toward the kitchen, where I had heard June rustling, and smelled coffee brewing. The one loose floorboard that usually squeaked when I stepped on it let out its old familiar cry and I decided it was going to be like any other ordinary day after all.

June was a librarian and worked at the Milton Library on Forty-Seventh Street. Dressed and ready for work, she was eating a bowl of oatmeal with a splash of cream, a sprinkle of brown sugar, and a few strawberries. Two bowls of steaming oatmeal were placed across from her, waiting for me and the departed Beth.

"Sorry June, no time to eat," I said. I pulled a light

overcoat from the hall closet.

"Mother always stressed the importance of eating in the morning."

"Mother also stressed the importance of burning trash in the middle of our living room."

"That's not funny, Oliver. I miss Beth. I'm so blue. This morning I made her a bowl of oats. I miss her doing my hair bun."

June's hair was pulled tight in the small bun she'd worn since my mother started messing around with fire. She reeked of the floral china musk Ralph had given her. She had such pearly white skin—clear without a blemish. Thin lines were forming beneath her eyes. As usual, she was dressed in earth tones, her clothing conservative and neat. She shopped only at Talbots.

I always felt sorry for June in the mornings. But today I felt devastated for her. I'm not sure if it was the way the sunlight streamed through our kitchen window and hit her face or if it was the methodically dutiful way she ate in the loneliness of our large kitchen, obediently finishing her oatmeal because our mother had always insisted that a hale and hearty breakfast ensured a hale and hearty day. Or perhaps it was the fact that I was a complete and utter fuck-up and was ruining everyone's life.

I took the bowls of oatmeal and tossed the contents out into the trash can. She heaved.

"June, I am so sorry. I don't know why I did that."

June was forty-two, and I know that each day, month, and year, she hoped for the improbable proposal of marriage from Ralph, never wavering from her dream to be married and with child. Ralph and June had been seeing each other for five years now, and I figured if he hadn't popped the question yet, he never would.

"I can't eat, June. That was Miss Macey on the phone. She

wants to see me before first session."

"I only want to say, Oliver, that I understand why Beth hated you going to that bar. Bar people are so beneath you, Oliver. You're an educated man, so knowledgeable. Yet you've always had this taste for people who are a bit sinister and suspicious. I don't understand you. I had hoped that Beth's leaving you would be an eye-opener."

"June, have a good day at the library. Please try and not be so hurt about this. We will get to the joy again, I promise."

"Ralph is coming to dinner. Bring Hank, if you like."

"Oh, June, why Ralph every night? I like him, but he talks so much."

"He tries so hard with you. Sometimes I think you don't even listen to him. Are you feeling all right this morning? You look disheveled. Divorce is at the top of the stress list. You're drinking too much. You're like Daddy."

"I really have to go, June."

"Please try and have a good day, Oliver," she said and stood quickly.

"Hey, June, I don't want you worrying about me. Okay?" I gave her a kiss on the cheek and left.

SEVEN

The walk to school was perfect. Ambling down Second Avenue, heading north, I passed Mrs. Edison, the florist. She was arranging roses—lovely red, yellow, and pink roses—in black pails.

"Hello, Oliver," she said coquettishly.

"Lovely colors, Mrs. Edison," I said.

She held a hand longingly against her heart as I walked by. She was seventy-nine. June once told me that Mrs. Edison had remarked that I was handsome, so I always went out of my way to be nice to her.

Taxis and cars beeped, and people chased busses. I passed Mr. Doodle, the grocer, on the corner of Eighty-Sixth Street. He also smiled and spoke to me each morning. On this day, he was arranging brussels sprouts on the wooden stand in front of his store.

"How about some nice brussels sprouts?" he asked.

"Not now, Mr. Doodle, thanks," I told him. "I'm sure June will be by later, though."

Although it still felt like summer, there was a tiny hint of fall in the air. I had noticed one lone, early pumpkin in the center of Mr. Doodle's display. I felt a sudden, overwhelming sadness. Beth loved the fall, and I remembered when we were first married how we'd carved our first pumpkin together. We'd roasted the seeds and made love into the night.

I walked on. I smiled tensely at the familiar faces of the small group of businesswomen who sipped coffee in front the deli on Eighty-Seventh and Second each morning. They always waved hello to me as I passed and always laughed after me as I walked on. I never knew whether or not they were making fun of me.

One morning, one of them shouted after me, "Shake that hot ass!"

I have felt self-conscious ever since.

When I told Beth about these women, she said they thought I was sexy and I should feel flattered. But I didn't. I just felt compelled to tighten my buttocks whenever I passed them, which may or may not have made me look genuinely foolish. At any rate, I felt myself walking awkwardly like that for half a block each day.

That was another gripe Beth had with me, that I was so naïve, so closed off in my inner world, that I was unaware of how "extraordinarily sexy" I was to women. In fact, she said, I trusted no one and was as bad as Hank. But I have never thought of myself as a man most people would find handsome, much less sexy.

I have always been in the habit of dressing conservatively and impeccably. Beth was constantly after me to buy new clothes and get a more up-to-date haircut. She'd said over and over that I had to break free from Brooks Brothers. She'd even started shopping for me at funky stores in the East Village. Once she'd brought home this "hip" colorful shirt she'd picked up at a trendy boutique and parachute pants from the Gap. I laughed hysterically at the very thought of trying them on. I was in my thirties, I told her, and needed to dress to fit the nature of my job. She grabbed the clothes, crumpled them into a ball, and slammed them down on the sofa. That had been only a few months after she told me she'd lost the baby.

When I was two blocks from the school, the real reason I'd been called in early suddenly struck me. Of course! Yes! Miss Macey had received another letter from a former student who now studied art in Florence or Paris, complimenting me and praising the influence I'd had on her life. There have been many letters like this in the past, praising me for a job well done. I began to strut now, and picked up my pace. I wondered who the letter would be from? Kathleen McCabe? Mary-Katherine Smith? Liz Yorker? Liz had been a fine student. She loved the French Impressionists.

Miss Macey had planned to take me to a congratulatory lunch at The Regency and had called me in early to show me the letter and to ask me to prepare for the afternoon sessions in the morning, so that we could lunch more leisurely. She'd taken me to lunch on several occasions. The last time was after she'd sat in on my lesson on the Sistine Chapel. She'd told me over lunch that my lecture was magnificent, one of the best she'd ever heard on Michelangelo's masterpiece.

When I was one block away from the school, two students—Sue Ruggan and Janice Carlton—ran toward me, giggling. Their blue uniforms were tidy and pressed, and the girls held their book bags in exactly the same way. These two, a blonde and a brunette, were nice girls, both in the tenth grade.

"Good morning, Mr. Pepper," Janice said. Her curly blond hair blew in the autumn wind. She tilted her head and smiled at me with her mouthful of braces.

"I'm almost done reading *Dear Theo*, and now I love Van Gogh even more! Can you recommend more books for me? Can you? Will you, please?"

"Yes, of course, Janice. I had a feeling you would love Van Gogh. Your sister Edith certainly did in her tenth grade year. I'll see you both in class. Run along, now," I said.

They ran ahead of me toward some boys from the Saint Paul School, two blocks south of Bolton, my Alma Mater. The boys shared their iPod headphones with the two girls, and they listened to, I'm sure, the very latest music. I wished I had been that happy when I was kid.

I stepped into a doorway of an apartment entrance,

huddled in a corner, and took a quick sip from my flask—to take the edge off. I turned to face Franco.

"Whoa! Hey! You scared me! Are you spying on me?" I asked.

"No. What are you drinking?"

"Orange Juice."

"You look like shit."

"Thank you," I said.

"Them girls you teach all rich?"

"I guess they are," I said. I walked onward. He walked by my side.

"They all rich. I want one of them iPods. Shit you know how much they cost?"

"I do not."

"I wish I had one of those things, Mister. I like music. You like music, Mister?"

"Who doesn't like music?"

"My aunt, I live with her, she hate music. She said it's bad influence."

"I disagree with your aunt. Music is art. It can bring you to places you've never been. It's good for the mind. It's inspirational," I said.

He smiled. "You talk all fancy and shit. But I feel the same way. My aunt is mean to me. She care only about her own baby. Not me."

"Well, I'm sure she loves and cares for you. I have to go. Have a good day."

" 'Bye Mister, and love got nothing to do with anything when nobody want you."

"I'm sure you are loved," I said. I picked up my pace.

"My father—he love me. But I don't got him no more."

"You don't have a father?" I stopped. My heart felt like it was going to leap out of my chest and crawl away. He had no father; perhaps that was what I had sensed about him.

"No. He in prison. You have a father?"

"I did. Once."

"Your father gone, too?"

"Yes." I sighed. A tinge of panic shot through my body. I saw my father's face before me.

"My father, too."

"One day he'll come home." I said.

"No, he got life in prison. I got no father no more. He locked away. I only got me. Who do you got? Where your father go?"

"My father died a long time ago. I was a boy," I said.

"How did he die?

"He was in an accident," I said. Franco put his head down and nervously skipped along the curb—one foot up, one foot down. There was an awkward silence until a speeding bike messenger flew by, yelling for Franco to get out of his way. Franco moved but then shouted an obscenity at the biker.

"Well, it's been very nice chatting with you. I have to go. I have a meeting. You take care of yourself."

He lifted his hand in a waving motion, and kicked in the direction of his school, head still bowed. I stood and watched him walk to his school, next door. Once there, he slumped against the wall and sat on the pavement. I was lanky like Franco when I was boy, and I had the same yearning in my eyes. His voice rang in my ear.

I entered Bolton. I walked into the foyer, sprayed my mouth with mint spray, and passed under the grand chandelier, shimmering gloriously in the early morning light. I passed the dining hall, which—the school's brochure boasted—was administered to accommodate each girl's individual dietary needs. That day was vegetable stew day, and I could smell tomatoes simmering. Most of the Bolton girls were vegetarians this year.

I climbed the curving staircase, my hand steady on the polished banister, passed the grand old library, with its carved mahogany, and then was pleasantly surprised by Miss Piper

Bergman, the school librarian.

Miss Bergman was standing in the doorway, her long arms extended across the wide entrance. She was wearing a flowery, green silk dress. Miss Berman had a sprightly air about her, unusual for the Bolton School faculty. Her hair was blond and curly, and her wide, blissful smile could suck you into her luscious mouth. She was hot.

"Hi, Oliver. How are you today?" she said.

"I have a meeting with Miss Macey. I'll let you know after."

"What is her problem now? What a pain!" Piper rolled her eyes.

"Who the hell knows?" I said.

I might have had an opportunity to kiss and make sweet love to Piper at last year's staff Christmas party, but being loyal to Beth, I had not explored the possibilities.

"You know, Mr. Pepper, that I am always very discreet," Piper Bergman had said to me at that Christmas party.

"Discreet?" I smiled at her. "Whatever can you be talking about?"

She was wearing a Santa hat, and her blond hair curled over its white edging. She held a Santa cookie in one hand and a glass of red punch in the other. She closed her red lips over Santa's head and bit it off.

I had sipped my eggnog casually while I buttoned my suit coat. I took one more whiff of her perfume. It was deep and musky—a mix of lemon and patchouli. She moved even closer to me. As I grinned tautly, I looked over, forbidding myself while letting myself long for her at the same time. But *fuck it*, I thought, this was all harmless play.

Miss Macey came out of her office, and Piper quickly disappeared back into the library.

"I'm ready Oliver, come into my office," Miss Macey said. Her voice was low.

I sat across from her and her large mahogany desk, which emphasized her authority. At seventy-four, Miss Macey was well-maintained. Her gray, shoulder-length hair was stiff with spray and as inflexible as her starched beige skirt. Her hands were folded over a yellow folder. She had no liver spots and wore no makeup. I'd lay odds that she'd never once in her life had sex.

"How are you today, Miss Macey?" I said. My voice was jolly. I'd managed to forget all about Amy Cumberland, and I was certain now that the letter of praise that was inside the folder Miss Macey held was from Joan Arcade.

Miss Macey's eyes were sad and shifted hastily away from mine. When she leaned over her desk, all the angst from earlier that morning rushed back into me, and I wished I'd drunk more than that tiny nip. Poor posture on Miss Macey's part was a genuine cause for alarm.

"Today is the day I'm showing the girls Tintoretto's Portraits," I said. My voice cracked. I coughed. I could hear the smaller girls below on the sidewalk playing and calling goodbyes to their parents for the day. My foot started to shake.

"Amy Cumberland claims she saw you drinking out of a sliver flask. She said after your lecture on Correggio's Frescoes in Parma, she went back to talk to you, for—she told me—she loved Correggio and wanted more information. That's when she saw you." Miss Macey pulled a sheet of paper from the yellow folder. "I now quote Amy, 'Mr. Pepper was drinking from a flask like a big drunk.' "

"A drunk! A drunk! I am not a drunk! That's absurd! You know as well as I, Miss Macey, that girl can be a rogue!" Calming down, I said, "Surely you don't believe this accusation. She couldn't care less about art or beauty, much less about Correggio. She's common and rude and, I now recall, slept through the entire lesson that day."

"Mr. Pepper, it is our mission at Bolton to prepare our

girls for an enriching life. Parents send their girls to Bolton to learn what some people refer to as 'old fashioned morals and manners' in addition to a good education that includes all of the fine arts. The world's morals and manners are disintegrating at an alarming rate. And we must be particularly vigilant. We must take care at all costs never to expose our girls to examples of inappropriate behavior. Furthermore, we must not forget their social stature," she said. "Clandestine alcohol consumption at Bolton is simply intolerable."

"Miss Macey," I said haughtily, "you know I have always maintained the standards required at Bolton. Now, with all due respect, if we are finished, I really must go. I have slides to prepare."

"No, Mr. Pepper, you may not. You see, Oliver ... this is rather uncomfortable." Miss Macey bowed her head and looked at the folder. She unfolded then refolded her hands and coughed to clear her throat.

"It is common knowledge among the teachers and myself that you do in fact drink from a small silver flask. It has been seen and reported before."

"Excuse me?"

"Oliver, please let's not make this more difficult than it need be. We ... I have wanted to approach you for some time now. You do a marvelous job, and the girls do look up to you. Also you've been exquisitely discreet until of late. But being seen and officially reported by a student ... I'd hoped it would never come to this, but it's out of my hands now. There is nothing I can do."

"I swear to you—"

"Please, let me finish. I have suggested to the Board that you be dismissed from the Bolton school for one year without pay. However, I recommend you get help with your problem, and next August we will review your progress. I'm sure we'll have you back with us in the fall. We all have problems, Mr.

Pepper. Make this your time to take stock of your life. I'm terribly, terribly sorry."

"I'm *fired*? You know this is about my giving Amy Cumberland a C in art history. This is about my reporting her smoking on the steps of the Metropolitan Museum of Art. It's about her refusal to keep up the standards of this school!"

"Oliver, I have always liked you. You're a fine young man, smart, well-educated, and dedicated. But we know. We all know. And we simply can't have it here. Perhaps you don't have a problem with alcohol, who can say for certain? I would be doing you a disservice to allow you to go on like this, Oliver. And I like you too much. It's simply gone beyond my control. I am sorry. I will personally supervise the packing of your classroom and have your things sent to your home. Now, let's do this with dignity."

As I stood outside Miss Macey's office, my heart was beating so quickly I thought it would jump out of my rib cage. I walked down the steps, my hands shaking, and as I passed the library, the girls were still waiting for the morning bell.

I stopped on the stairwell. *Fired fired fired fired!* It ran through my head. It swallowed me up. I went up to the library. Piper Bergman was reading *Memoirs of a Geisha*. She stood up upon seeing me. Her deep brown eyes scanned me; she shifted her lower jaw.

"I wanted to come by and say goodbye," I said. I told her what had happened, and she promised she would harass Amy Cumberland in her Library Science class. I thanked her for that.

Miss Bergman's eyes had pity in them; she took my hand and brought me to a small back room filled with old books. She locked the door behind us. The sun streamed through a small single window, and dust mites danced in its beam. Miss Bergman's face was half lit. I kept my eyes on her as she slipped off her dress, and I whispered, "God!" She came toward me, her body half in darkness and the other half lit in the right places, mainly her lovely breasts and full hips.

Her hands were as cool and soft as a bowl of whipped cream. She twirled her willowy tongue in my mouth, and we made love, if you want to call it that—all I know is that, to keep her quiet, I had to put a scored copy of *Wuthering Heights* over her mouth.

When the morning bell rang, she left me alone in the backroom. I waited for the girls to be in their classrooms. I sat, bare-assed and numb, feeling only the wetness run down my thigh. After having sex with the same person for all those years, there is some nameless power in the universe that can make those parts you thought were dead come alive again and thrill you into joy. I cleaned up and left.

As I briskly made my way down the stairs, Miss Bergman chased after me.

"Oliver! Is this yours? It was on the floor! I think it fell out of your pocket!" She knew she was being loud. She quickly covered her mouth and handed me the castration book.

"I heard this book was wonderful, Oliver," she said.

"Thanks."

"You're wonderful."

"You are too, Piper."

She smiled at me.

I looked around; the girls were all in their classes now. I pulled Piper Bergman close to me. I kissed her lovely lips, and I left.

As I exited the school, Franco approached me.

"Hey Mister," he said.

"How come you're not in class?"

"None of your business, whitey. How come you not in school?"

"None of your business," I said.

"You crazy, you know that?"

"Come with me," I said.

"Where you going?"

"Come with me," I said. He stood and followed me.

"You aren't no queer or nothing, right? I don't go that way."

"No, I am not a homosexual. Behave."

We walked down Lexington Ave. I pointed to the iPod he'd looked at days before. I walked in the store, and Franco followed. I asked the clerk to give me an iPod. The clerk handed it to me. I handed it to Franco. I handed my credit card to the clerk, who was eyeing me suspiciously. I signed my name and walked out with Franco following me.

"This for me? For real? I didn't do nothing for this."

"Yes, that's right; you did nothing. And I am being nice or maybe I'm just crazy, whatever."

How could I tell this kid that I saw myself in him?

"What you want from me?"

"I don't want anything."

"You a good whitey."

"You'll need a computer for that. You know that right?"

"Why, you think I'm dumb? Shit, I know. Mr. Clark, he teach computer lab; he'll help me put songs on it."

"Very good. Go back to school. People do care. People are good. Or at least I like to think so. I mean they are good. I don't know what I'm saying. Be happy or good or whatever it is … good for you. Find joy in your life."

"What? What you saying? You crying, Mister?"

"My eyes get watery."

"No, you crying bitch."

"You're young; you have your whole life ahead of you. Make the right choices. Be good, and every time you listen to music, remember that someone cared about you. You don't want to walk around feeling lonely and desperate and unloved even when people love you."

"What the hell you saying?" he asked.

"Enjoy the music. That's all," I said.

I walked onward to Central Park, and he shouted to me.

"Hey Mister! Mister!" I turned and looked his way.

"Thanks, Mister. You a good person. You real good! You crazy, but you good." Franco jumped happily and the sun made long multiple shadows on his dancing body.

I turned and walked. My eyes were streaming. I wanted my father more than anything right then.

EIGHT

There in the park, I sat watching people going about their daily lives: a mother with her crying child, a dog-walker with five dogs on his leash, a young couple snuggling in each other's arms.

I felt the *Castration* book in my back pocket. It was pressing against my butt, nagging at me, saying to me, "Pull me out and read me."

Then I thought about the sex I just had. I felt guilty. Was it my Catholic upbringing? Had I objectified a woman whom I respected? Had she objectified me? Why was the sex so animalistic?

I felt weird. Was it that book that was stirring all these raw emotions in me? Beth. Damn Beth!

I pulled the book out of my pocket and looked up my concerns: sex; aggression, animalistic, as a weapon, stress release: 40, 44, 45, 47, 49. Most of the stuff was in "Chapter Four: Sexual Politics and Penis Size." In brief, the chapter claims we raise our boys to believe that their penis is a spear, an aggressive weapon to poke woman with so we can rid ourselves of repressed anger toward womanhood, e.g., our mothers. That's why the average man penetrates a woman for only about three minutes, six seconds and screams out *Mommy!* when he climaxes. Also, the penis is dehumanized and used as a competitive apparatus for power, i.e., the bigger the penis in the locker room, the more powerful the man.

I didn't know what to think. I had had hot sex. It felt

good. I felt guilty. It was all normal thinking for a Catholic boy like me. I put the book away.

I tilted my head back and looked toward the sky, wondering if I could see the face of God. *What the Hell is with you, God? Huh? What the Hell is going on?* But I saw only the twisted branches of trees.

Then the sun broke though, and sparkled so brightly through the branches I was blinded. A hopeful sight, yet so incongruous, because I was shivering uncontrollably, horrified at the reality that I'd been cuckolded, dumped, and canned. I opened my briefcase, took out the silver flask, and examined it carefully. How awfully clever I'd thought I was being when I'd bought it! It was unusually small, as far as flasks go, but large enough for my needs. I never dreamed that this lovely little silver flask—my friend the flask—would become the vessel of my disgrace.

They knew. They all knew. My co-workers, my fellow teachers, and now, my students, all of them knew!

I was no common drunk. I merely nipped to take the edge off, to improve my ability to function, no more than that. I didn't *need* to drink.

I tossed the flask into the trash bin, stood and walked away a few feet, ran back to the trash bin and dug through it, snagging a few dirty diapers. I stopped myself. I was going mad! People were looking. I would buy another flask.

I decided to go to The Lincoln Center Campus. I headed west. I wanted to see the Chagalls. Perhaps, in my father's favorite paintings, I could find his spirit and ask for some sort of answer, some hope.

Walking through the park, I suddenly realized that I was passing the bench under the Japanese Maple that, when I was a little boy, my father had told me was "our bench." That Maple's red leaves seemed vibrant as they blew in the breeze that day, and I noticed that the tree had grown quite large. It saddened me to realize how quickly time passed.

The times that my dad and I had spent sitting on that bench are some of the few memories I have of him, and I felt them stirring so I sat down.

We'd feed the pigeons and eat hot dogs, always with extra mustard. We'd toss acorns at unsuspecting bicyclists and look away innocently if we actually hit one of them. Dad taught me how to whistle at ladies in skirts. Sometimes he whistled at men in business suits. Sometimes his sexual catcalls earned him nasty looks, sometimes glowing smiles. My father's whistling at men only baffled me. I never thought of my father as a queen.

My father was a handsome man, a combination of Marlon Brando and Dennis Hopper, with a touch of Agnes Moorhead around the eyes. When I was about three months old, my father, who was then a lieutenant in the United States Air Force, was sent to Vietnam. My mother decided we would stay in New York City. I don't remember that at all. But June told me later that our mother read his letters to us and that she thought that maybe he'd had to stay in a hospital for a while when he was back in the States. He wasn't in the Air Force any more, and when he got home, he began his law practice. She also told me that she thought that it was after that that he started drinking too much.

One day, my dad and I discovered a baby sparrow beneath "our bench." It had fallen from its nest in the Japanese Maple. I was sure the tiny bird was dead, but my father sensed the life in it. He gently cupped the bird in his hand and decided we had to take it straight away to the zoo to see if they could save its life. I told him it was useless, that it was going to die, and I started to cry.

"You always have to have hope, kid," he told me, "H-O-P-E!"

I went on crying, and he took a swig from *his* flask.

"Look, kid, I believe that in every living thing there's a little light, like a flame, and if we see it going out, we have to try to keep it lit. We have to keep the blaze of life going." He knelt down and told me to take a good look at the bird.

"This bird here has some life in it still. Look, Oliver."

I looked closely at the tiny bird with its half-opened, beady black eyes, and then looked away.

"Look at its eyes; see the light in its eyes," he said.

I looked again, and then I saw it. There *was* a light, a tiny glimmer.

"Daddy! I see the light!" I said, and my Dad smiled at me. I knew he was proud.

We marched through Central Park and headed for the zoo. We were on a life-saving mission. We were ready to rekindle the spark of the bird's life back into a flame, with the aid of the Central Park Zoo.

As we marched along, my father told me, "An old friend of mine in 'Nam once taught me that when we see a spark of life begin to dim, it's our duty to save it. He taught me that every life is worth saving. He was a man of great wisdom, Oliver. And I want you always to remember what he taught me."

"I won't forget, Daddy," I said.

"Then, move it, Oliver! We're almost there."

The staff at the Central Park Zoo saved the bird. We visited it, and saw that it was developing strong, sturdy wings. It would fly, after all, because my Dad and I saved its life. And it did fly, the zoo keeper told us one day, but it flew right into a snake den and was immediately swallowed up whole.

I fainted dead away, and my father carried me home.

He was still holding me when I came to.

NINE

When at last I was in front of Chagall's *The Sources of Music* hanging at Lincoln Center, I studied it carefully. I looked at *King David*. I looked at *Orpheus* rendered in vibrant yellows, blues, and greens—such life, color. I looked at the *Triumph of Music*, the musicians floating in a sea of swirling reds. How I wished I were floating with those musicians! How I yearned to escape permanently from my world and live with them in theirs. Safe from harm, lost in abstraction. Never to be seen again. Never to be heard from again.

I could never do that to June.

I briskly made my way down Ninth Avenue and, without thinking, walked into a liquor store. I went to the cash register and I eyed the shelf with the whiskeys and the scotches and admired their amber tones. I asked for a *Maker's Mark*. The clerk handed me the bottle, and I paid him.

But as I walked out of the store, the bottle slipped from my hands and smashed on the tile floor.

Everyone turned to look at me. I stood, bewildered.

"Hey, man? What the hell?" the man behind the counter shouted.

"I am terribly sorry," I told him.

"Goddamn it!"

I could take no more embarrassment that day. Or maybe I could? It felt kind of freeing. I was definitely losing it; something was going. My mind? My senses?

My heart pounded.

I darted from the store, went to the curb, and summoned a taxi. I stepped onto the street. A car, honking and beeping, came within inches of running me down.

I backed away from the curb. Sweat was running down my face. I bumped into a man, who gave me a shove and shouted some obscenity at me.

I tried to catch my breath. Then a taxi pulled to the curb, and I climbed in, not realizing that my pants and coat were sprayed with the whiskey I'd dropped in the bodega. As the taxi crossed over Forty-Second Street to the East Side, the brawny smell of the whiskey filled the back seat.

On my way to see June at the library, I once again felt a nagging press from that book in my back pocket. I took the book out. In the index I found …

> Sisters: mother image, friends, playing with her Barbies, depending on, trusting of: 13, 12, 64, 67, 90;

The book claims sisters and brothers are the healthiest female/male relationship a man can have: it's safe, and usually full of trust. However, if there are fantasies or intercourse between the two, these siblings should seek professional help.

For the record, I had no fantasies about my sister of a sexual nature. But did that qualify my relationship with June as "healthy"?

TEN

I looked into the window at the Milton Library. I watched June at her large desk cataloging books. Everything she did was methodical. She was fully engrossed in her safe world. She moved her head slowly from left to right, ran her hands over her head; she was so even-tempered when she was in public. Sitting there at her desk, she reminded me of small ladybug going about its business on the petal of a flower.

I wiped the perspiration from my forehead, took a deep breath, and walked into the library.

"June," I whispered. She looked up, surprised, happy to see me at first. But after one glance, I could see from her expression that she knew something was horribly wrong.

"Oh, my God! What happened?"

In a diner that claims to make the best grilled burgers in New York City, we sat in silence. Two cups of hot coffee sat before us. I searched for words to tell June while my eyes scanned the diner. It was a dirty little place, lime-green vinyl seats and black scratches on the white Formica. The place smelled like last week's deep frying oil and grilled burgers. It was filled with customers.

After I told her I was fired, she didn't speak for a long time. She only looked down at her coffee.

"You think you hide your drinking, but you only fool yourself," she said finally, "and you spend so much time with

Hank that I'm also beginning to wonder if you're not of the same persuasion as Daddy. Not that I don't love you both. Are you gay? There are studies that show homosexuality is genetic," she said.

Eight years after my father had died, my mother received a package from the Walter Reed Hospital in Washington, DC, with a short letter of apology and my father's war diary, which had been recently found there. She had no idea that the diary existed. It seemed like a message our father had sent from the afterlife. We were all anxious to know what my father had written long ago; I was able to save a few pages as my mother ripped them out and tossed them into a fire she'd started in a small trash barrel in the middle of our living room. Finally I managed to take the diary out of her hands, although she was in the throes of anger.

"I knew it! I knew he was a faggot! I knew it! Fucking queer! Queer! Faggot!"

My father wrote of an affair with a Vietnamese man. My father had a lot of secrets; the one about Mom's engagement ring was a doozy. This was way before I knew he was gay. But different memories of my father came back to me on occasion.

I recall when I was about seven years old, when I woke up in the middle of the night and found my father sitting alone on the sofa in his bathrobe. He was drunk and stared straight ahead of him, as if he could see some invisible being. Tears were streaming down his face and he whispered over and over, "Dac Kein. Dac Kein."

Dac Kein, we later learned, was his Vietnamese lover.

I sat close to my Dad.

He started to tell me about the Tet Offensive, about the things he saw after the bombing.

It was a gruesome story, the kind little boys love, and whenever he stopped, I begged him to tell me more.

"Burnt-out tanks and turned-up cars were smoldering all

around. Body parts were everywhere. I couldn't get away from the smoke and the stench," he told me, "and I knew at any minute anything might happen. I walked around for days. I was delusional. Underneath a wrecked motorcycle I found a lady's finger with a Jade ring still on it."

"Wow."

He took a long drink and went on, "It was still shining in the sun. And all I could think of was your mother and how when we were first married and I was still in law school I didn't have enough money for an engagement ring for her."

He looked at me closely, "Your mother was very beautiful then, Ollie. So beautiful."

"Tell me about the finger, Dad."

"I had always promised your mother that one day I'd buy her a ring like the one on that finger. So I took that ring off that finger. That's the ring she wears now."

Then he started to cry again and said, "Dac Kein, Dac Kein."

I had no idea what he meant.

"Don't you ever tell your mother about that ring, Oliver," he said. "Promise me."

"I promise, Daddy," I hugged him and lay by his side.

"Never tell her about it. It would kill her. Dac Kein! Dac Kein! Don't tell your mother, Ollie."

I looked up, and June was sipping her coffee.

"Oliver, what's going on? You zoned out?" she asked.

`"I don't know how I feel about all these recent disappointments in my life."

"Ralph has been predicting your decline for some time now," she said. She looked toward the kitchen. Large flames were coming off the grill. She held her head and kept her eyes on the kitchen.

"June, I'm hurting here. Stop it with the fire stuff. You do that to manipulate me. Concentrate on me, now."

"Oliver, Ralph is an alcoholic, too. You need to speak to

him." She ran her hands over her head and lifted her bun. She started to fidget in her seat.

"Too? I am not an alcoholic, June."

"You should have gotten help years ago. Do you blame yourself for Daddy's death?"

My jaw dropped.

When she finally took her eyes off the flames in the kitchen and looked at me, our eyes met. We couldn't speak, or we'd both start bawling. She sniffled. I hated myself for hurting June. I knew she worried about me, missed Beth, missed our parents. I somehow thought everything was my fault.

"You break my heart, Oliver. I know you're in pain. Poor mother worried so much about you. She knew you'd self-destruct one day. Personally, I am hoping that you're only a drunk. I don't know if I can tolerate 'crazy' after mother."

"Thanks a lot!" I said.

June covered her face. Her body heaved. A woman with spiked purple and green hair, dressed in black leather, with a small spike the size of a pencil through her nose, looked our way and gave me a darting, hateful look.

"Stop crying, for Christ's sake! These people think I'm abusing you," I said.

"I'm forty-two! I want to get married and have a baby," she wailed.

"Where is this coming from?"

"We're a couple of misfits; let's face it," June said.

"I'm sorry, June. I'm ashamed. I shouldn't do this to you."

"Ralph can help you. I have to get back to work."

She stood and kissed me, wrapping her long arms around my neck. I watched June leave the diner, her head hung low, arms folded over her chest.

I threw the cash on the table. I looked out the window and at the bar across the street. One tiny drink. Only one.

I looked at the awful spiked hair woman and waved my

book to her; if anyone would know about this book, that woman would. I wanted to show her I was indeed okay and cool. Unsurprisingly, she smiled at me, gave me the thumbs up.

"Keep reading!" she shouted after me.

ELEVEN

The next morning, I received a letter with a Vancouver postmark. I knew inside the envelope was a letter that expressed the thoughts of the woman I still loved but thought was a lousy bitch.

The letter, I imagined, contained one of either of the two following pronouncements: one that stated the ugly truth of who I was—even grosser, harsher than the ones she declared the day she left me—or an apology and a declaration of enduring love, ending with her beseeching me to come to her and bring her home.

I didn't have the courage to read it. Instead, I kept it near me or on my person, periodically patting it to reassure myself that it was still there.

In the days that followed, I locked myself in my room and continued to drink. I think I was having a nervous breakdown. But I wasn't sure; people who have nervous breakdowns in my family tend to start fires in odd places. I had no desire to do that; I never have. So I comforted myself by thinking that as long as I didn't have the desire to go buy a blow torch I was okay. However, I did have the desire to have a bottle of Bushmills injected into my arm. Getting up to drink was becoming an effort.

For the next week I drank myself into a stumbling stupor. June pleaded with me to come out. She even tried to get Ralph to talk to me, but I refused. I only came out when June went off to work. I didn't want to see anyone.

Every time Ralph pounded on my door, he would say things like, "I'm an alcoholic too, remember? We're the same, really. I know what you're going through. Let me in. Come on, Oliver. Let's talk."

For a few weeks, I didn't want to talk to anyone, for I'd started to hit the bottle really hard. I couldn't live with my newly unemployed, newly divorced life; I had officially become a pizza-eating, doughnut-scarfing, bathrobe-wearing, unshaven, ripe, bed-ridden pig. I had no desire to search for a job—despite June's repeated requests that I do so and quickly, too, because the bills were becoming harder and harder for her to pay on her salary alone, and I was depleting my savings on pizza, frozen foods, and *Krispy Kremes*.

June had been pleading for me to come out every chance she had. One night Ralph pounded and pleaded for about twenty minutes, and I heard his heavy nasal breathing between his pleas through the cracks of my bedroom door. I would rather have been hung upside down from a tree and doused with gasoline and have lit matches thrown at me than sit and "chat" with Ralph about his philosophy on alcoholism in general and my own drunken life in particular.

"I appreciate it Ralph, really I do. But I am fine. Honest."

June must have become desperate because she even called Hank to come and bang on my door.

"Ollie! It's me, Hanky," he said. "I haven't seen you in weeks. Come on, let's go for a walk. Hey, I know! We'll go get Mexican down at Maya's. Hey, I'll treat, even. You know how you love Camarones al Chipotle."

"Thanks, Hanky, I'll call you tomorrow. I'm fine, I mean it. Thanks for coming by! Don't worry about me. I appreciate you coming by, honest," I said.

At reliable intervals, June had been knocking sharply,

incisively, with one knuckle, speaking quietly in her motherly voice. She had always played mother to me, even while our mother was still alive. I hated knowing how much I was upsetting her, but I couldn't snap out of my funk, not even for her.

"Oliver," June called to me. "Guess what? I made your favorite—Spanish Rice."

"Thanks June," I said, "I'm fine. Please stop worrying about me." I couldn't be mean to June.

"I'll eat in a bit," I shouted after her.

Later that night I finally came out if my room and wandered into my study with a bowl of June's Spanish rice, my head spinning a bit as I sat on the center of the floor. I had covered the walls and the ceiling of my study with fine art prints over the years. Everything from Da Vinci to Van Gogh to Pollack. Everyone I knew hated my study. It was too overwhelming. Only I loved it. It soothed me.

There was a slight knock on the door.

"May I come in?" Ralph asked.

"Sure." I said. I felt embarrassed, even in front of him. He looked around my study. Ralph was a handsome guy in his own way. His body was rawboned, his hair a sandy grayish-brown. His lenses were the thickest I'd seen, and the black rims rested awkwardly on his irregular nose. When he did take them off, his magnified eyes were attractive—small and crinkly.

"Amazing," he said. He closely inspected all the prints on the wall.

Ralph was wearing June's bathrobe. He looked ridiculous. He was starting to spend the night at the house. I was happy for June. It seemed my decline coincided with her ascent.

Ralph held a book in his hand.

"I like this room. June would never let me in here. She says it's your private sanctuary."

"You're the first person to say that," I said. "Beth always hated it."

"I know passion when I see it."

"Look, Ralph, I'm sorry. I don't want to talk about me. I'll be okay. I'm fine."

"Well, let's talk about June, shall we? Quite frankly, Oliver, June is not fine, and neither am I. We're worried."

Ralph sat on my desk and his big hairy balls peeked out from a crack in the front of his robe.

"I don't know what to say," I said, unable to focus on anything but his balls.

He then smiled at me and handed me the book he'd brought in with him: The Castration of the 20th Century Man: How to Grow a New Set for the 21st Century.

"It changed my life," he said.

"I've kind of been reading it. Beth gave it to me."

"There is much truth in this book." He patted the book firmly. "Men are under attack nowadays. It's not our fault. It's the fault of our forefathers, and of war, and of being pushed away from our mother's love, and fear of homosexuality," he said. Then he put his arm around me. I froze.

"God you're so tense! I'm only showing you some affection. Did you read the part about the all-male nudist camps in Vermont? I was thinking about going. It's not a gay thing. It's a bunch of man walking around naked, touching each other in loving ways to help get rid of the fear of homosexuality—all so you can have more solid relationships with men. It sounds wonderful."

"It sounds scary, Ralph."

"I care for you, Ollie, because June loves you. And if she loves you, I love you. It's all right to be sensitive with another man. How about a hug?" I couldn't help but feel uneasy and amused.

"I'm all set for now, Ralph."

"Okay, but before I go, I need to tell you that you need to grow a new set of balls. You need to admit you're an alcoholic and allow me to help. But I can't force you."

I started to walk back to my room. I needed a big drink now.

"Wait, Oliver. I think you ought to know one more thing,

but June must never know I told you. I think it's important you know that I'm going to marry June one day. We've already talked about it." He pulled his robe tightly around his body.

"You're going to marry June? Really? You mean it, Ralph?"

"She uses you as an excuse. She won't leave you. Because you're a lonely, emotional cripple, and she's afraid you can't handle much."

This can't possibly be true, I thought. Poor June. Damn it!

Ralph went on, "She told me you had both promised your mother that no matter what, you would both take care of each other. Maybe you're both afraid to move on, I don't know. But I suggest you do some soul searching today, and I hope you do it quickly, preferably by this evening at eight. I have an AA meeting to go to, and I'd like you to come along with me. I have plans for June and me and, quite frankly, you're messing them up. You need to show her that you can survive without her. You can, can't you?"

I took a long look at Ralph, at his expectant face.

"Okay. I'll probably go to a meeting with you. Okay?" I whispered. Ralph then took me by my arm and looked directly at me. I stepped back a bit. Was he going to kiss me? Between him and Hank, I had my worries.

Ralph's eyes left my face and looked around the study, "Any human being who can see beauty as you do, can certainly feel beauty and be beautiful. You've chosen not to reveal yourself, to keep Oliver Pepper hidden away somewhere. Now, for the love of God, let him go. Grow up ..."

"What the hell does that mean?"

"Don't you see that your study is a reflection of your interior self? It's yearning to come out, but you keep it covered up every day with all your bullshit. And that's all it is, Oliver, bullshit. PLAIN BULLSHIT!"

"You're yelling."

"I know, and I know you'll go to the meeting with me. Oliver, you're finding your balls."

He left my study.

I took a deep sigh, went back to my bedroom and looked out my window. But the window only bounced my own reflection back at me.

TWELVE

That evening I went reluctantly with Ralph to my first AA meeting, but first I ate dinner with June and Ralph. While we ate June's burnt pork roast, she bawled. According to her, I looked worn and beat up. Then, soon after dinner, June played with the gas pilots on the stove; this was a clear indication she was beyond upset or manipulating me.

I told June I would officially stop drinking. My boozing days were finished! Finis! Rifinito! Acabado!—Done! Over!—God give me the strength. June walked away from the stove and cleared the tears from her eyes. Ralph smiled.

We sat together in the damp church basement on Ninety-Sixth Street, and I kept my head down, humiliated and ashamed, even though Ralph told me no one there would judge me. I felt pathetic. The people around me, seventeen in all, reminded me of the losers I'd spent hours boozing it up with at The Stone, and it was hard for me not to judge them—even if this group hadn't slept with my wife. I was trying to be humble, but I thought most of them looked like deadbeats and freaks. I even laughed a bit when people told their tragic stories, but that's okay, Ralph told me, it was all part of "The Recovery."

Every night I went back to the meetings with Ralph. June was thrilled. Every time, as we walked toward the church basement, Ralph would encourage me to speak.

"I'm not ready, Ralph," I would say.

"Okay. When you're ready, I'm all ears, buddy."

"Ralph, I appreciate it, really I do."

Ralph lived a few blocks away on Seventy-Ninth and First. He'd go home after work, shower, and show up at our place with a jug of cranberry juice. Ralph said that after years of binge alcohol consumption, cranberry juice was the best juice to nurse his kidneys. After dinner, we both would be off to an eight o'clock meeting. June was in a cooking frenzy. She made homemade chicken pies, fish stew, pasta primavera, even a roast duck. She was getting better at not burning things, too, but there were times June must have purposefully burnt things when she missed our Mother or thought she was on the verge of insanity.

During the day I watched television. My favorite show was *The Price Is Right*. At first, I thought the show ridiculous, but after a while, I actually enjoyed it. I played along and did not like to miss my program. I guessed the prices, and when I was wrong, I'd throw my slippers or any handy item at the television screen. I gave myself bonus points if I hit Bob Barker's face. Sometimes I read my art books. Other times, now that I'd discovered the many uses of the Internet, I'd go online and enter chat rooms. That didn't last long, after I accidentally entered a site for men who enjoyed having sex with butchered whole goats. (There was an entire page about where to buy the goat, too; some place in Queens where they kept the innards intact if asked.) It made me vomit. This was a good thing because afterwards I didn't feel so bad about eating my second family size tray of Stouffers Macaroni and Cheese and a pan of brownies and a package of Kaiser Rolls and half a jar of Marshmallow fluff.

Hank called me non-stop, but I never returned his calls. One afternoon, I finally decided it was time to call him back.

"Hank, it's me, Oliver. I'm sorry I haven't returned your calls."

"It's okay. I've been going through stuff too. It's been

weird not seeing you all the time. Do you realize we've seen each other almost every day since we were kids? This is the longest I've gone without seeing you. I think it's been almost four weeks! Are you having a nervous breakdown? I feel bad you haven't opened up to me."

"We never open up to each other because all we do is drink and complain. And you say you want the truth but you really don't."

"That's not true. You know me; I call it as I see it."

"Only when it doesn't pertain to you! Now listen, Hank, here it is. I'm … I'm an alcoholic."

"Come on, stop that!"

"If we hang out again, Hank, it's got to be with no alcohol."

"That's extreme. We should go get a beer and talk about this."

"Hank, I can't drink anymore. This is the truth."

"Not even beer?"

"No, Hank, not even beer."

"Cut the shit."

"I'm serious."

"What, are you in a cult? You're going be all judgmental and shit?"

"I'm going to try it for a while."

"Damn, Ollie!"

"I fucked up, Hank. I lost everything that matters to me. I think I did it on purpose. I sabotaged myself, and what's worse, I'm screwing things up for June."

"You're being too hard on yourself. Beth is history and so is that job," he said.

"I need some order in my life. I took Beth losing the baby worse than I thought I would. I really wanted … Oh, fuck shit Hank."

"What? Wanted what?"

"I really wanted to be a father."

There was a long silence. Hank coughed. "You'll find

another job. And be honest with me—do you really want another wife? Relish your freedom. Kids carry colds and other diseases. This is the truth."

"Hank, this conversation is going nowhere, and you're not understanding me. I know you're trying to make me feel better, but I'm telling you that I am hurting. I want to be a father and all you can say is that kids carry diseases?"

"I'm sorry, pal. Can you meet me in ten minutes? Eighty-third and Second? Let's hang out, and we can talk. I miss you, old boy."

"Okay. But I can't drink."

"Can I?"

"You can do what you want, Hank. See you in a few."

"Looking forward to grabbing that hot ass of yours!" Hank said. He laughed. I forced a snicker. But I was scared. I hung up the phone. I looked over at *Growing A New Set for the 21ˢᵗ Century*. I recalled seeing something in the back of the book about straight men and 'ass grabbing.' It reminded me of Hank and how he always managed to pat my ass or grab my balls in a "No worries, I'm your straight buddy" way.

I found what I was looking for: Chapter Three. I read it. Hank would have to wait.

The chapter's title was "Football, Baseball, Basketball, and that Pat on the Ass." I rapidly read about balls and more balls. How sports relate to the balls and scrotum. The book says that passing a ball around a field is a metaphor for manly bonding over the celebration of how the scrotum holds two balls forever in a basket of safety. That throwing and bouncing a ball around a field is a way of expressing an inner need for freedom from balls, i.e., a fantasy of owning a vagina, thus relieving the pressures of manhood, if only momentarily. The chapter also examines how it's only safe for most men to show emotion toward other men on a playing field involving balls. It suggests allowing men to touch you.

Interesting, I thought, but all the same, I wanted Hank to keep his damn hands to himself.

THIRTEEN

Hank came toward me with a big gleeful smile and a slight limp. When we were teenagers, we went skid-hopping on a garbage truck on East End Avenue on a snowy day. He was pulled under, and his leg was twisted. Hank was self-conscious about his limp, but it wasn't that bad. It was the scar that was the real killer. It ran up his calf and spiraled around his leg like a corkscrew.

We found a new place on Third Avenue called The Corn Whole Restaurant and Tavern. One side of the wall was covered in art work made from corn and corn products, and the restaurant specialized in country-fried catfish. Not that Hank cared about the chow, so long as they had a decent bar, a dart board, and a pool table. The winning factor—the real reason we stayed—was that they played Faith Hill incessantly.

Hank and I loved Faith Hill.

By the time I finished my ginger ale, Hank was on his second Makers Mark Neat. By the time I finished my second ginger ale, Faith Hill was singing "Mississippi Girl," and I gave into temptation. I took one sip of Hank's drink, then another sip, than another, and then yet another. Then I said fuck it and ordered one for myself, and then I ordered another. Six in total. I was sloshed.

By the end of that night, we had made new friends. They were a group of men from Germany who spoke no English but nodded a lot and bought us drinks. When Hank starting reciting and shouting German Cuisine—"Schnitzel!" and

"Jäger Schnitzel!"—we all laughed. They thought he was charming. I knew it was time to go when Hank started humping the leg of the biggest guy in the crowd, who was no longer laughing nor thought Hank was charming. Hank finally backed off when I yanked him from the guy's leg. "I'm just joking! Scherzen, Scherzen, Scherzen!" Hank slurred drunkenly. I apologized in German: *Wir bedauern, Wir bedauern,* and they nodded and shrugged. Keeping my hands on Hank's shoulders I pulled him toward the door, and we left singing along to Faith Hill's angelic voice, which followed us out onto the sidewalk. Our arms around each other, we stumbled along in a stupor.

We laughed and sang our way home, swearing our devoted love and friendship for each another. We hugged and kissed and forgave each other everything we ever did wrong, and we reminisced about our sometimes fun, sometimes lousy, but always tragic childhoods.

But when we turned onto York, I got a bit nervous, because as Hank hugged me goodbye, he grabbed my testicles.

"Gotcha!" he said. He laughed, but his hand was still on my balls and the other had found its way to my ass. To tell you the truth, it began to feel like sex to me, but I was in no position to call him on it at that point.

I felt it was time to go home, but I stayed a moment too long, maybe, trying to determine if I had learned something new about Hank.

"You feel like taking a walk down to the river?" he asked.

"Why not?" I said. We started walking down Eighty-Fourth toward the river. When Hank was drunk, his limp was more pronounced, and because the street was quiet, his shoes made a clobbering sound on the pavement.

"You never talk about those guys at the Stone," Hank said. "You still mad at them? It was kind of Beth's fault." His clobbering was getting steadily louder. He almost fell onto me.

"Damn, Hank, who's fooling who? You never have friends in a bar, only drinking buddies who'll pretend to commiserate about your lifeless life, shoot darts, watch a football game, maybe buy you a drink once in a blue moon, and share a bowl of pretzels. They are a bunch of losers."

I suggested Hank run up to his place and grab a bottle of Chivas before we sat by the East River and got totally, rip-roaring blasted. The next thing I knew, Hank and I were swigging from a bottle and watching the River's current. The sun was rising. It was Saturday morning—Hank's Scalp Breathing Day—so he tore his hair off, and the rising sun shone on his bald head. His puffy, sad eyes shifted, and he coughed after each gulp.

"Why do you drink like that? Damn, Hank, like a drunk or something," I said. I laughed but wanted to cry. We sat down on a bench. The bridges of New York expanded up and down the river. There was always a nasty current in the East River, and it scared me. The air carried a slight chill.

"You know what, Hank?" I said, "You should let your scalp breathe every day. That toupee is mangy. You're a great looking guy, Hanky."

"Regrettably, Ollie, I do own a mirror."

"Remember that chick we met that night? She said you had great lips and killer eyes. She thought you were hot."

"She had warts on her eyelids," he reminded me.

"Those were beauty marks," I lied.

"I know what I look like; I know I limp. I know I have an ugly scar on my leg. I know I'm a fat pig. I know how to face the truth," he said.

"Your limp is not even noticeable and, come on, women find scars really hot! And big bellies are hot on bald guys."

"You're too good to me, Oliver." He put his arm around me. I bit my lip.

Then, as if we'd been talking about something else all along, his face brightened. "Hey, remember how we used to ride our bikes along here? My mother always freaked out because we'd go toward the street."

I looked at the cobblestone at our feet and my eyes followed each familiar stone. They were like old friends, loyal and consistent. They couldn't talk, couldn't hurt, they supported you, and even though they made your ride bumpy, it was a sturdy ride, all the same.

"How's your mom doing?" I asked.

I adored his mother. She now lived in Naples, Florida, with Hank's dad. My mother and Betty Darby were friends. The Darbys lived across the hall from us growing up. After my mother started having her issues with fire, and June had had to send her away to the psychiatric ward, Mrs. Darby would send over pots of chili and platters of celery stuffed with cream cheese and pimento. My sister disparaged such food and, after thanking Mrs. Darby, tossed it straight into the trash as soon as she'd left.

"Mom is doing fine. Dad's doing well, too. Both of them are perfect in their perfect world. How can two such perfect people give birth to the biggest loser in the universe?"

"You're being kind of hard on yourself," I said.

"I've been having these dreams about kicking people's asses. Like last night I dreamed I was kicking the shit out of Sister Eunice, our first grade teacher. It was fucked up. I was pulling on her hair and kicking her in the face," Hank took another sip from the bottle. "I was calling her an ugly bitch and beating her to a pulp."

"That's not right," I said, loving it. I took the bottle from him and swigged.

"I still hate her. And it's been, what, like thirty years? But she humiliated me because I couldn't make a fucking 'S.' She yelled at me in front of the entire class!"

"I don't remember," I said, lying again.

"Sure, you do! I shit my pants, and everyone laughed at me."

"So you're saying Sister Eunice ruined your life."

"All I'm saying is that when we're born, the doctor should brand our butts, 'HANDLE WITH CARE.' Fuck, sometimes I think I'm a misfit. Let's face it."

"June said the same thing to me. She said she and I were a couple of misfits. Damn. Maybe I should jump into the river," I said.

"Fuck, you're perfect, Oliver. Always were, always will be."

Suddenly, there was a strange silence between us, and when I finally looked over at Hank, his face had changed completely. Tears were streaming down his cheeks. I hadn't seen him look that upset since he lifted Marie Carmichael's dress to take a peek. And I hadn't seen him cry like that since Marie had beat him up in front of the entire school while her younger sister, Ellen, peed in his Scooby-Doo lunch box. And this was after Father Robert had already beaten him with a ruler.

He turned away from me so I couldn't see his face. "Look, Ollie, I fucked up. I fucked up really bad." I patted his limp leg, and he turned his face back to me. He was really bawling.

"I wanted to be perfect for one minute. Maybe even half an hour," he said. Something about his voice was starting to give me a knot in my stomach.

He wiped his nose on his sleeve. He stood up, too quickly, his face covered in tears. His limp was really bad now; he held onto the cast iron rail overlooking the river.

"I thought this night was about me," I said. I grabbed the bottle from his hand and took a long swig.

"Fuck it!" he screamed. "I tried to fuck Beth, too, at The Stone. I'm a shit, lower than shit, the crusty old shit around a subway toilet. I'm sorry, man. I wanted to be with the perfect girl who belonged to the perfect guy. So I tried to fuck Beth.

But I couldn't even get it up. I fucked that up, too."

He backed away from me with every word he spoke. I knew why he was afraid of me. I had kicked his ass over twenty years ago. I forget why, but he had begged me to stop beating him. I had to stop; he refused to hit me back. But now, I only looked at him. I couldn't speak.

He hung his head over the iron fence, shaking, whimpering, spitting globs of phlegm into the East River.

"Too short, too fat, bald, small dick, limp-legged. I'm a fucking loser and a bad fuck. I couldn't even get it up! She laughed at me. Fucking laughed at me! So I didn't officially fuck her, but I tried, and that's as bad." He went on, repeating his pitiful mantra. I let him go on.

I sat in awestruck silence. I couldn't feel my buzz anymore. I couldn't feel my feet, my hands, my face, or my ears. I was less than non-existent. I was that ball of phlegm shot from Hank's mouth, floating on the surface of the East River.

"There is no excuse." I heard myself saying this over and over, louder and louder. "There is no excuse." I stuffed my fists in my pocket. A cool, sharp wind hit my face. The lights on the Roosevelt Island Bridge were off now that the sun had fully risen. The river was luring me to come jump in. The sunlight trickled off the water. A million lights, a million tiny deaths, years and years of friendship were dying before me. Hank. Hanky. Fuck, Hank.

I stood and walked away from Hank, my former best friend.

"So that's it?" he asked, desperately tagging along at my side. "That's it? You walk away? For weeks, I have this anxiety, I finally come clean and you walk away, like that?"

I crossed to the other side of East End Avenue. Hank was right. He was a loser. And I was as bad as he was. Hank finally managed to grab my shoulder and turn me around in his pitiful Bruce Willis-type action-hero fashion. We stood on the corner of East End and Eighty-Fourth. Aside from a man walking his Doberman, we were alone on the street.

"I demand you punch me. For the sake of our friendship, punch me," Hank was shouting. The man and the Doberman passed us by; apparently there was nothing new here for them to see, and neither of them looked back as they went on down the street.

I walked back to him. He backed away a bit, but I embraced him firmly. He started crying again, like a sniveling baby. He let go of me and looked at me directly in the eye for what seemed like hours.

I wondered so much about Hank at that moment. Beth had always said Hank was gay; I wondered if his "thing" for Elizabeth Montgomery was real or if it was really for the actor who played Darren? I began to wonder if he had tried to screw Beth to be close to me. I would never tell June or Ralph about this current slip from sobriety; at that moment I was more than eager to go back to the meetings. I clenched my fist. Hank spoke, breaking my stare.

"I knew you wouldn't hit me. My friend. My best friend. I love you," he said.

I hauled off and hit him so hard I heard his nose crack. Then I heard a release of air from his mouth, like the little whoosh you hear when you break the vacuum seal on a can of Planter's Peanuts.

FOURTEEN

My life was all going to change now. No more drinking and no more Hank!

I'd begun to loathe Bob Barker, have long fantasies about enjoying a ménage à trois with Lucy and Ethel, and crave large glasses of whiskey. My loneliness was inconsolable. I was horny as a barnyard dog, angry, obsessively masturbating, and plotting ways in which I could lynch Hank in Central Park and get away with it. However, the masturbating obsessively part was kind of worrying me. So I looked in my book.

Masturbation; obsessive, jerking meat, choking the chicken: 12, 19, 21, 43, 78.

The book said it was an ego thing, but perfectly normal, more prevalent in men who were under a lot of stress. Using objects like bottles, JELL-O, melons, meat, and animal byproducts was considered perverted. Phew, I was cool. I only used my hand. I smiled with relief, for if the only thing that was making me feel good was going to make me feel bad, I would surely lose it. The book said not to feel guilty, to feel free, to feel good about touching your penis. It was part of becoming a whole and sensitive man. The book suggested telling a few people you masturbate, to come out and be free of the guilt. But that was something I would never do. Never.

I walked to the AA meeting with Ralph by my side,

feeling normal and assured about my masturbation habit. We went up Eighty-Fifth Street, onto Second Avenue, and straight up to Ninety-Sixth Street. It was early October. The bodegas were selling mums, and the small vegetable stands on the streets held an array of squashes. The streets were permeated with the earthy smell of leaves, propelled along in clusters by cool, dry gusts of wind from Central Park.

When we were almost at the church, Ralph started in with his rhetoric.

"You must be feeling a little better."

"Those AA people depress me."

"It's because they're like you. And you're afraid to see yourself. You'll get there."

Ralph opened the church basement door, and I entered Alcoholicville. I was greeted by the same smiling faces I had seen the past few weeks. I took my seat. And as soon as I did, *she* sat next to me. Rosa. Then I felt a sharp nudge in my rib cage.

"Oh, excuse me, did I hurt you?" she said.

"I'm fine, it's okay," I said.

"I was trying to find my cell phone and I can't find it; it was ringing. My name is Rosa. Found it!"

She pulled it out of her pocket book. More people entered and got situated in the circle. Rosa's cell phone rang again, and she answered it. I listened to her. She had a thick Bronx accent. Her voice was throaty and sexy. Still on the phone, she pulled out a pack of gum and held it out to me. I shook my head, but she pushed it to me insistently, all the while speaking on her phone. I took a piece, and she motioned for me to pass the pack of gum around.

"I fucking can't deal with you now. Goodbye." Rosa hung up.

"Thanks, Rosa!" Ralph whispered. He put the gum in his mouth.

"What's your name?" Rosa said. She was tapping me on my shoulder.

"Oliver. Oliver Pepper," I said.

"Oliver Pepper?–Oh! Ralph's friend!" Ralph leaned over and smiled at both of us.

"Rosa, I'm sorry," Ralph said, "this is the guy I was telling you about. June's brother. Oliver, this is Rosa, Rosa, this is Oliver." He winked at me.

"You work at the school next to mine? You work at Bolton. Or did. Right? You were fired or something?"

"Ralph, why did you tell everyone my business? So much for being anonymous!" I said. Ralph was at a loss for words. He nervously bit the top of his index finger. He looked like a small child who had made a grave mistake. He looked over at Rosa for help.

"I'm the principal at the school next door to Bolton. I would see you around. Then I didn't, and one day Ralph and I talked. One thing lead to another, and you know how it goes, six degrees of separation and all that stuff. It's New York. It's a small town. No big deal."

"Yes," I said. My face started to heat up. I glared at Ralph. I felt like I was being set up for something.

"He's a wonderful teacher, Rosa" Ralph beamed. *Bingo*, I thought.

"Oh, and that was nice of you to buy Franco that iPod. He came into school with it. I was angry. But he told me some teacher at the 'rich girls' school' bought it for him, 'some guy called Pepper.' I was worried. I thought he stole it. Terrible of me to think that way, but I guess I have to. So, you see, when Ralph mentioned your name it all came together, don't be angry. It's cool. Really." She smiled.

"What a fascinating coincidence this all is," I said. I looked at Ralph, who shrugged his shoulders sheepishly. He'd had this all planned out.

"And Franco thinks you're pretty cool too. Here, take my card. If you ever want to substitute, call me," Rosa said.

The chairperson started the meeting, but I couldn't keep my eyes off Rosa. Her curly black hair fell over her face, and she kept putting it behind her ears as she spoke. Her skin was an even, light olive brown. Her eyes were a velvety golden-brown and had a warm glint. Her body was tiny and fit. Her black leather boots had sharp pointy toes. Her jeans were lusciously tight. I could smell her perfume—something fruity, like mango. It excited me beyond what I could imagine in this damp dungeon of a place.

I glanced over at her breasts. They stuck out nicely from her blue sweater and looked firm to me, nicely sized. I knew I had to stop looking at her before people noticed my staring, but it wasn't easy. I felt so attracted to her, I couldn't snap out of it. I begin to perspire and shut my eyes. I tried to concentrate on her voice—not on that body, which was making me hard. Her voice was soft at first but became elevated as she spoke.

"My name is Rosa and I'm an alcoholic." All eyes looked her way. She remained in her seat in the circle.

"Hi, Rosa!" everyone replied in unison.

Except for me. I hated that unity thing. It was all too freaky. Too personal.

"Tonight I need to talk about boundaries. I have to. I hope you guys don't mind. I know this meeting is about the seventh step, but I need to get it out," Rosa said.

I looked over, and I became paranoid. Was I too obvious? I found my head automatically turning to her, as if some unknown force had possessed me.

I tried to concentrate on the large coffee pot in the corner, then the plate of old doughnuts that were covered in black and orange sprinkles—a sign that Halloween was three weeks away—but her voice kept drawing me back to her face, *that face.*

She's so beautiful.

"My sister, who is still a drunk, comes to my house last night with her three kids in tow, she drags them all the way from the Bronx on the train. I'm in Soho for crying out loud!

'I mean they're little kids. One is in a backpack, another she carries in one hand, and the other holds her waist. They look like something out of skid row. And it's ten thirty at night, mind you, and she's a mess, and the kids are a mess. They're crying and stuff. She tells me her drug addict boyfriend has moved out again. She tells me that she needs money to pay her rent. It's always the same thing with her. So I write her a check and she says to me, 'Is that all?'

"She thinks I work to support her. She starts telling me she's a single mother and she knows I have a lot of money, which I don't, but she thinks I do, and I find myself continuously enabling her. I struggle sometimes to take care of myself and get my life in order. She's my sister, and I love her. It's really hard for me to say 'No!' to her, especially when her kids are looking up at me all dog-eyed. I know half the money I give her goes to booze.

"She can't go to my parents because they're drunks, too. I feel like I'm the only one in my family that's sane. Then at work I try really hard to pull it together and people take advantage of me. They call in sick all the time, they complain and complain.

"I'm starting to think, 'I'm taking too much on.' I have to say to myself, 'Hey, hold up, take a step back and take care of you, one step at a time.'

"But when I do that I feel all self-centered. Catholic guilt stuff. I live in a really nice place, I worked hard for it, but I feel guilty because my sister lives in a shitty place. I have to check in with myself and remind myself I'm taking care of me so I can help those I love, but that doesn't mean enabling anyone. So anyway, I was really proud of myself today for about an hour."

Everyone laughed, and I found myself still laughing after everyone had finished. Rosa looked at me and smiled. She patted my knee.

"If you think that's funny, wait till you hear the rest!"

Rosa winked at me, and there was more laughter. I looked over and I saw Ralph looking at me, smiling that humble *I'm proud that you're participating smile.* I wanted to flip him the bird, but of course I didn't because that would be low class. But I sure thought about it. Rosa continued.

"I called my sister up this morning. I made the decision because I knew her visit last night would burn at me all day and I wouldn't be able to let it go. I told my sister she was ungrateful. I told her she went beyond my boundaries and for the first time I told her I wasn't going to help her anymore until she helped herself. And now I feel like shit. But I did it! She needs to get a job and take care of herself and her kids. Anyway, she started screaming at me, told me I was selfish, I mean she really attacked me, brought up things from our childhood I had forgotten about, and it creeped me out. And that's when I realized the insanity of this disease. When I hung up from her, I was really scared I was going to pick up a drink, and this is one of the reasons I can't deal with my family. I want to pick up a drink every time I have dealings with them. It's damn hard for me to keep sane. When my sister and I were teenagers, we would party together, and it was rough. She would pass out on her bed, and I would keep drinking until I blacked out. Then I started drinking alone, completely alienated myself from the world. I knew I needed help.

"I think my sister is pissed at me because she can't accept the fact that her drinking partner is gone. I can't indulge her nonsense. Thanks for listening. I really needed to come here tonight. Thanks everyone."

We all applauded.

Rosa had no shame, only a humbleness that wasn't vulgar or showy to me; it was refreshing, and she didn't evoke any pity. She only stated the way her life was at the moment and she was trying to fix what needed to be fixed.

And she had an outstanding ass.

How could I tell everyone about my family? I could never!

Hello my name is Oliver.

Hello Oliver.

What a joke, me talking to these strangers. I couldn't imagine doing it!

Or could I? I closed my eyes and imagined myself speaking—a slight, sad smile on my face.

Hello everyone. I'm Oliver.

My mother, Louise Wojciechowski Pepper, was a beautiful woman. Tiny and slim, but imposing and stately. Mother was so regal in manner that no one would guess her working-class roots. Her black hair was perfectly straight. She'd had her hairdresser cut and style it in the same way that Jacqueline Kennedy Onassis wore hers. Mother's hair was softer, though, and less thick, really uniquely her own, and so she'd kept it that way ever after. Mother's eyes were an intense green. In the summer they became almost lime green, like two pieces of beach glass under shallow ocean water.

Mother adored her Chanel, Givenchy, and Christian Dior suits, and was always immaculate. Her speech was impeccable, remarkable in tone, her consonants clear and crisp, her vowels musical. She had taught herself to speak with a slight New England accent, so no one would know she'd grown up in Queens, but her accent, like her hair, was uniquely her own. Her nails were always perfectly manicured, and she kept herself fit, watching her diet carefully. I remember she ate mostly poached salmon and thin slices of pineapple; she believed the acid in the fruit helped keep her thin. When I was a little boy, I thought my mother should be a Countess. And to me, she was.

"You and June are my miracles," she always told us, "my two, lovely, miracles! What have I done to be so blessed by God with you?" She'd stroke my face and kiss the top of my head and pull me close to her small body. I noticed, sometimes, that she shook like a nervous Chihuahua.

After my father died, *my* mother would spend days watching cartoons. She was very fond of Bugs Bunny. It seemed that only good old Bugs could make my mother smile. And when we saw our mother smile, we thanked God for *Looney Tunes.*

One day, our mother confessed to us that our father's death was entirely her fault. This was the first time since his death, three years before, that she'd ever spoken of it. She told us that she'd wanted more and more from our father when there was no more to give. He had given her all he had. It was her insecurities, her shortcomings that had ruined their marriage.

"When you come from poverty and you find yourself out of it, you never want to go back," Mother told us.

This all happened on Good Friday, and Mother wanted to color Easter eggs with us. She had come to the decision that our life must go on. She didn't care about *her* life anymore, because she had robbed us of our father.

So, still in her bathrobe, dark circles under her eyes from lack of sleep, she sat in the corner of our kitchen, watching June and me at the table, pretending to be excited about coloring eggs. Then she began to pull the petals off of the daffodil June had bought her.

Mother looked on as we placed white eggs into the colored water—blue, green, and red—and spoke to us, each word sad and measured, her voice soft and peaceful.

"I hated being poor," she said and tossed a daffodil petal into the air.

"I hated being average," she went on, and sent another petal flying.

"I wanted the world," she said, and another yellow petal flew.

June looked at our mother and then fished out a green egg.

I fished out a red one and plopped another white egg into the red bowl.

"It's all my fault your father is gone," she wept into the remains of the daffodil.

"Mama, stop," June said. "Daddy is in a better place."

I'd be damned before I looked at my mother. It *was* her fault. I hated her. I wanted to throw my egg in her face. But I couldn't.

"Remember," she droned on, "no matter where you go, or who you become, you two must always take care of each other. Always stay together. Never allow anything or anyone to tear you apart. You must promise me this."

"I promise, Mommy," June said.

"Me, too."

"I need to know that you both will always be well taken care of. You are my two little miracles, remember?"

June and I looked at each other.

"You two are the only proof of any good that I've done in my life."

Then she left us to color the eggs by ourselves. It was time for Bugs Bunny.

Some weeks after that peculiar Easter, on a Saturday, my mother took me to the Metropolitan Museum of Art. She held my hand as if I were a small boy. She wanted me to see one of Van Gogh's sunflower paintings. She whispered into my ear, "If you look at a painting long enough, you can disappear in its beauty. Your father told me that once, a long time ago." She'd never spoken to me like this before. "You can be anything and go anywhere you want, Oliver." I was still speechless. "The spirit of your father lives in beautiful paintings. He's alive in them because he was everything beautiful and good."

She held me close to her as we strolled the long hallways. Finally we sat in front of Leutze's painting of *Washington Crossing the Delaware*.

She looked deep into my eyes as if searching for something. "I know you hate me. Oliver, but I love you so much. I only wanted to improve our life. I didn't mean to take your father away." She pointed to the painting of *Washington* and his men on a dilapidated-looking row boat crossing the Delaware while massive waves come toward them.

"See how brave President Washington looks in the painting? So steadfast and determined. Oliver, in life, even if the boat you're rowing hits massive waves, you must remain brave."

"Okay, Mom," I said.

"Do you hate me very much, Oliver?"

"Yes," I told her, "Some days."

"Do you hate me today?"

I looked at her, my mother, waiting for my answer, afraid that I'd tell her the truth.

"No, Mom," I lied to her, "I don't hate you today."

"You adored your father, Oliver," she said, "You never adored me. But you adored your father."

We stood in silence. I was drowning in the river of my mother's guilt.

"I forgive you, Mom," I said. I wanted to mean it, but I knew that she knew better. I took her by the hand. "I love you, Mom," I told her. Then I led her out of the Met and brought her home.

A few years later, after she received my father's Vietnam War diary, things, as they say, *went up in smoke.*

Things grew so bad that June and I slept with fire extinguishers in our beds, and toward the end, took turns sleeping so that we could stand watch.

When Mother wasn't setting fires, she talked about what her life should have been. She should have married that nice German man, she told us, who said she reminded him of Katherine Hepburn. They would have been rich, she said, and lived in Seabrook, Connecticut, probably next door to

Katherine Hepburn's family.

June and I had no idea who or what she was talking about. Still later, Mother decided to live only for June and me, hardly spending a cent on herself. Money, she insisted, was the root of all evil. She refused to buy herself new clothes and ate only meager portions of her meals. Since we each had a college trust fund, when the time came, June went to Barnard College so that she could stay at home and take care of Mom. When my turn came, however, I went off to Boston College to major in art History.

Thank you all for listening to my unbelievably fucked up life story.

Thank you, Oliver, group applause, group applause, group applause.

The truth was, I felt like I would never be able to speak about my life so openly.

When the meeting was over, Rosa left hurriedly. I followed her out as quickly as I could. I wanted to see more of her, maybe talk to her. However, Ralph was right by my side.

As we walked onto the street Ralph spoke.

"That was a great meeting. It goes to show, Oliver, that everyone needs love and that everyone has his own pain."

"Yeah, I guess," I said. I saw Rosa up the street. She crossed Ninety-Fifth Street and was heading south.

"What's *your* pain, Oliver?"

"Ralph, please don't look at me like I'm some pathetic puppy dog. And please don't stand in my way. It makes me nervous. Look Ralph, I need to take a walk alone. I'm grumpy. Tell June I will be home in a while."

"But I was hoping we could hang out a bit, you know, take a walk, get some coffee at Starbucks. We could split a white chocolate chip pumpkin-artichoke-loganberry muffin? Maybe talk about the castration book? What do you say?"

"Nah, I need to be alone. Thanks Ralph." My eyes were scanning for Rosa.

"Come on."

"No, really, Ralph, I want to be alone." I was losing sight of Rosa.

"Come on," he said. His expression was full of longing and supplication.

"You and June need some time alone," I said. Couldn't he see I was trying to get rid of him? Fuck!

"Come on. Please?"

"Ralph, no."

"Oliver. I have to tell you something."

"What? I want to go. I don't mean to be rude," I said.

"I masturbate," Ralph said. I was stunned. *What the hell*, I thought.

"Ralph. I have to go now."

"I wanted to be out with it. It's okay. June and I hear your bed board hitting the wall like a freight train more than three times a night and, well, we know you masturbate, a lot. It's okay. I do, too." Ralph put a tender, brotherly hand on my shoulder. I took a deep breath and looked away. I couldn't speak for what seemed a very long time. I turned to him. I still couldn't speak.

"You okay, Oliver?" Ralph asked.

"I have to go. I want to talk to Rosa, let me go. Go home to June," I said.

"Really. Rosa? Go for it! Why didn't you say so? Well, okay, Good idea," Ralph finally said. "And make sure you knock when you come home!" Ralph laughed and ran across Lexington Avenue.

"That's gross, Ralph. That's my sister!"

He screamed at me from across the street, and everyone turned to look: "Love is not gross, Oliver! And I love your sister! I LOVE HER!" He shouted to the autumn sky and laughed with joy. He was so loud I turned and started to walk up the street, pretending not to know him.

I waited to be sure Ralph was out of sight and then I ran

up Lex, hoping to still find Rosa. I wanted to bump into her causally. But she was nowhere in sight.

I looked at the clear sky, my stomach in knots. People passed me, and I kept my head down.

As I looked for signs of Rosa, the New York sidewalks were illuminated with colorful lights from restaurants and stores; people talking in the cafés were wearing sweaters and drinking cappuccinos.

I walked down Second Avenue to Eighty-Sixth, then crossed to First. I repeated my path twice. Still no sign of Rosa. I headed toward East End Avenue. I wanted to sit by the East River and think.

As I passed the Mansion diner on the corner of Eighty-Sixth and York, I saw Rosa sitting alone eating a dessert glass filled with red JELL-O and taking quick sips from a mug. Seeing her eat JELL-O was reassuring. If we became an item, maybe I wouldn't have to hide the fact that I like fried Spam on toast. I stopped for a brief moment to look at her. She took a mouthful of the JELL-O and examined a chart, keeping the spoon in her mouth. She checked things off and wrote quickly. She must be working on some sort of project. I wanted to go in and talk to her, but I couldn't. I felt insecure and awkward. Would she think I was stalking her? I walked on and then stopped. I thought about walking back to the diner and asking if she wanted to have coffee with me. But I couldn't. I walked a full block. I stopped again. Why not go in, right? I had nothing to lose. I could sit alone, get a cup of coffee, and if she saw me, she saw me; I could act like I hadn't seen her. I turned around again. I peeked in the diner's window. She was getting up to leave, counting cash for her check. I tried to pull back before she saw me looking at her, but it was too late. *Damn!* I began a nervous shuffle. I gave her a sad grimace. She smiled back and waved hello and continued to count her money for the bill. *Oh, well*, I thought, I'd made fool of myself. I headed down to the East River. It was a dumb idea, anyway.

I was a full block away when I heard her voice, "Hey! Pepper!"

I turned around and Rosa strutted toward me, "Wait up, Pepper! Why didn't you wait?" Her lips were full and pink and they turned up at the top like a small rose bud.

"I didn't want to bother you; you looked busy," I said.

"I'm always busy. Some dingbat teacher called in sick, and I'm trying to get someone. And well, here you are."

"Yes. Here I am."

She laughed. "I need teachers badly. So what do think?"

"At that school? Really?"

"You want to give it a try?"

"Do I have to make the decision now?"

"Well, I'm desperate."

"I need time to think about it. Okay?."

"Where are you going now?" she asked.

"I was going to the river to sit."

"Want some company?" she asked. A police car rushed past us, blue lights flashing and siren going full hilt; the sound jarred Rosa.

"My nerves are a wreck!" she said.

We walked to East End Avenue in silence. The street was dark, except for the street lights that intermingled our shadows. When we came to the park, we found a bench and sat. I looked at the lights of the Roosevelt Island Bridge, and for a moment, I thought of a few weeks ago when I'd slugged Hank. I thought about giving him a call. Poor Hank. I sighed, and Rosa laughed nervously to herself. We sat in silence. She glanced over at me.

"You look worried. It all gets better. You have to go back to the start of things," Rosa said.

"The start of what?"

"Your life. You have to recognize the shit that went down and go to the start and begin again."

JOHN C. PICARDI

"Trust me, I don't want to do that."

"Who the hell does?" She laughed robustly, and then she was silent for a moment. She looked at me and smirked.

"The meetings help, and so do the drugs." She roared with laughter.

"Drugs?" I asked.

"Prescription drugs. Anti-depressants. Everyone is on them nowadays."

"Do they help the cravings?"

"Hell no, nothing does."

"I want to drink so badly."

"It's tough. I'm new to the program, too, only four months. But I'm glad. I feel I have more clarity."

"Me, too. It's very clear how much I like to drink," I said.

She laughed. "You're a funny guy. I like that. I think you'd be good where I work. It's tough, but a sense of humor makes it much easier."

"Okay, let's make a deal … If you agree to go to a movie with me, I'll teach one day at your school."

"No dice! I don't make deals like that." She gave me a dark look that made me feel like I was a horny, menacing old dog. She had me pegged. I didn't want to screw this up. I was enjoying being with someone new. I was sick of June and Ralph, day after day.

"I'm sorry," I said, "that was inappropriate."

"It's okay. Not that I wouldn't go to the movies with you, but I don't barter for my time."

"I understand." I smiled the best I could and looked away from her. What an ass I was!

"Look, I have to split. I'm glad we had the chance to talk." She held out her hand, and I shook it. Her hands, for her size, were surprisingly large and thin. Her nails were painted a frosty pink. I looked into her eyes; they reflected the lights, and when she smiled slightly, the slight space between her two front teeth made her more alluring.

"Can I have your phone number? Could I call you for work?" she asked.

"Sure," I said. I felt scared giving her my number. I didn't think I could teach at her school; however, I really liked her and, for the first time in these past gloomy weeks, she had made me feel something good and real.

I gave her my phone number, and she scribbled it down on her clipboard. She shoved the board back into her bag with difficulty. "I carry too much shit." She stood, and I remained seated.

"I'll be in touch. If not, I'll see you tomorrow night at the meeting," she said. She walked away from me. God, her figure was perfect—small but an ideal form for a woman.

She disappeared into the night, and I felt more alone than I ever had. I wished she had stayed with me.

FIFTEEN

I lay in bed staring at the ceiling. I had put a pillow behind my bed board to make sure it didn't bang against the wall anymore. I then contemplated whether to eat a bagel loaded with cream cheese or an English muffin thickly spread with peanut butter. Or maybe I should sleep directly through to lunchtime and order pizza. I listened to the rainstorm outside, along with the noisy confusion that comes with a rainy day in New York: an overabundance of car horns and the extensive cries of bus engines.

The phone by my bed rang, startling me. I sat up, thinking, in my warped mind, that it had to be Miss Macey calling to beg me to come back and teach at Bolton.

"Hello," I said, prepared to hear Miss Macey's voice on the other end of the line.

"Look, I'm sorry for calling so early, but I'm desperate. I need a teacher. Can you come in today? I need someone for a few weeks. No teacher wants to come here."

"Hello? Who is this?"

"It's Rosa. Come on. Give it a shot. I need you. I'll return the favor. I'll hold your hand at a meeting some night." She laughed. "Okay, bad joke, but can you come in anyway?"

"I don't barter for my time," I said.

"Very funny. Please, Oliver, it's not as bad as you may think."

"I've heard nightmares about those schools."

"Are you a teacher or a mouse?"

"I'm a mouse who was a teacher at a privileged girl's school. Okay. I'll come in for … for a few weeks, until you find a steady teacher. Okay?"

"Be here at eight. I have a parent here now. See you in a few." Rosa hung up. There was a knock at my bedroom door.

"Oliver? You up? Who was that who called?" June poked her head into my bedroom.

"I have a teaching job for a few weeks. I met this woman. Well, Ralph of course said something to her, and she probably feels bad for me."

"Why would anyone feel bad for you? Stop all this paranoid nonsense. You found a job, and that's terrific, Oliver. Ralph!" June shouted down the hallway. "Oliver has found a job—someone he met at the AA meeting!"

I heard Ralph coming down the hallway. He stood next to June at the door of my room and said, "It's a start. Congratulations, Oliver! What did I tell you? Everything works out for the best. It's all in the attitude. The grace of God and the miracles performed each day."

"Ralph, come on; you planned this entire thing. I'm not a complete idiot."

He came fully into my bedroom, sat next to me, and hugged me.

"It doesn't matter. It all worked out," he said. I immediately stood up. The wind and rain outside picked up in velocity. I put on my best discontented expression.

"We're all rooting for you!" Ralph said. And he left the room. June winked at me and followed Ralph.

I laid out my navy suit, my shirt and tie, ran a hot shower and stood under the pulsating water as it ran down my back. I thought of Rosa. I put VO-5 in my hair, pulled on my rubber galoshes, reassured myself that the unopened letter from Beth was in my pocket, skipped my oatmeal, and split. June called after me: "Mom and Dad would be proud of you!"

During the walk to school I thought about when June and

I were very small. Our parents took us to the Hamptons in a red Mustang convertible they'd rented in the City. My mother's musky perfume intermingled with my Dad's spicy aftershave, and the smell made me feel safe.

I poked my head between the bucket seats and noticed they were holding hands. I knew they loved each other.

That day, for some reason, it occurred to me to ask, "How did you fall in love?"

They both laughed and said, at the same time, "Chanel No. 5."

"Huh?"

"Your father's first words to me were, 'Chanel No. 5.' "

"I was at a jazz club downtown. I smelled Chanel No. 5 and turned around, looking for the gal who had it on. I saw a beautiful woman standing alone a few feet away. I walked over to her and swept her off her feet. The first thing I said to her was, 'Chanel No. 5.' "

"I was so impressed. But to tell you the truth," my mother said, blushing. She spoke directly to our father, "I chased you. I followed you around all night. I didn't think you would ever look my way." She leaned closer to my father, her fingers tickling his ear. He laughed, and my mother smiled. "I thought your father looked like a movie star. Like Rock Hudson," she said, "I adored him. Your father was so good looking. He and his cornflower blue eyes, his beautiful black hair, his broad shoulders and oh, that sharp, perfect nose!" She tapped the end of my Dad's nose.

My father wrinkled his nose at her.

"I'm driving!" he said, giggling.

June held a can of orange soda between her legs, "Tell us more!"

So my mother continued, "Your father had a great gentleness about him, a softness. Most men don't have that.

He made sure I got home safely that night. He always, always wanted to be sure I was safe and happy. I thought he was the most sophisticated man in world!" She laughed and blushed a little.

"And your mother made me feel needed. Besides, she looked like a movie star. Rita Hayworth, maybe!"

"Rita Hayworth?" My mother was frowning. "She was so vulgar."

"Louise! Rita Hayworth was gorgeous in her day. Did you ever see that old movie, *Gilda*?" my father asked. He looked over at me and winked, his smile confident. I gave him a wide smile back. I loved that they loved each other.

"Who is Rita Hayworth?" June asked, and Mom and Dad sniggered.

The rest of the ride I looked out at fields of towering and sturdy corn plants while sipping the rest of June's orange soda; she slept in a curled ball next to me. As my father drove, he sang happily the song from *Gilda*; my mother snapped her fingers and hummed along with him.

> Put the blame on Mame, boys, put the blame on mame …

If that wasn't enough indication for my loving mother that my Dad was a raving closet queen, then she must have been deaf, dumb, and blind.

Still, I am absolutely, one hundred percent certain that there was genuine love in our family until, of course, my Dad couldn't suppress his sexuality any longer. Our own private earthquake hit our family hard, and it wasn't Mame's fault. There was no one to put the blame on. Except when it came to my father's death.

SIXTEEN

Multiple choice.

1. The absolutely, positively horrifying experience of teaching at Rosa's school for those two weeks was worse than:
a) My mother's pyromania
b) The circumstances of my father's death
c) My former wife's nymphomania
d) My best friend's cuckolding me
e) Being fired from the finest teaching position in the City
f) Having to spend so much time with Ralph
g) All of the above

The correct answer is G.

2. The best solution to get out of teaching at Rosa's school was:
a) Suicide by hanging
b) Suicide by gunshot
c) Suicide by self-immolation
d) All of the above

The correct answer is D.

Remember the worst nightmare you've ever experienced.

Now double that terror. Still, I did not commit suicide. I was learning to trust myself more each day. Learning who you are is called clarity. Learning to love yourself is a line from a Whitney Houston song.

Either way, it's a way to find the greatest love of all. Well, that and learning to express your feelings without fearing that other men will laugh and point at you.

During classes, I read the *Castration* book. I read one section after a student called me a "fucking weak motherfucking faggot, cock-sucking pussy." The book says men are afraid of other men viewing them as weak. Men go to great lengths, even so far as to sacrifice who they really are, all in the name of *not* coming off as weak to other men. This is why most men are repulsed by gay men; they view gay men as women, i.e., the stereotypical image of submission, weakness, the receiver of the penis—the human sword. The book says weakness is the only way to open your heart and let in love. Indulge in your weakness. Celebrate it!

The book is entertaining and so I sat and read it while my students, all boys aged twelve to thirteen, pitched paper balls at my head and called me a variety of names that I tried not to pay attention to, because if I did, I'd be in a high security mental institution receiving treatments for primary identity issues. The students said the most awful things to me with such utter conviction and indelible hatred, there was no doubt that these words came from the very core of their beings. Plainly put, they hated their lives. Bluntly speaking, they hated white people with a passion, and I can't say I blamed them.

According to these boys, I have a variety of names: faggot, queer, nigga, bitch, ho, whitey, motherfucker, da Man, fuck-head, cracker, zebra, and shay whitey. When they want to ask me something, they address me by any of the above names, always preceded by "Yo!"

That first day I arrived at the school soaking wet. The wind was strong. It blew my rain coat wide open and my umbrella inside out. I wanted to kill someone because I wanted my old life and my flask back. The school is a cement building with two fenced-in playgrounds alongside. It looks like a satellite building from Rikers Island. It was that depressing. I couldn't imagine how the children felt.

I fully expected to be clobbered over the head, have my liver cut out of me, and then have my dead body pimped out by the local necrophilia specialist.

All for Rosa.

I entered the school, showed my identification at the security desk, and walked up the stairwell to the third floor. I felt Beth's letter in my breast suit pocket. At least Beth was with me in a way.

On the stairwell doors and walls was written in black and red marker the usual various vulgar words: fuck off, eat shit, motherfucker school, this school sucks, your Mama, your brother, your sister, sit on my face, fuck me, fuck you, fuck your mother.

I was tempted to add my favorite, *fuck off and die.*

I continued up the stairs, and a young boy of twelve came running down. He stopped and looked at me, and I nodded hello to him.

"Good Morning," I said.

The boy eyed at me with gross animosity, "What the fuck are you looking at chicken head? I'll put three bullets in your face," and continued down the stairs.

I was about to return back home—after all there are plenty of Rosas in the sea—when, wouldn't you know it, Rosa came running down the stairs toward me. Her hair was flying wildly in wavy curls, her face red with fury, her breasts practically bouncing in my face.

"Hi! Hey, did you see a boy come down this way?"

"Yes, he passed me and called me a chicken head. What does that mean?"

"It means you suck dick," Rosa said. She shrugged her shoulders. "I'll deal with that kid later."

We continued to climb the stairs, and two more boys came running up toward us. They wore extra-large sweatshirts, baseball caps put on backwards, and jeans that hung low on their hips.

One boy shouted at the other boy ahead of him, "I'm gonna put the smack down on your ass!"

They were both so fast and quick, their running startled me. I stood back as one boy passed by. Rosa grabbed the other boy by his shirttail, and she lost her balance. I caught her in my arms. She felt tough, firm, hard, very sexy ... and I didn't want to let go.

"I'm going to kick your ass, nigga!" the first boy yelled down to the second. Rosa then told me to hold the second boy by his arm, which I did hesitantly.

He whispered, "Get your fucking cracker hands off me, shay whitey. I'll kick your ass."

Rosa chased the first boy down the stairwell and screamed after him, "Manuel, get back here right now!"

I firmly gripped the second boy, and my body trembled. I'd never held a child in that manner before, and I didn't like it.

"Manuel! Get up here now! NOW!" Rosa's voice echoed throughout the stairwell.

Rosa came back up the stairs holding Manuel. She held both boys against the wall and leaned her small frame full force into them. Their eyes stared blankly like those of a couple of dead fish.

Manuel, trying to divert Rosa's attention, pointed at me, "Who dat sorry ass man?"

Rosa pushed them both against the wall with even more force. "I'm not joking with you guys! You're both supposed to be in the cafeteria with your class until your teacher comes to get you. Now go back down."

The boys turned around and started to run back down the stairs, laughing. "Damn, Miss Rosa, chalk it, will ya? Chill!"

"WALK!" Rosa screamed after them. She ran her hand through her hair and let out a dog-tired sigh; she then hit her forehead.

"Damn, Oliver! You have to go to the cafeteria and get your class and bring them up to the classroom. You're after Mrs. Hadley's class. Ask for help. I have to get back to the office."

"Is Franco here?" I asked. He would make this ordeal easier for me.

"He's been out sick. Lord only knows when he'll be back. Talk later." Rosa left my side and scuttled up the stairs.

I descended the stairs with a worried sigh.

In the cafeteria I found absolute pandemonium. The students, most of them boys of multiracial backgrounds, were leaning over tables, shouting, slapping, swearing, and spitting. All the while teachers and para-professionals were grabbing at students and trying to control them. The noise was all-consuming.

One boy passed me with his breakfast tray and gave me a once-over. "You fucking homo," he said.

Then Miss Lancer, the science teacher, with her slow eyes and quivering lips, came to my side. Her hair was a golden brown, coiled and flowing. She gave me a lumpish look. Her voice sounded like an out of tune piano.

"Your name?" she asked me.

"Mr. Pepper."

"Hi there. I'm Miss Lancer, but you can call me Lucy. This is your class. Lovely, aren't they? Little darlings. Don't let them get to you too much, honey-buns. You got kids?"

"No."

"You married?

"No.

"Gay?"

"No." What was with all the questions? I thought.

"Oh, well, if you need any help, let me know. Good luck. And look, baby, you look like a deer in headlights. If you show these kids you're scared shitless of them—pardon my French—you'll be totally fucked, got me?" Miss Lancer walked away and, as she did, she eyed me up and down and then shouted to Hector to come assist me. He was my para-professional.

"Hector, get over here, help this guy out!" she screamed.

"LINE UP!" Hector barked at the six boys who would be in my class.

"Easy there, crack-head. No need to shout, damn nigga!" one of the boys said to Hector. Then the boy came over and stood very close in front of me. His big expressive brown eyes looked up at mine.

"I'm Anthony. Who the fuck are you?" Anthony was a small-framed boy with a shaved head—his eyes were a bit crossed—and he had a pug nose. He held a cup of berry yogurt.

"I'm Mr. Pepper. I'm your teacher for today."

"What the fuck is that kind of name? I don't mean to be rude or anything but that name is whack."

"Please don't use that language. It's vulgar."

"What the fuck does vulgar mean?" Anthony asked.

I didn't speak. I turned and walked onward, following Hector, who had all the boys in line. They were proceeding to the classroom.

As we walked up the stairs, the six boys shouted at me, "What the fuck is your name? Hey, Mr. Whitey teacher, what the fuck is your name? Hey, nigga, I'm talking to you!" Along with the universally popular *faggot, homo, and queer.*

The boys slapped, punched, kicked, and nudged one another until Hector stopped and threw a boy against the wall; they hooted, howled, and clapped. It was like being at a basketball game at Madison Square Garden.

As the class climbed the stairs and crossed into the hallway, I saw a big bold sign with the red letters "EXIT" above a door.

Leave, run out, go, and never return.

Hector stopped at the classroom door.

Then the reason for my being there at all walked toward me with her big, wide, sexy, inviting smile. "How's it going, Mr. Pepper?" Rosa asked. "Is the class behaving?"

"Yes, fine."

"Good!" She turned to the class, "If I hear any complaints today, you're all in major trouble, you understand?"

They all laughed at her.

"You think it's funny? Roberto, take your hat off. Now!"

"I'm cold," Roberto shouted back.

"Take it off or its mine!" Rosa screeched.

Roberto took his hat off and said in a low voice, "Fucking bitch."

When Rosa heard this, she ran after him and grabbed him by his shirt and pulled him close to her face, "I'm calling your father, and you will repeat to him what you said to me!"

"Get your hands off me, bitch. Don't be getting in my lunch, fuck."

"What are you going to do? Huh? Huh?" My ears ached. But all the same, it was very sexy and hot. She was one bad-ass lady.

Rosa looked at me and told me if there were any more problems to call her on the classroom phone. She dragged Roberto to the office.

And there were more problems, endless problems. I was passive and numb and wanted to die my first hour there. But I did like one thing.

After Rosa left me with the class, Anthony said to me, "Yum yum gimmie sum, she's got a fine butt on her!"

I tried to act authoritative, but I'm not a very good actor, and besides it was the truth. All the same I was the teacher; I needed to set an example. So I shamefacedly turned my head away from Anthony so he wouldn't see my wholehearted concurrence and I looked out the window at the closed-shaded Bolton across the way. A longing, pitiful feeling consumed me.

SEVENTEEN

I tried to teach the kids about Monet. I brought in a recycled lecture from Bolton. I made worksheets and brought in a few prints. The boys had absolutely no interest in what I was saying. I gave up.

Then Franco walked in. I sat up and beamed.

"You're in this class? Where have you been? I'm glad to see you."

"I was out sick." The boys shouted obscenities at him. He sat down, put his face in his hands, and curled up his lips. He looked over at the other boys when they wouldn't stop, and yelled, "Shut the fuck up, motherfucker." They all laughed, whistled and howled.

I went on about Monet.

Franco looked up at me and asked me if Monet was a "French dude." When I was about to reply, I received a spit ball on my forehead, accompanied by roars of laughter.

I couldn't take the humiliation anymore, so I packed my lesson away. I sat at the desk while the students beat one another up and called me a "fucking faggot." I think one kid tried to smoke some crack in class. Hector said something like, "Put the crack pipe away." I don't know; I might have been dreaming because I slept for an hour at the desk.

I was spending my days waiting for Rosa to appear in the class. I only saw her for a minute in the morning. When I was not thinking of Rosa, I thought of Beth's letter by my bed. I couldn't bring myself to open and read it. Then, when I couldn't tolerate the thoughts of that letter, I wondered what June would make for dinner. A few of her last meals had given me terrible indigestion. I'd been having the most awful burping fits after eating two of her standard weekly meals. I usually had no problem with her Texas style meatloaf or noodle casserole with tuna, peas, and pineapple. But my burping offended June terribly. Ralph told me I needed to read Chapter Four. He said my burping was a cover-up for other issues that I wasn't dealing with. I made a face at both of them, rolled my eyes and went to my room to quietly read the book.

"Chapter Four: Showing Emotions through Farting and Burping": More metaphors. Men are fearful of showing emotions, so they do so through expulsions of gas. This is a clear indication of the repulsion men feel about outwardly expressing themselves, so they do so in the most disgusting way possible. This brings to the surface the fear of homosexuality and how it relates to the rectum and mouth, the two main orifices of homosexual sex, e.g., anal and oral sex.

What was going on?

Maybe I was missing Hank. I contemplated calling him. Nah.

Instead I burped.

EIGHTEEN

I took a long look at the classroom. It was a depressing barren space with light puke-green walls. A table in the back was covered with books. I told Rosa I thought the room was depressing. She told me I could paint it if I wanted to, but I would have to do it with my own money and on my own time. I needed to make that classroom more conducive to learning; perhaps that was the reason the kids didn't care. The students' desks were scattered haphazardly, crumpled paper balls on the floor. My desk was gray metal, and on top lay piles of incomplete work sheets. One side of the room was lined with yellow lockers.

I went to the windows and looked across at my old school. There it was, Bolton, in all its glory: brick and sturdy. And there was the window to my old classroom, shade shut tightly, blinded to my new world. I missed some of those girls. But I couldn't face them. I did everything I could to avoid them, even taking an alternate route home.

What the hell, maybe I would ask Franco to help me paint this lousy looking classroom. I trusted him to help me.

When the boys entered the class, they went straight to their lockers, pushing and shoving one another.

They murmured, "Fuck off," to me as they passed.

I returned their greeting with, "Good morning!"

I overheard one student say that I was nothing but a "rich cracker" and he hoped I would die. Or he may have called me a *Ritz Cracker*, I'm not sure.

Again, I did nothing, I sat through the bedlam in amazement, arms crossed.

After school, I asked Franco if he would paint the classroom with me. He looked at me with a brooding expression and shrugged.

"You pay me?" he asked.

"I bought you an iPod!" I said.

"You said that was a gift!"

"Okay. You're right. I'll pay you."

On the walk home, I bought some paint, brushes, and rollers. I picked out a light blue.

June thought what I was doing was great; however, she could be negative about it and to my surprise, a little snotty. She told me a friend had related a tragic story about a teacher who taught in an "undesirable school." The teacher's father was a CEO for an investment company on Wall Street. This teacher could have had anything he wanted in life, but his passion was to work with disadvantaged kids. He had mentioned to his students that he came from money and that he was at the school because he cared for them. One day, his former students came to his house. He let them in and they tied him up, cut him all over his body, robbed him, and finally killed him.

Ralph warned June to back off and not tell me such things. I was a man and could make my own decisions. They shouldn't treat me like their feeble son.

On the nights June and Ralph got on my nerves I would go to bed early and hope for good dreams. Sometimes my hoping worked. Once I dreamed that Rosa and I had sex all over my apartment. It was fast, furious, and animalistic. In the morning I remembered thinking I might be in love with her. I felt like an adolescent.

Anyway, the boys began to fight over a padlock. "Motherfucker, get you hands off my shit."

"Stop this bullshit!" I yelled. For a brief moment they howled and hooted at me but eventually went back to their usual routine.

One boy pushed another boy, and he went flying across the desks. The class began to egg the boys on to fight. I stood frozen. I was not going to get accidentally punched. No way. Hector took one of the boys and carried him to his seat. The other boys laughed. As they sat, they turned their desks any way they pleased, ignored me, and chatted amongst themselves.

It occurred to me that I didn't know any of their names, only Anthony and Roberto. And Franco, who was mild-mannered and sad-looking. Sometimes he talked to me, and other times he acted as if he didn't know me.

NINETEEN

Yesterday a student told Rosa another student had a gun. I was scared out of my wits. The police came, and the school had a "lockdown." The boys were very excited about it. I wanted to quit, but I couldn't. I didn't care what the book says about the male ego; I couldn't show Rosa I was a complete wimp. I acted pretty brave for the most part, even though I didn't leave the classroom all day. When the boys went to lunch, I peed in the classroom sink. I had no choice. It was either that or take my chances at being gunned down on the way to the men's room.

It turned out no one had a gun. It was only a knife or some kind of sword.

After one of the boys blew out an enormous fart that made the classroom smell like the depths of hell and the windows went flying open, Franco approached me.

"I'm not like these boys. I'm here because I stabbed my teacher with a pencil. I was angry because my father gone away in prison. I only stabbed my teacher in her hand. They say I can be angry and shit. But I'm good. I'm going to get out of this school."

I believed him. He wanted to do the right thing and his hope and claims of worthiness tore at me. I wanted the best for this kid.

Franco sat down and placed his desk in the front of the classroom. He looked at me with anticipation. It was math period. I looked over at the four boys who were now playing with a small computer game. Hector stood over them.

"It's math period. Take out your books," I said.

"Fuck off!" someone shouted. That proclamation was followed by laughter.

"Can you teach me math?'" Franco asked me. His voice was low.

"Sure, of course." I found the teacher's edition of the math book. I sat next to him and leaned over his desk. I wrote down multiplication problems from the book. He kept confusing his numbers: eights were threes, and fours were sevens. The other boys looked over at us every so often and went back to their computer game.

"Can you see this clearly?" I asked.

"Yes. I can see it," he said.

"But that's an eight."

"I know."

"But you wrote down a three," I said.

"Fuck this. I want to draw." Franco shut his Math book. "Teach me how to draw something."

"Like what?" I asked.

"I don't know. A lion. You know how to draw a lion?"

"I can try," I said. I was a lousy artist, but I did my best, and Franco followed along with me. It was pretty clear the Metropolitan Museum of Art was not going to call either one of us any time soon, but I felt like I was a teacher. I was master of all subjects.

Well, I pretended to be.

TWENTY

I waited for Franco for a half hour after school. I figured he was pulling a *no show*. I put all the desks in the middle of the classroom and covered them in a canvas the janitor had given me.

I was washing down the walls when Franco came in.

"Wassup dawg?" he said. He carried a radio and plugged it into his iPod.

"Did you tell your Aunt you were going to be helping me?"

"Yup."

On his radio, some rap star sang about a dirty ho (that means whore) and her dirty pimp "doing the nasty" doggie style in a parking lot at a *White Castle* burger joint. The song played on and on.

I did not approve. But I let him listen to his music as long as he worked.

Together we washed down the walls and painted the room.

Then Franco gave me all kinds of grief because I wouldn't allow him up on the ladder.

"I only want to be up high. Why won't you let me go up, Dog, share the high?" he pleaded.

"Stop bugging me. We have a lot of work to do."

"Shit. You one bossy white ass." He went back to painting, dancing a bit in place as the rap music went on. I smiled. I liked this kid.

After a while, he stopped and looked up at me.

"If you try and teach these mother-fucking kids something, maybe they listen to your white honky ass," Franco said.

"I don't know. They don't listen to anything I say. And stop that swearing," I said.

"Shit. Why you come here?"

Franco was right. What the hell was I doing at this school?

Was I a dedicated teacher? Did I care about these disturbed boys? Or was I that hard-up and desperate to prove to Rosa, the woman I thought I was falling in love with, that I wasn't a quitter, a first-class loser?

The answer was, yes, I was that hard-up. But I did care, a little. I was painting the classroom wasn't I?

Was that enough, though?

I had visions of old movies. They ran through my head: *To Sir with Love, Goodbye Mr. Chips, The Prime of Miss Jean Brodie,* and *The Dead Poets' Society.* The boys would grow to love and adore me. I would change them.

"These kids—they know you don't care for them. No one care," Franco said. He dunked his roller in the paint.

"You said that the first time I met you. I care," I said. I looked down at him. Paint dripped off my roller and onto the floor. I stepped off the ladder and cleaned up my spill. The scent of the paint was thick and chemically noxious. My insides churned.

"Shit, you don't care! You sit there on your ass. You don't care. No one care." Franco spoke with conviction as he rolled paint on the wall. He sniffled and wiped his nose. The blue paint made a streak across his face. I looked right at him.

"We did math together. I'm painting the classroom, aren't I?"

"Shit, who care about some damn room being painted?"

"I want to make it nice for you and the other students," I said.

"We need a teacher. No nice room. You gonna pay me, right?"

"Yes. Of course," I said. I looked down at him as he busily painted. There was a glumness and longing in his face that made me ache inside.

"Are you mad at me, Franco?"

"I know what's going to happen. You're here helping the poor black kids, and when you get sick of it, you go and we never see you again. It happens all the time. Shit you white people famous for that shit. It's all to make you feel good about being snotty rich people."

"Do you really think these kids care if I go or not?"

"I don't fucking know."

"Maybe it's you who cares if I go."

"I ain't saying that. Did I say that? Shit."

"It's okay to tell me if you feel that way."

"I'm not talking about no feelings."

"We're a lot alike, you and I."

"I'm black. You white. We nothing alike."

"We are more alike than you know."

"Shut the hell up. I'm trying to paint. Damn! You talk too much. Talk. Talk. Talk. All you want to do is talk. Damn. You messed up."

I smiled to myself and went back to painting.

When we were done, it was about eight pm. I gave Franco my cell phone to call his mother. He laughed.

"I told you, I got no mother. I live with my aunt. Why you a'ks me about my mother? Shit! She left when I was small. I don't even remember her. I got an Aunt Ethel. My father's sister. She's working. She don't mind where I at. She don't like me. She say I'm like my father. *Trouble* she call me. You don't listen to my shit. Damn."

"I'm taking you home anyway," I insisted.

"I can take the train home. I ain't scared of nothing.'"

"I'm taking the train home with you," I said.

"You ain't taking nothing wit me. You ain't the boss of me."

"I'm not letting you walk in the streets alone at this hour, so I guess I am the boss of you," I said. He laughed at me.

"You are one silly motherfucker. You're like a pushy whitey to say he's the boss of the black boy." He laughed even more.

"Franco, you shouldn't talk like that. Come on; let's go."

We rode on the train in silence. He sat away from me as if he were ashamed.

After the train ride, Franco insisted I leave him, and I said I was going to walk him to his house. He mumbled something about me being a stupid *cracker*.

"You gonna get your white ass kicked there for sure," he said.

The neighborhood where he lived was in a cluster of massive project buildings built in the late 1960s. Graffiti was painted on the side of the buildings and on the front doors; in the distance I could hear the thump thump of rap music. People stood in groups under the yellow lights that surrounded the buildings. I had seen too many movies about this neighborhood, and I was scared out of my wits. The occasional police cruiser passed; its alarm sounded only for a quick second, warning all those around. One car drove past us, stopped. The group of people inside looked us up and down, laughed, and sped off. The thump thump thump of rap music blasted out of their car.

I could only imagine what was going to happen to me.

I was the only white guy in the neighborhood. The boys at the school had told me on several occasions, *In my hood you'd get your ass kicked cause you got a white ass, motherfucker.*

Franco's building was on a side street; it was a small brownstone. There was no one around. The street lights glared brightly. Garbage barrels were chained to an iron gate in front of his house.

"You can go now," he said.

"I want to see you go inside. I'm not leaving you on the street."

"What is your problem? Shit," he said.

"You said no one cares. I care. Okay?"

"You are one crazy motherfucker." Franco laughed to himself.

We walked up to the front of the gate that blocked the front door. And as we did, a woman swung open the iron gate. It made a piercing sound that raked my ears.

Aunt Ethel started screaming at Franco. She held a small baby girl, who was crying. Aunt Ethel was buxom, pneumatic, and had a powerful, intimidating presence. I was scared of her. I can only imagine how Franco felt. She was angry. Her hair, which was braided into small beautifully beaded cornrows, swung from left to right as she spoke. She had a fierce look in her eyes.

"I told you, Franco, you had to watch Cantrice! I gotta work. You think I'm playing games here? Do you? When I say you be home to watch Cantrice, you be home! Where you been?! And who the hell are you?" She looked me up and down.

"I'm his teacher; he was helping me paint our classroom."

"Paint? What he doing that for? This boy, he nothing but trouble, you can't be taking him away. Franco, you get your ass in here before I whoop it."

"He gonna pay me Aunt Ethel," Franco said. I handed Franco forty bucks. His Aunt grabbed it out of his hands.

"I warn you for the last time, Franco. I'm having you live with me only for my brother. You start acting up with your shit, you ain't coming wit me when I leave here. I'm going to Chicago. I'm telling you the truth. I am going, so you best listen to me! I am going, and you best hope you do better, if not, you not coming nowhere. God knows your Mama had the good sense to leave both of you. Damn fool your father is.

My Mama put up with his trouble all her life, and I'm telling you now I ain't putting up with any of your trouble. I am tired, boy. I am tired!"

She handed Cantrice to Franco, and she kissed her goodbye. She spoke softly to her.

"You be good baby. Mama be home soon," she said. Aunt Ethel then looked at me.

"You heard me warn him, Mr. Teacher. He mess up, he not staying with me. I have my own life to live and my own child now." She walked off.

I looked up at Franco, who was now holding Cantrice.

"Sorry Franco. You should have told me. Bring the baby inside. It's too cold out here for her."

Franco went into the house.

" 'Bye, Pepper," he said.

Franco left the apartment door open. I went up to shut it. I peeked inside. It was an old but clean space. Large piles of *People* and *Ebony* magazines lay stacked by a big easy chair. One large photo of Cantrice was on a small table. There was a strong scent of pine cleanser. I could see Franco's reflection in a mirror in the hallway. He stood very still, holding Cantrice as she cried. His eyes looked sullen and they blinked quickly as he bounced her in his arms.

I shut the door. I ached from the depths of my gut as I walked to the train.

TWENTY-ONE

The next day in the freshly painted classroom I was determined to try harder.

"Can I have your attention please?" I said softly. They ignored me.

"The motherfucker is trying to fucking talk!" Franco yelled over to the boys.

"Sorry, Doctor Pepper, that I swore," Franco said to me.

"Shut the fuck up!" one boy yelled over to Franco.

"Hey! Turn your desk around and pay attention to the teacher!" Hector screamed. He took the small computer game out of one of the boy's hands. They all groaned, and they looked at me, eyes squinted, mouths twisted. *God, they hated my white ass.*

Well, that's what one of the boys told me, "We hate your white ass. Get out of here."

"As you know, my name is Mr. Pepper and I have been your teacher for one week and well, we never had a chance to talk." The class roared. They all slapped each other hands, hooted and howled.

"Do you like the new classroom?" Not one student had remarked about the fresh paint. I'd stacked the books, arranged the desks nicely.

"I want to make this classroom more conducive to learning" I said.

"What the hell does that mean? Con-what?" one boy shouted.

I wrote it on the chalkboard. The boys all laughed. I picked up a dictionary and gave it to Franco.

"Look the word up."

"I don't want to," Franco said.

"Because he stupid!" one boy shouted. The class howled. Franco stood and ran out of the classroom.

"Franco!" I called after him. But he was gone. I told Hector to let him go. I looked over at the class.

"Why do you guys do shit like that?" I asked. They went crazy because I said "shit."

"QUIET DOWN!" I shouted. They banged their desks and went wild with laughter.

"What's your name again?" one boy asked.

"Mr. Pepper," I said.

"I'm going to call you motherfucker," another said, and everyone laughed.

"And what should I call you?" I asked the boy.

"You can call me motherfucker, too." The boys all laughed again.

"His name is Toby, Doctor Pepper." This boy's voice was low, cautionary.

"Shut the fuck up you retard!" Toby shouted. Toby was short, round, his skin a cocoa black—eyes bright, slanted, and big. I think he was stoned.

There was another voice; my head turned.

"I'm Anthony; you met me. You remember me?"

"Yes, I remember you, Anthony."

"And what is your name, sir?" I pointed to another boy.

"He called me 'sir'! That's fucking whack!"

The boys laughed again.

"My name is Chris, but everyone calls me Rissy." Rissy had deep red hair and dark freckles all over his face.

"And he's fucked up! He got this Irish-'Rican thing going on. He's one freaky looking motherfucker, isn't he?" Toby said to me.

"Shut the fuck up! I'll kick your nigga ass!" Rissy said.

"Quiet, please," I said. They ignored me.

Hector intervened in the brewing fight between Rissy and Toby. "Both of you stop!" Hector stood in between them, and the boys stopped for a moment.

"You forgot about me? What the fuck is up with that?" one boy in the back yelled.

"I'm sorry. You are?" I asked.

"I'm Bunky." Bunky was small and very thin; his black hair was bristly.

"They call him Bunky because he used to be a fat shit," Toby said.

"Shut up, asshole!" Bunky said.

"But because he's a psycho, they put him on Ritalin, and he got all lanky," Toby continued. Then he sat on my desk.

"Please, sit in your seat," I asked.

"Says who?"

"I'm asking you to please sit in your seat."

"SIT DOWN!" Hector screamed.

"FUCK OFF!" Toby shouted.

Hector grabbed Toby by the collar, and he began to kick like wild, and then the boys scattered from their desks.

Toby screamed, "Fuck off! Fuck off you stupid spic! Fuck off!"

Hector grabbed him and dragged him toward the door, and as he did, Toby's foot hit Bunky's mouth. Bunky began to bleed, and then he dove onto Toby. Toby started punching Bunky.

Meanwhile Hector was still trying to drag Toby away from the fight and out the classroom door.

The other boys clapped with joy and rattled their desks, egging the fight on. The noise was so loud that students in the surrounding classrooms came running out and peaked inside the small window on my classroom door. Some were entering my classroom. I quickly led them out and locked the door.

They screamed for me to unlock the door so they could see the fight.

Rosa then appeared with Franco. She unlocked my classroom with the keys that she wore around her neck and entered.

"Sit down all of you!" Rosa shouted. Franco sat back in his seat.

But the boys continued to fight, and Hector continued to drag Toby toward the door. Bunky's face and the floor were covered in blood.

"Don't worry about it, Mr. Pepper; stay calm," Rosa said. I only nodded at her and wondered how she continued to avoid being a raging drunk. All I could think of was downing a gallon of bourbon.

After Rosa exited with Bunky, Hector was left holding Toby. Franco took paper towels from above the sink and cleaned up the blood. Franco approached my desk.

"I'm a good boy, Mr. Pepper. See how good I am. You think I'm stupid?" Franco said.

"No Franco, I don't think you're stupid," I said quietly.

The other boys commented on the fight.

"Please boys, sit down," I said. I looked over at Roberto, who was nodding off.

"Young man, what is your name?" I asked.

"Roberto. Fuck off," he mumbled.

"Can you boys please try and not use that language?"

"Mr. Pepper, if we behave, will you buy us Burger King?" Anthony asked.

"No!" I barked. But on my lunch break I bought myself a Whopper and read my *Castration* book, the section about men fighting, and what it all meant. We raise our boys to be aggressive, competitive, and insensitive—all in order be war-ready. My new job was kind of like going into a war zone, and I was ready to wave the white flag.

TWENTY-TWO

While I was picking the boys up from the gym, Miss Lancer came over to me. We both watched as the gym teacher helped Anthony out of the basketball net. The other boys had found a ladder on casters, lifted Anthony up, and used him as a basketball.

"Most of these boys are good kids, but they have serious problems. Didn't anyone tell you that? Not everyone can do this." Miss Lancer crossed her arms, one leg forward. She stared at the gym teacher lifting Anthony out.

"I certainly can't," I said.

"It's tough. I lost a former student of mine the other day. Nice girl, believe it or not."

"She was killed?" I asked. I felt my eyes widen for the fifth time that day. I scratched my forehead. Was this real? Was I this naïve to the things that went on in the city in which I lived?

"No, she was sent to Rikers Island. Last year she was trying to get into the 'Bloods,' and she killed someone. Good kid, too."

"The Bloods?" Miss Lancer looked over at my class. They were shouting to her that they could smell her "pussy." I wanted to cry from sheer embarrassment.

"If you boys don't shut up, I'll make you all stand at your desks when I have you for science!"

"Wash that thung!" a boy yelled, and we ignored him.

"Anyway," she continued, "the Bloods is a gang, and to

113

belong you have to slice someone's face and kill them. This girl got into a cab, sliced the driver's face, then told him to go to *Kentucky Fried Chicken*. He did. Then she shot him. When the judge asked her why she did it, she said she didn't like the way the cab driver drove. I'm going to Rikers to see her this weekend. She's eighteen years old."

"Eighteen." I was stunned.

"Your class is pretty bad. Rissy was raped by his stepfather, and the next day he threw a chair at his teacher. That teacher lost an eye. Toby was caught having anal sex with another boy in the bathroom last week. Franco's father is doing a life sentence for murder. The kids pick on him. He's a very sensitive kid."

"Seems kind of hopeless," I said.

"For us or for them?"

I shrugged. "I don't know."

She turned to look at me. "This stuff horrifies you, I can tell. I guess I'm immune to it all. I understand these kids. They trust me. It's about gaining their trust. But I'm telling you, if you're not into being here, you have to tell Rosa, because it gets bad."

"How much worse can it get?"

"Oh, it can get worse."

"Great," I said. I looked at her darkly. She pulled on her ear then scratched it.

"What are you doing for lunch?" she asked. "I go at one."

"I go at twelve."

"Too bad," she said and walked away.

I felt in my suit pocket for Beth's letter; I was looking for a little twisted comfort.

I felt bad still thinking of Beth when I was obviously having a big sexy love affair with Rosa, who didn't know that I was having this big sexy affair with her.

TWENTY-THREE

I had to tell Rosa I couldn't do this anymore. I had to simply confess and say, *Look, I'm a first class loser, I can't handle the class*. I was no miracle worker. I was a spoiled middle-class guy who was not into saving the world. I'd tell her that it takes great strength to recognize one's weaknesses. I'd do whatever it took.

But still, through all the ridicule, I was drawn to stay. I couldn't tell if I was only staying for Rosa anymore. Maybe it was self hatred and a sick need to be punished.

Franco sat there most of the day, his hands folded on his desk. He tried so hard to behave. Sometimes he talked, too; other times he acted as if he didn't know me. I'd been buying him a bag of chips or soda and slipping it to him. He wouldn't say much, only a murmur of thanks. Sometimes he kept his head down on his desk and covered his head, slept, or appeared to be in his own world of inner pain.

I was telling Ralph and June about Franco. I told them I felt frustrated because just when I thought I had reached Franco, he'd pull away from me. He wouldn't trust me. Sometimes I thought he hated me. I didn't understand. June's attitude about me teaching at the alternative school surprised me. Whenever I would talk about the students, especially Franco, she would tell me not to get attached. She said I had enough problems of my own.

Was this my charitable sister talking?

I didn't understand her, either, sometimes. However,

Ralph thought what I was doing was great and told June it was taking my mind off myself. I tended to agree with Ralph.

I tried to be the bigger person and not drop to the level of those boys. After all, I was a thirty-six-year-old educated person. But this constant steady stream of degradation day in and day out was getting to me.

TWENTY-FOUR

I decided it was time to read Beth's letter. But I was scared. I couldn't bring myself to do it.

Instead, I pulled out my book and looked up ...

> Scared: woman attacking you, calling you weak, cutting your balls off, reading letters from a scornful woman: 32, 45, 47, 55, 62, 67, 89, 91, 102, 104.

The book claimed that meditating on your first sexual experience, gay or straight, would help revive feelings of being the conqueror, which would lead to bravery and the certainty that you are king of your own world. However, the book warned, these feelings will only help you do something painful, like breaking up with your girlfriend or telling her you cheated with her best friend. Sexy, slinky women and hunky men were not objects to be conquered sexually anymore. This was simply an exercise in feeling good about one's self in order to face a painful and fearful situation.

Okay, so I decided to think about my first time. I wanted to feel fearless; I wanted to be the king of my own world, and I wanted to face that letter that Beth sent me.

I have always been shy with women, and I had been eighteen—old by the standards of those days—when I first had sex.

I was in my sophomore year at Boston College, and, like every guy on campus, I walked around looking for girls. My hormones were in overdrive, when I finally had my first sexual experience with a girl named Clara Woodsman. She was a graduate student assisting my English professor, a bit chubby—not my ideal—but she had a great smile and a tender manner. She always held a cup of coffee in her hand. I liked the way she sipped from the cup. Her full lips kissed the edge of the cup's rim and her eyes would look up at me and blink innocently, while she made a slight slurping sound. It made me wild.

The spring of my freshman year, I received a "D" on a paper about Ibsen's *A Doll House*. I was a young healthy man, and I wanted to make love to women. I was not particularly interested in writing about their oppression. Anyway, Clara offered to help me rewrite the paper. When I arrived at her small off-campus apartment, she answered the door in a pink fluffy bathrobe. I knew right away she had more in mind for me than a discussion about Ibsen's oppressed Nora.

We didn't speak much at all. In fact the only thing she said was, "I love the way you look. You're very handsome. Don't speak, not one word. I'll write your paper so you can pass that boring class. I only want you to call me Nora when you're ready to cum, okay?"

Shit, I would have called her *Bozo The Clown* and sewed my mouth shut with a needle and thread if she had wanted me to. I took my clothes off, and I did what was requested of me. When I came, I felt as if millions of butterflies were flying out of me.

Norrrrrrra!

We did it over and over that night, and the next day. I was so sore that I had to go to the local drug store and buy some *Ponds Cold Cream* and wrap my privates in gauze.

Clara and I knew our relationship was only sex, and sex it was. When she passed me on the campus green, I would nervously nod at her, and she'd brush up close and feel me through my pants. We'd mess around for hours, and I would go home sore and limping. For a while I was in heaven.

But then I thought I needed to branch out from Clara. I mean, hey, there were a lot more girls out there with different sizes, shapes, smells, and techniques. And so I had a field day, humping and grinding through college. It was the nature of my beast.

The downside was that every time the urge for sex came upon me, I couldn't concentrate until I was released, and it became a bit of a distraction.

Once I graduated and was back in New York, Hank and I would go to bars, pick up girls, have sex, drink all night—the usual triad of youth. Hank never got lucky, but he had his share of some pretty hot hookers who ran a place out of the Upper East Side. At least that's what he told me.

But Beth was the first woman I could connect to on a higher level. And she stole my heart away. I was twenty-three and scared.

It was a May evening when the trees on upper York Avenue were starting to bud and the air was warm, and people took to the streets, heavy with anticipation of spring. It was the end of my first year teaching at Bolton, and I wanted to frame a small print of Degas' *Blue Dancers* as a graduation gift for one of my students.

When I walked into Beth's frame store on Second Avenue, I knew she was the one for me. I watched her as she enthusiastically leaned over her work table, showing me the different frames that would go with the print. When she put her auburn hair behind her ears, it moved me in such a way that I even surprised myself by asking, "What time do you get off of work?"

Beth later told me she'd liked my bluntness, but she didn't know from that first encounter that bluntness was not a normal part of my personality. It was unusual. A sudden aberration.

That evening we walked through the park. It was dark, and the lights made the grass look deep and lush. The trees with their sappy buds called small flies to swarm into the spring air, and as they danced in our path, I swatted them away as if I were swatting away some other kind of obstacle that had stopped me from living.

I was young, and my entire life consisted of the Bolton School and June. That night I felt happy because I believed a magical spell had been cast over me and made me clairvoyant, because in my heart I knew I would marry Beth. We found a bench in the park, and we talked for hours about art, life, hopes, dreams, everything young couples talk about. My mother had died that past winter and I was trying to change things and get on with my life. We married weeks later, and for the next fifteen years, Beth told me that she wondered who I was and *where* was that "bold man" who came into her shop that spring night? Where did he go? she would ask. Still, I thought we were happy. We did so many great things together. We had a life together.

The day I opened Beth's letter, it was one of those long and cold October days when the air was becoming chilly and I wanted to get plastered so badly my body shook with panic. I was alone. Ralph and June were out at a dinner and a presentation of scenes from *Madame Butterfly* at the Asian Society. Ralph's obsession with all things Asian was expanding beyond his hankering for Chinese food lunches every day, and I think in a strange way, June liked it because it brought her close to our father, who had a double life in Asia.

In any event, that afternoon I spent a lot of time asking God for strength so I wouldn't drink. I didn't feel like going to a meeting. I decided to walk through the park. I remember looking at the trees and feeling rather down because they were almost bare, but taking solace in the fact that at least a week remained before all the leaves would be gone. As I walked around the water basin, my hands buried in my coat, I had those familiar pangs of dread from the deepest part of my being.

I knew I couldn't continue at the school. I was avoiding all real adult commitment in my life. Being at that school was about seeing Rosa, my new obsession. I would have to make some sort of change after the holidays. I knew Rosa was desperate for a teacher, but she would have to understand, and I would have to swallow my pride and give up my interest in her. She had no romantic interest in me, and it was time I grew up and stopped living in my obsessive fantasy world.

I sat on a bench and took out the letter and read what I hoped would provide some closure in the form of an apology.

Dear Oliver,

I know you will think I'm crude and harsh saying what I have to say to you. But in time I know you will find in your heart some kind of understanding.

The day I discovered I was pregnant I became scared. Most women, I imagine, feel happiness when they discover they're pregnant by the man they love, but I felt only dread. I refused to be like those other women, caught in a marriage because of a baby, trapped in desperation. I wanted to be loved. I was tired of fighting for conversation, tired of feeling like a failure, tired of competing with your students, your sister, Hank, and your passion for art. And I was sick of feeling as if I was trying to invade that world that you keep so tightly guarded. The worst part of it was, I thought, that you seemed happy when I told you about the baby. But as the days went on, you withdrew from me more than you ever had before. Then I blamed myself again, as I always did. It was all my fault. I wanted too much; I was pestering and needy; my thoughts began to conflict.

We all need to hear voices of assurance that we are loved; you gave that to me only once, and through the years, I grew to sadly believe that you're incapable of love beyond that spring night when we first met and sat for hours on that bench in Central Park. Maybe for you love is a fleeting moment, but for me it is a collection of fleeting moments that tally up to hours, days, months, and years.

The day I told you I lost the baby, I had actually gone to a clinic downtown. I aborted our baby. After the procedure was over, I had this overwhelming feeling of euphoria. I felt that I had woken from a ten year nightmare, that I was free to be touched and loved and that I had something to look forward to. Do you understand what I am saying? Damn it, Oliver, everyone needs to be needed, and I realized you're incapable of giving the proper attention to a child, to me or to anyone, except maybe your sister. You're an emotional cripple, Oliver. I will always love you and I will always fantasize about what we could have been. You were my first love.

On a recent counseling session over the phone with Moonbeam, we both came to the conclusion that my sexual promiscuity was a way to escape from you; it delivered me to a new life of personal freedom in Vancouver with my new lover, Jon Luke.

By the way you would really like him. He paints mountains and moose in his spare time.

Moonbeam has suggested we continue to be friends, and when you feel like you can see me, Jon Luke and I would love for you to come out for a visit.

Take care of yourself, and if you're still drinking, please try and stop.

Love, Beth

TWENTY-FIVE

King of my world? Fearless? No! I tore that letter to shreds. My hands seemed not to be a part of me but of some unknown, angry, fire-eating beast that had taken over my being. I scrunched the small pieces of the shredded letter in my hand, and I threw them into the air with such force I almost snapped my shoulder out of joint. I was done with Beth and done with that book! I tore each page out of *The Castration of the 20th Century Man: How to Grow a New Set for the 21st Century* and crumpled each page. I threw them behind me as I walked. A gust of wind caught the bits and blew them up, around and into the water basin. I imagined they were the droppings falling from a flock of wild vultures flying over head, the product of birds of prey defecating into the dirty waters of humanity.

A *nouveau-riche* Fifth Avenue woman in tight leather pants and a face that looked as if it had been pulled back and wrapped around her head three times came over and pointed one of her crimson claws at me, "You ignoramus! We drink that water, respect our city!" She then went on her way.

I covered my face, I was going to explode any minute.

Then this Neanderthal who was jogging around the basin, stopped and came over to me, pushed me on my shoulder, yelling, "I ought to make you fish that out, you moron!"

I lost it. I barked back a furious "Fuck off!" and he ran off.

There's no doubt that the sound came from the depths of my despair. I could feel my face heating up and my eyeballs jumping out of my head.

After the jogger had disappeared into the park, I stood in that same space where I shouted at him, remaining very still. I screamed *fuck off* to the open fall air. I repeated *fuck off* about twenty times. But then this great sadness erupted from my gut, and as much as I wanted to bawl, I wouldn't do it. I walked through the park with my head bowed so low you would think it was being swallowed by my chest.

I could have been a father.

And then I ran through the park. I ran for all I was worth, and all I could think was that *I could have been a father,* but I was never given the option. She had no right. It was her body, but she had no right.

I found that bench where my father and I sat when I was a child, and I shivered in the cold, holding back tears, panicking and thinking of my father; this would have been a great time to have a father to sit and talk to.

Then came the predictable panic, threatening to overcome me entirely. It was a familiar panic that I had been living with since I was a child, a panic that would come whenever my parents fought.

For a long time, our parents were apparently very careful to shield their problems from us. They became increasingly frustrated and, I think, actually hated each other by the time my father died. I know neither of them would have hurt us for all the world, but we didn't understand that it was their shielding us, the unspoken anger between them, that caused us to hurt so badly.

So, when we first heard our mother shriek obscenities, it came to us as from out of the blue.

And it was a doozy.

June and I were sitting in the living room, and our parents were behind the closed door of their bedroom. We eventually realized that they were actually having an argument, and, as it became wildly fierce and their voices rose, we became more and more frightened, but also more and more intrigued.

June whispered to me that they were arguing about S-E-X.

"They have sex?" This was the last thing I wanted to know, and I covered my ears. But nothing could have prepared us for what we heard next.

"Where do you go? I demand to know!" Mother screamed.

"I told you I go to the village and walk around!" my father said.

"But why there? What do you have in common with artists and homosexuals?"

"Stop it Louise," he said.

"GOD DAMN IT! I WANT TO KNOW WHY YOU DON'T FUCK ME ANYMORE!"

Our mother had said that? Our perfect, pristine mother?

"You can take the girl out of Queens, but you can't take Queens out of the girl," my father said.

That's when we heard the first of many items that my mother would throw at my father during the rest of their marriage smash against their bedroom wall. That time it was a jar of cold cream. Half an hour later, our mother stormed out of the room, and my father followed, his face covered in cold cream, shards of broken glass cupped in his hand.

I knew that if I thought any more of my childhood, the ultimate nightmare of my father's death would come to me, but I couldn't stop myself. Once home, I went straight to my small study, my sanctuary of beauty. I shut the door, laid myself out on the floor, and looked all around. I enjoyed the feeling of being consumed and taken away to another world, created by others, but brought together by my use of Scotch tape and tacks. I sat up. I glanced over at the cork board above my maple desk. I looked at all the index cards that I had pinned to it with colored tacks earlier that summer before I was to return to Bolton, only to be fired weeks after.

I always prepared early for the upcoming school year. Miss Macey gave me the list of new girls without hesitation; she loved my enthusiasm. On each card was written a student's name and, as the year unfolded, I would note down her progress. In the past I would make specific personal notes on the bottom of each index card about the girl, for I felt it important to know them, how they learned and who they were. My notes were simple: *more help, understands well, loves art, troubled girl, needs more encouragement, explain carefully, inspire her, lost girl, shy girl, insecure girl.* I took each card down, piled them in a small stack, and tossed them into my trash barrel.

I wondered what my father would think if he knew what I had made of my life. I reached into the bottom drawer of my desk and found the pages of my father's war diary. I didn't know what I was looking for in my father's writing; however, I surmised, while I read the only two pages I saved from my mother's fits with flames, that I was looking for some sign of hope exposed through his writing, a secret code for surviving life that would jump out at me. Once found, I would feel safe and exclaim, "Yes that was it! I knew all along!"

January 12, 1968—Saigon

It will be very difficult for me to leave Dac Kien. I think back to the day I hired him. A slight Vietnamese man who had a way with sheer curtains and bamboo shoots. I never dreamed I would fall in love with him or that he would turn out to be my best friend and lover. He has a wisdom that I can only call profound. And how charitable he is! How kind. He makes one hell of a *Gỏi sứa đồ biển*, to boot! His culinary skills are magnificent. I never dreamed I would enjoy jelly fish so much! This war makes me so sick that sometimes I don't even care. And then I remember Louise and June and Oliver. And I think of Dac Kein, too. I love them all so very much. Dac Kein and I are always careful. Still, I'm always afraid. Dac Kein's advice is to remain optimistic.

I trust his wisdom entirely.

February 12, 1968—Washington DC Walter Reed Hospital/ Psychiatric Ward

During the Tet Offensive, Saigon was blown to smithereens. After one night of heavy bombing, Dac Kein and I lay in bed. I worried about the men. What would happen to Louise and my kids if I were killed? But Dac Kein told me that we must get up. It was our duty to find people in need. I told him it would be a waste of time; everyone was dead. We were safe and comfortable. But Dac Kein told me comfort makes a heart sleep and that every living thing carries a little light within. When that light begins to fail, it is our duty to rekindle it, to keep the blaze of life going.

On the streets there was rubble everywhere, burnt bodies, blown-up automobiles, people crying for help. I couldn't take the devastation and destruction. It overwhelmed me. I fainted in Dac Kein's arms. He held me lovingly. Then we saw North Vietnamese and South Vietnamese fighters as well. I thought that we'd be killed in the crossfire. The American Soldiers asked me if I was okay. And I didn't say anything. Then they turned on Dac Kein. They'd seen us. They knew what we were.

From across the street, a Viet-Cong shot Dac Kein dead. I fell to my knees, paralyzed with grief. The American Soldiers, my comrades in arms—those assholes—they left me to grovel in my shame and guilt. Later I had a massive breakdown. The numbskulls in this hospital told me that I was found wandering the streets of Saigon, days later. I now believe that Dac Kein's light had somehow made its way to me in the shape of that Jade ring. When I get out of this lousy hellhole of a place and get back to my family, I'm giving the ring to Louise. What better way to honor Dac Kein than to have the wife that I love wear the light of the man I loved on her finger?

God is good. I have one more week of therapy—they are experimenting with a cure for homosexuality that has me viewing photographs of naked men. Whenever I become aroused, I receive an electric shock. Soon, they say, I will forget everything and be able to go home and be with my family. But I keep this journal to remember.

I put my father's diary away. I laid down in the center of the study and spread my body out.

"Mom? Dad? Help me," I whispered.

Then the night my father was killed came back to me. I started to hyperventilate.

I was nine. My parents had gone to a cocktail party at the Council for Foreign Affairs, and someone asked Mom if her accent was British.

She replied "Yes, how observant." My father laughed so relentlessly he choked on his crab canapé, and from what I could tell from my mother's screaming, my dad was making an absolute spectacle of himself.

"You're despicable and low class," she shouted.

They fought all night. June came into my room and we huddled together. We heard their shouts and various objects being thrown across the living room: plants, vases, glasses, and books. For hours there were crashing sounds and declarations of hatred.

Then we heard a huge resounding thump come from the great room. We snuck out of the bedroom and peeked. We saw our mother standing over our drunken father, who was huddled in a ball on the red and gold oriental carpet, laughing hysterically as my mother cried and beat him with her Gucci umbrella.

"Why are you telling people you're Ivy League educated? Louise, you've never stepped foot on a college campus!" my father roared.

"Get out, get out! You're a disgrace to your children, and to me. You are a common drunk!"

"And you, my dear," my father laughed, "are a common fraud!"

June held me tightly to prevent me from going into the room. I wanted to save my father even though he was laughing. I began to cry quietly and tried to remain calm.

"It will be okay. Mother knows best."

"Let me go! I want to get Daddy. Please June, let me save Daddy!"

"Shhh! Please Oliver, be quiet, it will make it worse."

When my father stood, with much difficulty, he leaned into mother's treasured French inlaid table, which displayed a crystal bowl she had purchased at Sotheby's.

"Oh, God not Mother's table and bowl!" June exclaimed. She held onto me for dear life.

When the table and bowl went crashing to the floor, both breaking into pieces, mother let out a blood-curdling scream, "GET UP! GET OUT!"

My father stood again and went into his bedroom, while mother, still in a fit of rage, followed him with one of the table's legs. June and I both quietly, but frantically, followed and watched as mother took his suitcase out from her large closet and pulled out my father's drawers from his dresser, dumping the contents into the open suitcase. She then crazily beat the bed with the leg of her French inlaid table.

"I want you out. OUT!"

I ran out of June's grip and into my parents' bedroom. I held my father by the waist. I was crying uncontrollably. June then entered the bedroom, where she watched as mother took me by the arm and tried to pull me away from my father.

"Don't make him go away!" I cried to my mother.

"He's a bum! A common drunk! See what you're doing to your children?" she screamed. Mother cried, and June went to comfort her.

"I'm leaving. This crap has gone to your head! I don't know who you are anymore!"

My father closed his suitcase and kissed June goodbye, and even though I was too big, he picked me up and hugged me tightly. The scent of his VO-5 made me cry even more. My father's large, safe hand rubbed my back.

And when he put me down, I ran to my bedroom, got my red suitcase, and packed it.

But I heard my father leave the apartment before I got back to him.

I chased after him. I missed the elevator, so I ran down the stairs.

In my pajamas—which had pictures of sheep jumping over glowing, hopeful moons, with slippers to match—I ran out into the winter night. It was snowing. I looked for my Dad and finally saw him standing on Eighty-Fifth Street, getting ready to cross Park Avenue. That is when Stan, the old Irish doorman with caterpillar eyebrows, tried to grab me.

"Daddy!" I kicked Stan the doorman, called him an old mick, and ran after my Dad.

"Get back here, you! You little Scallywag, I'm callin' your Ma!" Stan hollered after me.

Dad hadn't heard me and began to cross the street. I ran so fast that I dropped my suitcase and my clothes blew around in the wind and snow.

I ran across Park Avenue, and I glided on black ice, falling in the middle of the busy street.

"Oh, Daddy!"

My dad turned around, finally, and saw me. I was so happy!

"Daddy!"

But he wasn't looking at me now. He was looking at the lights of a taxi, heading for me, only yards away.

He dropped his suitcase and lunged for me. Flying through the air, he landed on top of me. He huddled around me, pulled me in, hid me in his large arms, and pressed me close to him as tightly as he could.

The taxi had slammed into my father's back with such force that we had both been sent crashing into the curbstone. The paramedics had literally pried my father's arms from around my small body. He had been holding me that tightly. We were both rushed to the hospital, but my father was already dead. He had died while I was curled within his body. His spine was crushed.

My father had saved me. I was not physically harmed. But I did not speak for weeks. The doctors called it traumatic shock.

My mother and sister never spoke about the accident. But they knew I blamed myself. I remembered the feeling of the black void. And the accident still rattled within me. I knew I was only a little boy, but I couldn't help feeling that way.

But that was then; now I was lying on the floor of my study, my hands trembling and perspiring. I felt my spirit leave my body. I found myself thinking of Hank. It was time to make peace with him. When I was seventeen-years-old, I had this hard spot on the tip of my nose. It was deep inside my skin and invisible on the surface. It wouldn't go away. My dermatologist told me it was an ingrown pimple and it would flare up periodically and possibly be a nuisance for the rest of my life. Although I would be able to feel its presence, I would be the only one who knew it existed as long as I didn't poke at it. I guess that's the best way to describe my relationship with Hank. He would always be an invisible entity that lived deep within me, and he would never go away; he would be a part of my life forever. He would go unnoticed by most people; he was short, bald, a poor conversationalist, had a hairy back, and was a drunk. But I was his only true friend and, like my pimple, I have become accustomed to him in a perverse way.

All our married life, Beth had nagged me about hanging around with Hank. Beth pronounced him a vile deadbeat idiot. And so, in spite of it all, I erased from my mind what he'd done with my wife. I also considered it was probably the first time in Hank's life he tried to have sex of any kind without paying for it.

TWENTY-SIX

I found myself in front of his door. I rang his buzzer.
"Who is it?"

"Open the door, it's me," I said.

"Who?" Hank said.

"Me! Damn it, buzz me in! I got this lousy letter from Beth!"

"Oliver? Is it really you? Hold—hold on!"

I entered Hank's apartment, sat in his brown vinyl easy chair, and leaned back. The foot-rest sprang up and caught my feet.

"I've wanted to call you for some time now," he said. "I didn't know whether it was okay. I'm really glad you're here. I have to talk about some stuff."

"Me, too," I whispered.

"You sound like shit."

"I feel like shit," I said. My voice was so low I could hardly hear myself.

Hank was eating out of containers from *Maya*, this modern Mexican food restaurant between 64th and 65th streets where we used to eat practically every Wednesday night.

"I miss hanging out at Maya's with you, buddy. But things are good now." He cut into his Chicken Mole. You want to talk first?"

"I dunno," I said.

"I missed you. A lot."

"I missed you, too." I leaned back in the chair and sighed.

I reached across the table to grab a corn chip and, in the process, put my elbow in a puddle of Mole sauce. I detonated into a hissy fit.

"Christ Hank, this is disgusting! Why do you have to get food everywhere when you eat?" I flung the chip on the table. "Fuck!" I took a napkin and wiped my elbow. "Fuck and shit!" I continued.

"So what's a little Mole sauce? Welcome back!" he said. His horse chewing and slurping were getting on my nerves. I took a deep breath. Under his coffee table, I spotted a bottle of whiskey and a lone glass.

"Want some guacamole?" Hank held up a container filled with the green dip.

"No thanks."

"Salsa? It's excellent. Fresh tomatoes, cilantro, jalapeños."

"No. Why do you have all this food here? It's like a Mexican banquet."

"It's my last big feed before I diet for good this time," he said as he jammed a handful of chips and salsa into his mouth.

"Congrats," I said keeping my eye on the bottle of whiskey.

"Are you still going to AA?" He crunched away and dipped steadily. I covered my face, and my body started heaving with agony over Beth's letter.

"Oh, shit, oh fuck. Shit. Shit. Shit. Fuck," I said. Not hysterically, but rather in a slow, sad, dangerous clamoring way that made my legs shake and my throat muscles go into overdrive.

Hank stopped eating; he shook his head at me.

"I know buddy, life sucks," he said. "Men are under attack. I've missed having you around so much. More than you know." He took a big bite of a Flauta; bits of chicken, chili sauce, tomatillo salsa and cotija cheese ran down the corner of his mouth. "You look like how I felt inside only a few weeks ago." He spoke softly. "Here—have some burrito, it will make you feel better. Go on," he said. His voice was dulcet and sincere.

"Nah," I said. "I'll be okay." I blew my nose.

"What's going on, old buddy?"

"Beth didn't lose the baby. She aborted it," I said. I couldn't even look at Hank. "She told me in a letter." I closed my eyes and crossed my arms over my chest.

"Fuck man, I am sorry." He stopped eating and looked away, face full of remorse. He closed his eyes for a moment and rubbed his forehead.

"That's awful, man. I am really sorry."

"I feel like I woke up and now I'm faced with this real nightmare called my life. I want a drink." Then out of habit, I reached under the coffee table and poured myself a glass of whiskey. I sat back down. Hank remained very still.

I could smell the whiskey's richness—a fermented, mash smell—and excitement roiled in my belly. I was hungry for the burning comfort that would bring relief. I swished the amber liquid around in the glass and studied it.

Hank watched me, puzzled. He then began, slowly, to cover up the containers of food. I looked at his walls. Photos of the Yankees. Young men, some my age, some younger. Successful. Strong.

As Hank put the last food containers away in his fridge, he looked over at me. It was Sunday, and his toupee was off. It lay on the coffee table next to the Chicken Mole, looking like a dead, wild, hairy animal that happened to fly by and land its ugly-self on top of the coffee table.

"Hank, it's Sunday. You don't have the rug on," I said.

"We're under attack Ollie," he said. He looked at me earnestly.

"What the hell does that mean?" I eyed the whiskey.

"It means we're under attack," he said again. He came

back down and sat on his sofa and looked over at me. His gut bulged out from under his shirt; I could see glimpses of his hairy belly.

"I want to drink. I have a lot of drinking to make up for." I leered at the glass in my hand. I felt naughty, and I liked it.

"Listen to me first. We're under attack."

"What the fuck are you talking about? Who is under attack?"

"Men. We're all under attack. And it's unfair. For generations men were assholes to chicks, but now things have changed and chicks are fighting back. But they're fighting the wrong guys. It's our fathers and their fathers before them and their fathers before that they should be fighting. Damn! No one considers the bullshit that today's middle-aged man has to cope with, and know what it's all about? I'll tell you, my friend, it's all melted down to three words: fear of homosexuality. I've been reading this book," he picked up a book by the side table. I recognized the cover: *Castration of the 20th Century Man: How to Grow a New Set for the 21st Century.*

"That book is for the weak and semi-retarded," I said. "It's all bullshit!"

"We *are* weak! Men are weak!"

"I'm leaving. The hell with that book. I would never read a book like that!" I said. I didn't want to admit I'd been reading it.

"No wait! Listen to me. Everybody is reading it. It's the hottest book, and it's changing men."

"I don't want to talk about that book, those books!" I said. "Huh! It's filled with all this gross unrealistic dogma, and before you know it, you're doing stuff you wish you never did like, like reading a letter from a former wife!"

"Don't get all defensive. Listen to me. You've changed my life."

"Me? Come on Hank. I'm in no mood—"

"This relates to you. Listen," Hank said with gross enthusiasm. "Take your dad, for instance. Big queer but nice guy right? He was brave and free. God bless him. He was free of all the macho bullshit!"

"I can't talk about my dad, not now!" I clenched my fist and shouted.

"Wait! Hear me out first." Hank waved the book in front of me.

"Now look, our fathers were raised to be rough and tough. They taught us how to fight and to be models of ideal men—you know, protect our territory, ready to fight the big wars, fuck our woman, keep the bitches under control, that type of thing. You would think we still lived in the Stone Age, right? Men are socialized to be insensitive egotistical beasts, and so our sensitive sides are repressed. We're as sensitive and as much in need of love as women, but it's assumed that if a man receives some tender love and care, it will make him 'weak and lady-like.' Thus the fear of creating a homosexual, and no matter how much people say they don't mind gay people, they do. Homosexuality is our biggest fear! Therefore, boys are torn apart from their mothers at a young age as to *not* create a 'mama's boy.' If you're a mama's boy, you're weak, and if you're weak, you're society's antiquated view of a woman—'weak and helpless.' And presto! You have a raging homo on your hands! But people don't realize you can't make a *homo*, you can only make a sexist pig. Most men grow up resenting their mothers for pushing them away at a young age, and so they look for women who closely resemble their mothers and marry them and then act like assholes to their wives to subconsciously get back at their mothers. It's complex, I know, but I've been really thinking about this book. I'll stop now by saying this—I think it's very cool we can express our feelings in front of each other. So keep on talking buddy. You let it all out. This is a new dawn for me, and I am taking charge. I deserve to be loved by men without the fear of homosexuality. This book says to come right out and say it—'the love of a man!'—and the minute I said it, I felt new balls growing."

"Hank this is too much," I said. I looked at the full glass hungrily, ready to toss it back.

"Wait! Hold on, before you do that. I'm not a completely soulless human being. Ollie, for crying out loud, don't drink it! I did the shittiest thing a friend can do to another friend. But trying to sleep with your wife was another revelation for me."

"I'm so happy that porking my wife has helped you!" I said.

"Look, these weeks haven't been easy. I wake up each morning, and I look in the mirror and think, what kind of person am I? I can't forgive myself, but now you've forgiven me or you wouldn't be here. I've had to take a long look at myself." He picked up his toupee, which had tortilla chip crumbs inside it, threw it on the floor and stomped on it.

"It's all bullshit. Drinking and toupees and saying that you fucked women like horny old dogs … it's all about covering up the real thing, the pain we carry, the ugliness that settles in our balls."

"I'll drink to that," I went to raise the glass, and Hank plummeted on me and slapped the glass of whiskey out of my hand, whiskey splattering on the wall. Hank's bald head landed in my crotch, his arms gripping my thighs, his doleful eyes looking up at me.

"Don't drink. Don't do it. You made the change; don't go back! You and this book inspired me."

"Jesus shit! Stand up, Hank. What is it with you?"

"I haven't had a drink this entire week, and I haven't been wearing my toupee."

"What?"

"I love you. Not in an 'I love you I want you to fuck me up the ass way,' but in a brotherly way. I love you, and the fact is, Beth brought us down and kicked our asses, I'm talking about cutting our balls off! It evoked change in you and now in me. This book says it's all a big chain linked to our balls."

"What the hell, Hank? Are you doing coke again?"

"No! This book says that every time a woman cuts your balls off and it brings a change in your life, you should have a ceremony. Burn something, run naked on a beach, whatever—something to celebrate the fact that once you're man enough to admit your wrongs, you will grow a new set of fresh man-balls. We can grow new balls! Damn it Oliver. We're practically kids. We have a lot of living to do. I'm going to lose weight, have my hairy back lasered, shave my head of the few strands I have left, and maybe lift weights and buy some really cool eyeglasses In fact … hold on a second! " Hank went into the kitchen and came back with a large silver bowl. He put his toupee in the bowl and covered it with whiskey.

"Let's make a ceremony out of this right fucking now!"

He lit a match and threw it into the bowl. A large puff of blue flame warmed our faces as we stood over his burning toupee while it smoked and crackled. We watched as it disintegrated into a small black lump of sizzling liquid. The smell was atrocious.

"Remember when we were kids and you used to be so upset by your mom's fires? Well, your mother's pyromaniac behavior was good for something. She taught me how to light fires."

"I'm so glad you're benefiting from all the crazy women in my life."

"Ollie, from now on, let's do what the book says: find the good in everything. You yourself always say, 'look for the joy'!"

The fire dwindled down, and all that was left was a small steady stream of thick white smoke that danced to the ceiling. Hank made small circles with his hands over the smoldering toupee. He looked like a Maharishi.

"Let's have a toast to growing a new set of fresh balls." Hank swigged from his Coke bottle and handed it to me. I saw some small green guacamole specks on the rim of the bottle and tortilla crumbs floating on the surface.

"We started drinking when?" I asked. "When we were ... how old were we anyway?"

"Twelve. My Dad had some really great scotch, remember? We got plastered and threw up and got some burgers and got drunk again and threw up some more." Hank was laughing. "Those were some good times."

"I wanted to be something then, and you wanted to be something then, too. I forget what you wanted."

"Play for the Yankees."

"Oh, yeah! You were obsessed! What happened?"

"I really sucked at baseball. That's the truth. As you know, I talk the truth."

"Ya, you're a regular honest Abe."

"Hey, if you don't want the truth, don't sit next to me. That's my motto," Hank said.

"Did I have a dream?" I asked. "I can't remember."

There was a long pause.

"I dunno."

"Come on."

"Forget it," he said.

"Tell me what it fucking was. I forget my dreams! Tell me the truth, Abe!"

"You always talked about wanting to die so you could be with your Dad. You used to freak me out. Especially when we had a good buzz going on, because you'd always cry. One time you said you wanted to hang yourself in Central Park or slice your throat in Central Park, I don't remember which."

And that's when I started to bawl.

Hank reached over and gave me a big hug.

"New balls new life; castrated no more!" he said. He held

me very close, his hand on the back of my head.

He laughed sadly and said, "We're going to make it; we're gonna grow new balls."

"Oh, damn it Hank."

"What?"

"I've been reading that dumb book, too. I hate it. I wish I never read Beth's letter. And I did, and I blame that fucking book." Hank gleamed. He hugged me again and, when he went to grab my ass, I caught his hand, smiled at him, and backed away.

"You're having a delayed reaction to the book," he said. "It's pretty common."

Then, quickly, without warning, Hank grabbed my ass. I giggled nervously. Hank looked at me—for a split second I could have sworn his eyes were full of longing—and then laughed, too.

TWENTY-SEVEN

The first part of the day was easy, believe it or not. I was free most of the morning. The students were in gym, then woodworking shop, then science. It was my lucky day. I roamed the halls a bit, heard students fighting and others telling teachers to *fuck off*.

I went to my classroom and cleaned up as best I could. I went back into the office a few times, hoping to catch a glimpse of Rosa. She was nowhere to be seen. Finally I went to the deli across from the school, bought her a cup of coffee and a Snickers Bar, and headed to the office, once more in hopes of seeing her.

Back at school, I coolly and casually wandered into the office, where Rosa was on the phone with a parent. She put her hands over the mouthpiece and said to me, "Some parent was thrown in jail and can't pick up her kid. Never a dull moment."

I handed her the coffee and the Snickers, and she glowed. She motioned for me to wait. She was wearing a sage-colored cashmere sweater, tight jeans, and black boots. Then Franco came running in the office crying, with the nurse following him.

"Franco, you have to go back to woodshop," the nurse said.

"No! They're trying to nail my hands to the bench! Don't you fucking listen to me?" Tears streamed down his face. I'd never seen him upset like this before.

Rosa asked me to take Franco out for pizza around the corner to try and calm him down. When we arrived at the pizza shop on First, he looked up at me and curled his lip.

"Can I get pepperoni on my slice?" Franco asked. His hands were deep in his pockets. He moved with a slow saunter.

"I don't see why not," I said, as I opened the door.

"You got some ugly ass shoes," Franco told me as we went into the pizza shop.

"I never thought about it much."

"You dress funny, too."

"Don't you own a suit?"

"No."

"Every young man should own a suit. It's only proper."

"What do I need a suit for?"

"Special occasions. Perhaps you'll find a young lady you would like to take to dinner or a movie, or perhaps, a party."

"Shit, I got no special nothing. Can I get a root beer too?"

"I don't see why not," I said.

"Do you think I'm good?" he asked.

"You seem very good. I worry about you. Do you sleep well at night? You sleep in class and sometimes you don't talk. Is everything okay?"

"I don't know," he said.

I didn't push him to speak.

Franco devoured the pizza and asked me for another slice, then a third and a fourth. Another root beer as well. The place smelled of garlic and tomatoes. We sat at an old wobbly table, and Franco ate quietly, as if I weren't with him. I sat upright and proper, my hands folded in front of him.

"You should eat slowly. You wouldn't want people to get the wrong idea."

"Wrong idea about what?"

"Good manners are important."

"For what?" Franco asked.

"That's a good question, Franco. Maybe so people won't get the wrong idea about you. I guess I don't know really." I chuckled.

"I'm black, everyone get the wrong idea about me. You know what I think? I think you need to get your hair cut and you need to change those damn clothes. You look like some kind of freak show. That's why the kids don't like your white ass. You look all whitey and shit. When you came into my neighborhood looking like that you lucky your ass didn't get kicked. People get the wrong idea about your ass."

"Then I guess I should stay out of your neighborhood."

"I think so, too." Franco started to laugh, kicked up his leg on a chair, and sipped his root beer, making slurping sounds.

"I'll buy you another root beer, if you like," I said. Franco shook his head no, so we sat in silence for a minute.

"I ain't being racist or nothin', but next school I go to, it's going to be all white." He crossed his arms.

"But you're African American," I said.

"What's the African-American bullshit? My granddaddy was from Jamaica. My father people I think are African. I dunno."

"I'm sorry," I said. I could feel my face turn red.

"What you sorry about? Jamaica's a nice place."

"No, I mean I'm sorry I said you were African."

"Why? Africa's probably a nice place."

"I'm sorry."

"Say I'm black, okay?"

"Okay."

"Let's go back to school," I said.

"No. I told you I ain't goin' back. I'm sick all this shit. I'm sick of my aunt, those kids, and this school bullshit."

"We have to go."

"Why do I have to go? I want to be good, that's all, and those kids fuck me up."

I stood. Franco didn't move. I looked at him, shifting my eyes, standing my ground, thinking that I could perhaps intimidate him with an authoritative pose. No dice. He was not scared of me.

"You get you hair cut and I'll go back."

"I don't need a haircut."

"You slick it down like something from the '80s or something. It should be more in the times," he told me. Franco turned his head and pointed to a small barber shop across the street.

"Come on, homie, I dare you."

"I don't need a haircut."

"I'm telling you, homie, you flossin' with the wrong look."

"Let's go back to school."

"You get your hair cut, I'll go back," he said.

"Why do you want me to get a haircut so badly?" I asked.

"Because you got some thick ass hair, and it looks freaky, and I can't stand looking at your hairy head freak show."

We both laughed, and I sat down. Franco laughed so hard that he knocked over his cans of root beer.

"Do I really look that bad?" I asked.

"Damn, man! Everything wrong with what you look like. You all wound up like some fucking tight ass white bitch. You got some fine looks going on but don't work with 'em."

I looked at myself in a small mirror that hung above us on the wall. The mirror had a *Coca-Cola* logo around it. My hair was overgrown.

"Take that tie off, too; you in the ghetto. My people don't like your white cracker face around here. You come here thinking people goin' to respect your white ass dressed like that?"

"I'm not going to be at this school much longer anyway. I have another job lined up," I said. I bit my upper lip.

"Why ain't you coming back?" He crossed his arms and rolled his tongue in his mouth. His eyes widened.

"I don't think I'm suited for this school?"

"You don't like black people?"

"Of course I do."

"Why ain't you coming back?

"I have another job."

"Then why the hell you wasting my time?"

"I'm trying to help you."

"I don't need your motherfuckin' help. I knew it. You people leave all the time."

"You were crying earlier because the other kids were giving you a hard time. Let's talk about that."

Franco stood and leaned over the table. A few of the customers looked over at us. "Shut up!" he shouted. "Shut up! I'm good! I'm good. I don't need to hear this shit from you!"

I was taken aback by Franco's emotional outburst.

"Please, stop this now!" said the Italian man who owned the restaurant. He had spots of flour on his face, and his gray hair was awry. "We want no trouble here. You take the boy out."

"Shut up, you old WOP!" Franco screamed.

I stood. The old man grabbed Franco by the shirt and lifted him up.

"Get your hands off me! I ain't bad. I ain't bad. You can't get me out of here. It's a public place!"

"Franco, stop!" I shouted, surprising myself at how loud my own voice was. The old man let go of Franco.

"We're only rehearsing for a play, Shakespeare's *Othello*. I'm his drama teacher. I'm sorry. We're going ... we're going across the street to get haircuts." I grinned nervously at Franco, and his dark eyes widened with glee.

"All right, Mr. Pepper, let's go!" Franco jumped up from his seat, and I followed him out.

I sat in a barber chair while a Hispanic man wrapped a blue smock over my body. There were photos of Jennifer Lopez and Mark Anthony on the walls. Spanish music played.

146

I leered at my reflection, in awe of what I was doing. I chuckled in spite of myself. I wasn't such a bore. I did have the ability to be unpredictable, a capacity for spontaneous behavior. And it was kind of fun. Franco was having a great time and all was cool.

Ah, hell, who was I trying to kid? This was the craziest thing I'd ever done, getting a haircut without planning for one.

I was a horrible bore.

Behind me sat old men speaking in Spanish, watching as the barber cut my hair. Franco stood close by giving the barber instructions, "Cut the back short, keep that long, trim this, cut that …"

The spicy smell of lotions and powders overwhelmed my senses, and I thought of the VO-5 my dad had used every morning.

How many times had Beth wanted me to have, what she called, a "decent hair cut, something updated"?

"Okay take a look!" Franco said with excitement.

I lifted my eyes and glanced at Franco. His arms were crossed over his lean chest, and his eyes were wide and fired up.

"You da bomb!" he said. I had to admit, I liked my haircut. I was, indeed, da bomb. It felt strange to have it cut short on the sides; it made me look younger. Franco beamed at me.

But I smiled sadly at Franco. What if Beth had had the baby, what would he be like when he was Franco's age? Would we have had other children? Would we have moved upstate, as we'd often talked about? Would we be living in a big house with lots of children?

Franco clapped his hands, held his stomach and laughed, "Mr. Pepper you goin' to get yourself lotsa Poo Nanny now!" he said.

"What does that mean?" I asked.

"Pussy," he told me. Then he gave me a big high five.

"Maybe you shouldn't talk like that." I tried not to show I was hoping that it was true—in particular, as it pertained to Rosa's Poo Nanny.

I bowed for all six of my observers and they all cheered, "*¡Muy bueno! ¡Muy bueno!*"

"Shit," Franco mumbled, "you a freak show."

"We have to get back to school now."

We began to walk back, and as we approached the school, Franco slowed down. He stopped at the playground's metal fence and started kicking it like mad. He began to cry.

"What are you doing?" I was stunned.

"Motherfucker, motherfucker, motherfucker!"

"What? What's wrong?" I asked.

"You don't understand, you don't get it, no one gets me!"

"Tell me. What's wrong?"

Franco then let go, sobbed uncontrollably, and slid down the fence. He curled himself into a ball, crossing his arms and tucking his head into his lap.

I knelt down to him. I wanted to touch him, comfort him, but I didn't know how, so my hands and my arms froze. I was petrified of his strong emotions. I held my hand out, and I tried to touch him, but I couldn't. Still, I knew I had to do something, so I put my hand onto Franco's shoulder, and I patted him hurriedly. Franco wept even more. This frightened me, so I pulled away and looked at him, almost as if I were angry or disgusted.

"Please, it's okay. Stop crying. Tell me. What's wrong?" I asked.

"They give me shit. My father is in prison. They say my father is getting fucked in the ass. They say all kinds of shit to me. They call me retard, and they pick on me. They don't stop."

"I'm sorry, Franco."

"I want to write him a letter."

"So why don't you?"

"I can't write so good. I got this thing."

"What thing?" I asked.

"I read like backwards and shit. I read things and they all jumble up on me."

"Dyslexia?"

"Yeah, that's it, that fucking thing you said. And they call me retard."

"I can help you write a letter."

"I don't know his address."

"Can you get it? We can write a letter right now and you can get his address. I'll mail it."

"You'll buy the stamp?"

"Yeah, sure."

"I don't want no one to know about this letter. They'll call me a pussy and shit."

"I won't tell anyone, I promise. Come with me; we'll sit over there, and we'll write it."

"Lunch is over," Franco said.

"Don't worry about it. It's your woodshop time, my free period. Come on," I said.

We walked over to a cement bench and chair in the playground where we sat across from each other. The cement seats were cold, and above us was an oak tree with golden leaves. One leaf fell from the tree and onto the table. As Franco picked it up and slowly tore it into pieces, I could smell its dry earthiness. I opened my briefcase and pulled out a pad of paper and a pen. Franco looked at the remnants of the leaf around his large feet. He wiped his tears with his sleeve and looked at me, eyes shifting quickly.

"I get mad sometimes, sorry. But I'm good. I am."

"Tell me what you want to say to your father," I said.

"I don't know."

"We can start off with 'Dear Dad.' "

"I call him Daddy. But don't tell anyone I still call him

149

Daddy, okay?"

"I promise I won't. Okay. *Dear Daddy.*" I started to write the words, and Franco rubbed his hands together and an untouchable essence of who I could have been as a father over came me. *"Dear Daddy."* My hands moved across the paper with a tentative ease as I listened to Franco dictate the letter. Franco kept an eye on me while his knees bounced nervously.

> When are you coming home? I miss you. Why do you have to be away? I want you to come home.

Franco's voice was hesitant at times, but he had control and knew what he wanted to say to his father; his voice was sincere, deep, and moving.

For a moment the letter sounded like a letter to my own father, one that I have imagined writing many times since his death, wondering if his spirit would read it over my shoulder. I felt an overwhelming sense of loss and sorrow. I stopped writing for a moment. I coughed as I often did when I became nervous and clasped my hands tightly.

You're having a nervous breakdown, asshole.

"What the hell is wrong with you?" Franco said.

"Nothing. I have a headache," I said. I clawed my face and felt my now short mane, and I picked up the pen. I was ready to write again, and as Franco dictated more words, it felt like his heart and voice belonged to my own inner voice. I looked up at the sun. A slight wind came our way, the pad of paper blew in flutters, and leaves fell on us. Franco looked up, and his eyes twinkled with joy. He started catching leaves as they fell, and he laughed. I imagined it was my dad speaking to me through the rays of sun and the golden leaves that leisurely pirouetted around this lost boy and me.

"I'm done. Why you sitting there looking all funny?" Franco asked.

"I was thinking that your letter is very good, right to the

point." I turned the pad of paper toward Franco, and he looked at it and nodded approvingly.

"It looks okay. I can't read it all that good anyway." Franco's eyes looked tired, but his body was jumpy; it indicated to me that he was ashamed of his sensitivity but excited all the same.

"How should we end the letter?" I asked.

"I don't know. Say, 'from your son,'" Franco said.

I looked down and I watched my hand write the ending to the letter,

> I love you Daddy. Please be well. Love from your son, Franco.

"I'll mail the letter in the morning. Bring me the address tomorrow." I folded the letter, found an envelope in my briefcase, and placed the letter inside.

"I thought you weren't coming back to this school?" Franco said.

"I'll come back tomorrow. But after that, I won't be back." I put the letter and my pen back into my briefcase and looked over at Franco.

"It's getting cold here; come, let's go inside."

We walked back into the school, and once again, silence encompassed us.

A part of me wanted to express to him my sorrow over losing a father, but I had that damn apprehension because I always maintained there should be a distance between student and teacher, all to preserve a certain amount of reverence. Too personal a relationship between student and teacher could lead to judgments about and misconceptions of a teacher's character, and that could all result in disrespect and distraction from learning on the student's part.

But at that moment I wondered if my beliefs applied in this case. Would it have been so improper to share with this broken-hearted boy my similar pain? Would it have helped Franco feel that he was not so alone and isolated? It seemed that everything I believed and trusted was proving to be dead-wrong during these past months. Everything I believed were illusions, mere falsities put forward in my mind that were supposed to help me live safely.

After my father's death, June retreated entirely into a world of books. And our mother lapsed into a world of guilt. She often spent her days alone, crying in bed. Other days she'd have spastic fits of energy. On those days, we were forced to walk the streets of the city for hours with my mother leading us like a mother duck. Having no particular destination, she'd talk to herself and walk hurriedly as if late for some grand event. She'd turn and call to us, frantically, "Quickly, children, we don't want to be late!" Then she'd pick up the pace even more and walk for hours more. Our feet became tired and swollen. Finally home, she'd retreat to her bedroom and sleep for days. June ended up taking care of me then. It was June who paid the bills and did the shopping and the cooking and the cleaning. That was how, as a young teenager, June became my mother.

Yes, I wished I'd shared my personal grief with Franco. So much for becoming a man for the Twenty-First Century. I was glad I'd gotten rid of that lousy book. I felt like I'd failed another human heart that day.

TWENTY-EIGHT

Franco got the address for his father's prison from his Aunt Ethel. He watched me address the envelope. On my break, I put it in a mailbox. Then during lunch period, it all came to an end. I walked out of the school that day, yup! I left. *Goodbye, Rosa.*

It was lunchtime at school. I stood and watched as food flew about the cafeteria and students screamed for no apparent reason. Other students were retained by paraprofessionals. Teachers yelled like lunatics. A Styrofoam cafeteria tray full of Sloppy Joe and iceberg lettuce swimming in fluorescent orange French dressing soared across the cafeteria and landed on me.

There was much laughter.

Teachers ran toward where the flying tray had came from. I furiously brushed lettuce from my shoulder.

"Pepper is a freak!" a student yelled.

And that's when I lost it. I'm talking bonkers.

It all came down on me: the divorce, the lost job, reading about my balls, that horrid dream. The fire that was building inside of me was now raging.

I dashed over to where the tray came from and grabbed the young boy who threw the tray by the shirt collar and pushed him against the wall.

"Look what you've done, you disrespectful rogue! Look at the mess you've made. You think you can say and do whatever you please. You think you can push people and push people and they're not going to react!" As I held the boy to the wall, I reached over to a table and picked up a pile of napkins.

"Clean up this mess now!" I pushed the napkins into the boy's chest.

"Get your fucking hands off me!" the boy screamed.

I shoved him against the wall again, and the boy gasped for air. The commotion in the cafeteria had stopped, and all eyes were on the boy and me. Rosa looked on from a distance. She made her way over to me slowly.

"Don't tell me what to do. Do you understand me? I am a teacher! Now clean up this mess." My voice, which seemed only to be an instrument of my rage lately, was so earth-shatteringly loud, so forceful, and authoritative, that the cafeteria became absolutely still.

"I said, clean up this mess!"

Again I shouted, and I took the boy by the collar and brought him to the mess. The boy tossed the napkins in my face. Most gasped and some snickered, and the teachers looked dismayed. But they allowed me to handle the situation. The boy ran from my grip, but I was determined to make him clean up his mess. I ran down the hallway, chasing the boy; he ran up stairs and down the stairs, through classrooms and out. The boy had a daunting energy, but I was resolved to catch him, and so, as I ran, I took off my suit coat and my tie.

The boy ran outside into the fall air and into the playground area, and still I ran after him. He was running out of breath. I was amazed I was still able to chase him, but my intense frustration over my life empowered me, and I would not stop. Before me, I could see my father, Beth, Miss Macey as she fired me, all those school boys who had disrespected me these weeks, and then that letter, that awful letter from Beth ... Her words ran through my mind:

I know you will think I'm crude and harsh saying what I have to say to you. But in time I know you will find in your heart some kind of understanding. The day I told you I lost the baby I had actually gone to a clinic downtown …

I ran after that boy until he stopped behind the swings and tried to dodge me, but I was too quick for him, caught him, and brought him back to the cafeteria.

"Leave me the fuck alone!" he screamed.

I brought the boy back into the school, to the mess, and made him kneel over it. I took the rag out of a bucket of water and threw it at the boy.

"Clean up this mess now!"

"Fuck off, asshole!"

"What did you say to me?"

"Nothing."

"Nothing what?"

"What!"

"My Name is Mr. Pepper! Not *asshole*, not *motherfucker*, not *freak*! My name is Mr. Pepper!"

"Leave me the fuck alone!"

"Clean this mess up now!"

The boy picked up the wet rag and whipped it into my face. It fell onto his head. The students laughed. I grabbed the rag and knelt down to the boy and took his hand and shoved the rag in it, and together we cleaned the mess, my hand on his.

"Clean this mess, clean this mess, clean this mess!" I repeated over and over. The boy began to clean the mess with my hand firmly on his. Our hands went backwards and forwards through the splattered ground meat and tomato mess, and they went in and out of the soapy bucket of water.

"Fucking bullshit." I took the rag from the boy's hand. "What did you say?"

"Nothing," he mumbled.

"Tell me your name," I snarled.

"Abe." He swirled the rag on the floor.

"You may not believe me, but you'll remember me. You'll remember me, and you'll know that there was someone in your life who cared enough to not let you get away with something indecent and wrong. Look at me," I said. Abe stopped mopping. He put his head at angle. He was irritated and humiliated as he looked up at me.

"What?" Abe said.

"Remember my face, and don't forget me."

I then walked past the kids, past Rosa and the other teachers, and then outside. I walked steadily with a resolve to only get home. I hailed a taxi and, as I was about to jump in, I heard Franco calling and running toward me.

"Mr. Pepper! Mr. Pepper! I got your briefcase! I got your briefcase!"

"Thank you," I said.

"That was pretty cool."

"Good luck, Franco." I put out my hand, and Franco shook it. His hand was small in mine, and only then did I realize he was only a kid like the other boys and girls at the school, though their physicality and personalities were incongruous. They did not have the joy or lightheartedness that most children I'd encountered in my life had; they all had heavy hearts and an offensiveness that saddened and overwhelmed me.

I had to leave. I went into the taxi and shut the door behind me.

"You're coming back, right?" I heard through the open window. "You're coming back, right?" Franco kept shouting after the taxi as it pulled away. "You coming back? You coming back here?!"

I took one last look out the back window then turned away.

TWENTY-NINE

When I got home, I could still feel Franco's small hand in mine. I wanted a drink so badly that when I gulped down a glass of water, I imagined the water was burning the back of my throat like whiskey. I thought fondly of that familiar burn that had given me the assurance that my nervous edge would soon be gone. I thought about searching my bedroom for a nip or a bottle that I had perhaps forgotten about. But I knew there was nothing. No *Lost Weekend* moment for me.

I wrote in my journal, hoping to help ease the cravings, but nothing worked. I wanted a big glass of forgetfulness so bad I would have drunk a bottle of Listerine. I stood and paced and clawed my face and took multiple deep sighs. I eyed June's small knickknacks on the windowsill—various animals and a small ark. I realized for the first time that there was no miniature Noah to lead the animals to safety.

I sat at the kitchen table. I can do this! I will not drink … I stood, I paced. For what? What reason? It was only a drink, one drink, what would be the big deal? Maybe I should call Hank, maybe he was back to drinking? Maybe June had some wine in the refrigerator? Wasn't there an old bottle in the fridge from months ago when she had a few of the girls from the Library over for dinner? I dove into the refrigerator, moving food out of the way.

Maybe June had hidden the bottle? Did the bottle even exist? *Damn it, June!* No, there was nothing in there. No wine.

I decided I would go outside and go to a bar, any bar, and get one drink, only to take off that horrible nervous edge that was hindering me from relaxing, no more, no less. After all, one little drink wouldn't harm me, and no one would have to know.

As I started to leave, the phone rang. I ignored it until I heard Rosa's voice on the machine.

"Ordinarily, if a teacher leaves a school, like you did today, it would be considered abandonment of students and you would be fired. Since you're a substitute, I don't know what they call it. Hey, I understand. It's not easy. Call me. You did a good thing today. I hope you're not feeling bad. These kids do a number on teachers, but it's going to be okay. Okay? Hey, Oliver, take it easy. Come to a meeting tonight. I'll be there. 'Be there or be square'—remember that saying? Hey, we'll have some coffee or something after. Okay? I'll see you tonight, I hope. 'Bye. Oh, it's me, Rosa, in case you forgot." Click.

I wanted a drink. *Fuck everything,* I thought, even Rosa. I picked up the phone and called Hank.

"It's me," I said.

"Oliver!"

"Look, fuck this—fuck everything; let's go back to when we drank and had fun. Let's stop this nonsense. I'm one of those people who can't handle much. And you know what? That's okay! Let's drink."

"Oliver, calm down, it's too late; we're like two speeding trains, our destiny is Transformation Island!" Hank said.

"Fuck that. I'm walking up Eighty-Sixth Street and heading to a bar, any bar on Manhattan Island."

"Don't do it! Don't pick up! You have to trust me on this, please Oliver! Nothing can ever be the same! Your not speaking to me for a while changed me. And I like it better with you not drinking. Please get a hold of yourself! Read the book. Be brave; be fearless. No one is going to laugh at you because you want to share your feelings."

"Look, Hanky, if you care to join me, call me. If not, fuck you, too! Fuck change and fuck this life! Fuck that book!" I hung up and left my apartment.

Damn Hank! I walked up First Avenue and stopped in front of a bar on the corner of Eighty-Sixth. I scratched my elbow. Damn Hank! I couldn't go inside, nothing could be the same now; I had to change; I had to try. Damn Hank! *What am I thinking! No, I can't do this!* I walked onward. *I can do this I can do this I can do this, I am not a weak man I am not a weak man, I will not let this control me. That letter, that horrible letter! I could change!* I walked and inhaled deeply to ease the panic. I stopped at another bar on Lexington. *No!* I went around the block and back down toward York. *Fuck!* I hoped for some kind of distraction, something that would keep my mind off the drink. Onward I walked.

Damn Hank! Damn Hank! Damn Hank! I shouldn't have called him.

I passed the funky clothing store that Beth and I would pass when we walked to the movie theater on First Avenue, and every time we passed it, she wanted to take me inside and buy me clothes. Of course I had always refused.

"But Oliver, you dress like an old man. You're young! Come on, let's go inside and buy you something more updated. Something funky and wild. Please, for me?"

I stood in front of the store. Its sign was in bold, swirling letters painted in deep indigo and a smooth ginger-orange. *Get Your Funk On.* I looked inside the window. The walls were orange with purple molding. Funky colorful clothes hung from the walls and colorful porcelain hooks. There were beaded framed mirrors all over the place. The place looked more like an East Village establishment than an Upper Eastside Store. It was empty, and I decided to go in. I could hear Beth's voice: *You're too conservative, too Upper East Side, too boring.* I was not a bore! I read the latest book about becoming a man, and it sucked. I could walk in this store, and

I could get my funk on!

As I entered the store, the scent of sweet Jasmine hit me. The music was soft and earthy: Carol King. I tried to appear calm and cool, as if I always went into stores like this. Actually, the last time I was in a store like this I was at college in Cambridge. I was looking for a knitted hat, and I swear the clerks mumbled that I looked nerdy.

I looked through a rack of shirts. Most of them were retro-1970s, with colorful psychedelic prints—stripes, dots, squares, and paisley. Then I went over to look at the jeans. One hundred and seventy-five dollars! I held them up. I picked up a soft, silky, black shirt. I put that down and picked up the jeans again. I felt a momentarily bewilderment over the price and the style. Could I wear something like this? Is this what people my age wore? I was thirty-six. A young man greeted me. He had a mouth full of too-white teeth, two ears pierced with slight golden rings, short brown hair, and a nose slightly off center. He wore tight jeans and a very tight t-shirt with a small tear over the right side of his chest.

"Those are Seven Jeans. The best Jeans you can buy. They'd look hot on you."

"I don't think so."

"Why not? You have the perfect body for them. I wish I had your ass."

"Oh. Thanks. I think." I felt my face turn red.

"Hi, I'm Gilbert. Welcome to Get Your Funk On. Is this your first time here?"

"Yes," I said, "it is."

"That sounds so phony. I've seen you walk by here in the mornings for, like, the past ten years. I could tell the time by it. I haven't seen you in the last few weeks, though."

"This used to be my path to work." My eyes shifted nervously.

"I'm glad you came in to check us out. I like your haircut, too. Hey, those jeans you're holding would look so amazing with this shirt!" Gilbert turned to the rack behind him and picked out a slinky blue shirt with horizontal lines in various shades of blue across the chest.

"You'd be the hit of the bar wearing this! Where do you hang out?"

"I don't go out."

"I hear you! The bar scene sucks. Sometimes I get so sick of gay men. Do you have a lover?"

"I am not gay."

"Come on, for real?"

"No, really."

"Damn! You ought to be with your good looks. Oh, well my loss. So let's get you some clothes!"

"I was just looking around," I said.

"Don't you watch TV? It's a new dawn. *The Queer Eye* is dressing the straight man! But don't be fooled by it. We don't all have good taste, trust me. See Ronnie over there?" Gilbert pointed to the man at the register, who looked half asleep. His head rested in his hands. He needed a shave, and looked like a lump of slop.

"He doesn't have a clue! He lives with his mother in Queens, and I think Mommy hems his blue jeans. I gave him a job because I felt bad for him. He's in the closet, too. I'm a sucker for a guy in denial, if he's cute of course. I feel so bad for Ronnie. I try and help him, but he insists he's asexual. How can anyone be asexual?" Gilbert rambled on as he went through the rack of clothes and piled things on his arm.

"So, tell me your story," Gilbert said. He held up a black shirt with white dots to my chest.

"My story?"

"Yeah, go on. Tell me everything," Gilbert said.

"I'm looking for a change. I guess I'm kind of boring. That's what I've been gathering from people lately. Well from my former wife, mostly," I said.

"We'll take care of that. You like blue? Blue would look nice on you." Gilbert put a blue shirt into the pile on my arms.

"I think this is plenty," I said. "Where can I try them on?"

"Well, it's buy-two-get-one-free on the shirts, and the jeans are buy-one-get-the second pair for twenty percent off, and these pants over here—come here—they're three pairs for one hundred one dollars. You might as well get it while it's hot."

For the next hour I tried on new clothes, while Gilbert waited outside the changing room and talked non-stop.

"So tell me more about this Rosa chick?" Gilbert asked. I had told him about school and Rosa.

"I am attracted to her and would like to go out with her. She's different."

"Tonight you get yourself all dressed up before your AA meeting, and you go up to this Rosa, and you ask her out for a cup of coffee and a piece of pie. Make sure you say 'pie.' Pie is a sexy word."

"Pie?" I asked.

"Trust me. Okay, so go on. You hate your new job. You like this Rosa chick. You want a change … what else?"

"I'm tired of being afraid of things."

"I hear you, Oliver! It's not really different for gay men. I finished reading this great book a few days ago, *The Castration of the 20th Century Man: How to Grow a New Set for the 21st Century*, and it's fabulous. It's based on society's fear of homosexuality and how we mess up our boys and all. Gay men are always trying to prove they're men, you know, that macho thing," Gilbert put on his best macho voice: "We're men, too; we only like to have dicks put into our orifices." He continued in his normal voice, "It doesn't mean we're 'fems.' Gay men are just as crazy when it comes to that macho stuff. It's so ridiculous." Gilbert let out a big bored sigh.

I came out of the dressing room. He was sitting down and resting his arms on the pile of clothes on his lap.

"I hated that book," I said.

"You didn't find it liberating?"

"No."

"How about the stuff about how straight men only enjoy homosexuality when it involves two women? And how men love their penises but want nothing to do with *other* penises? The lone penis, no matter how small or big, is a non-threatening unit at the opening of a vagina, but at a man's mouth or rectum, another erect penis is almost always nearby and ready for comparison."

"I think I skipped that part. The book wasn't my thing. At first I was intrigued. But it didn't work for me."

"I heard the book can have delayed reactions on some men. Maybe you're having a delayed reaction. Maybe you need to relax," he said. He frowned with concern, and his eyes became sad.

"I just didn't like the book, that's all," I said.

"Gosh, I love it! In fact, I'm going to start hosting a discussion group on the book. Right here in the store every Tuesday night. You should come. Maybe it would change your mind. It's not only gay men. It's straight men, too. I think it is going to be a very healing time in America. This book is changing men. A few boys who used to beat me up when I was a kid because I was a fem came in here and apologized and hugged me. It was weird to see those boys as full-grown, sensitive men. It was so therapeutic. Then, before they left, I gave them all blow jobs. Ha, only kidding! Don't look so horrified," Gilbert said.

"You got me, that was, uh, very funny," I said. Gilbert's face became serious.

"I want to say something. I might regret it, but what the heck! The book claims men are afraid to express their feelings to other men. Gay and straight men are very much alike, so here goes, I'm going to express myself."

"Uh, okay."

"I used to watch you walk by every morning, and I knew

you were not like everyone else. I knew you were different."

"Me? How?" I asked.

"Well, I live one floor up from this store, and sometimes in the morning after I come in from my jog, I eat yogurt and granola, and I'll sit by my kitchen window and crunch away and look down on the sidewalk, you know, watch the people pass. I usually see the same people every day, and I make up stories about them. I kind of get to know their lives by watching them. It's a little game I play by myself to pass the time. When you used to pass every morning at seven forty-five a.m. and then pass the store at three fifty p.m. almost every day for the last ten years, well, you always looked the same; in fact, it sounds funny, but you were one of the most consistent things in my life." Gilbert laughed.

"Is that good?" I asked.

"Consistency is good to a degree. I did wonder what happened to you, though, these past few months. God! You were like clockwork."

"You said you make up stories about people who pass by. What was my story?" I asked, and I smiled.

"Well, the people I see everyday are either smiling, laughing, crying, running for a bus, walking slowly. It's fun to see their changing moods and urgencies every day."

"What are you saying?"

"Yes, well, I shouldn't say this. But remember how the book says men have to help one another? Well, I guess it's ironic that you're here."

"Why?"

"When you passed every day I would say to myself, 'there goes the saddest person in the world.' I would smile at you, hoping you would look my way, but you only looked forward or downward, always stern and deep in thought, preoccupied and burdened. When you came in today, you can only imagine my surprise. While I was reading that book, in fact, you would be passing the store whenever I looked up. Life is funny, with its weird coincidences, isn't it?"

"I'm not sad," I said. My voice was a whisper.

"Oh, who cares what I think! I'm a drama queen! Hey, I think you should leave the store wearing your new clothes. Wear the jeans and the orange shirt. Don't wear a t-shirt, that's very '80s. Listen, I have some hair gel in the back, I can fluff up that fabulous new haircut of yours a bit, too. Then when you walk home, you'll see the way people look at you. I mean, you were always hot. Now you are on fire!"

"Okay," I reluctantly agreed.

After I put my new outfit on, I went over to the register and paid Gilbert. I knew I shouldn't be spending the money, but I did anyway.

Before I left, Gilbert straightened out my clothes then rubbed some hair gel in my hair and fixed it. I saw in his face his sincerity, gentleness, and happiness. He had balls.

"Thank you," I said. "I had a really bad day and this was good. Thanks."

"I had a really great time, too," Gilbert said. "Stop in and see me, and remember don't forget when you ask her out tonight, say coffee and 'pie.' "

"I won't forget, Gilbert. Goodbye."

"See you later. And smile, it looks good on you," he said as I left the store.

"Hey!"

"What?"

"How 'bout some sugar?"

I went back to him. He hugged me, and I hugged him back.

"You're growing a new set of balls, Ollie! You hugged a gay man."

"My father was gay, too," I said proudly.

"My luck it doesn't run in the family. Or does it, a little, perhaps, maybe?"

"No. I'm sorry." I winked at him and left the store.

I stood in front of the store, a bit paralyzed with fear over the newly clothed me. *Fuck*. I *was* a sad person. But I admitted to myself standing there, holding the bags and wearing my new outfit, that I felt more alive and sexy than ever. I noticed the glances from women and some men as they passed me. I wondered if I looked younger than thirty-six. I combed my hand through my hair. I wondered how June would react. With intense scrutiny? Or would she approve? Or would she be vaguely embarrassed for me? I didn't care, because I didn't want a drink anymore. Whatever I'd done, it had worked. When I started to walk away from the store, there was Hanky, running toward me, his belly bouncing.

"Oliver, Oliver! Wait, wait!" He was huffing and puffing.

"Hank, you're going to give yourself a heart attack. What the hell are you doing?"

"Did—Did—Did you drink? Did you do it?" He was perspiring heavily.

"No, I didn't," I said. Then he hugged me tightly, too tightly in fact. He felt like a vinyl, smelly bean bag chair that had been put on the curb for pick-up.

"Thank … thank Christ. Thank Christ! I've been in every bar from here to First Avenue searching for you." Hank let go of me. He took a step back and looked me over. He had this astonished expression on his face.

"What?" I asked.

"Your clothes, your hair. God you're … you're … wow, you're a super model. Work it girl."

"What? What did you say?"

"Nothing. You look good, like a new person. Wow!"

"I bought them at that store." I motioned to the store behind me.

"Get Your Funk On?" Hank read the sign. "Well, you certainly did get your funk on," he said. He crossed his arms, and he looked at me with glassy, puppy-dog eyes. It was scaring me.

"Do you know Gilbert?" he asked.

"Yeah, do you?" I said.

"Not really, kind of, I guess. I met him at a book signing for *Castration* the other day at Barnes and Noble." Hank coughed like crazy.

"You okay?" I asked.

"Sure. I'd like to buy some new clothes, but to be honest with you, I thought you'd laugh at me."

"I wouldn't laugh at you," I said.

"The book says that men are afraid to experiment with new clothes. It's about fear of our feminine sides and what our buddies would say. Plus I'm still fat and I can't fit in those clothes. But I will! I'm exercising and I'm taking *Trim-Forever*, these dietary supplement pills. It's a new dawn for me. Wanna grab an ostrich burger with me? They're very low in fat."

"You're obsessed with that lousy book," I said.

"I am not," Hank said. He put his hands on his hips and stamped his foot.

"Look, Hank I need to be alone and figure things out."

Gilbert came out of the store.

"Hey Hank, how are you?" Gilbert asked.

"Hi, Gilbert, what's up?" Hank said. He gave me a quick, darting, nervous smile.

"You're losing weight! I can tell, come on in. I have a shirt that would look good on you.

Don't be insulted. It's an extra large, but it's funky. I ordered it for you."

"Go in, Hanky, I have to be alone." I said.

Hank rolled his eyes and hit me on the shoulder in a loving way.

"I think he's gay," Hank whispered to me.

"So what? Grow up Hank," I said.

"I dunno. I was only making a statement. No big deal."

"Hank, I need to go. 'Bye," I said. Was Hank exploring his

feminine side? Or was he a raving queen on a fast moving train to Buttfuckville?

I couldn't think of that anymore; besides, I didn't care where Hank did or did not want to stick his penis.

When I arrived on my block, I saw Rosa sitting on my stoop. I didn't know what to expect from her, but I was excited all the same.

"Hi there. You okay?" she said. She shielded her eyes from the bright afternoon sun.

"I know it was unprofessional of me to leave, but I couldn't do it anymore. I know my limitations. I knew them the first day I was at the school. It's not fair to the students or to you or me."

"You're being way too hard on yourself." She patted the step next to her, indicating that I should sit. "I like your clothes and your haircut." Rosa smiled. "They made fun of you, didn't they?"

"Yeah, the way I dressed, my hair, everything."

"They made you feel old."

"I was cool at one time; at least I think I was. Hell, who am I trying to fool? I was never cool," I said.

"It's a bitch—getting old. Look, the first time I lost my temper with one of these kids, I felt like a total monster. I went home, and I cried myself to sleep. This kid, he pissed me off and was testing me all day. You see, these kids feel awful about themselves, and they want us to confirm it. They want us to dislike them. But I can't and I won't give up on them."

"I give you lot of credit. I can't do it," I said.

"You won't come back?"

"I'm sorry."

"What if I told you I had another class that I think you would like?"

"I'm not capable of teaching those kids. I would be doing them a disservice."

"I think it's great you know your limitations, but this

other class, well, they're smaller kids and their teacher has to leave. She's pregnant, and she's not coming back. It would be a great help to me, the kids, the school."

"I don't think so."

"I think you would really like it. You like children, don't you? I think you'd be good with little kids."

"Yes, I like children, why would you ask me that? Does it appear that I don't like children?" I asked.

"No, I was only wondering," Rosa said.

"Because I do like children, and I think people get the wrong idea about me."

"You like Italian food?" she asked.

"What?"

"Italian food. You like it?"

"Yeah, I guess," I said.

"Let's go to little Italy."

"I wanted to go to a meeting tonight," I said.

"We'll have our own meeting. Let's go now, come on."

I left a note for June, and soon Rosa and I were on the Number Four downtown. We walked along Canal Street heading toward Mulberry, stopping and looking at a few items in front of the Chinese markets. Rosa thought about buying a pair of Asian slippers, and we both looked at the fresh fish. Rosa was terrified of one large slimy-looking fish sitting in chipped ice; the fish had a thorny body and a mouth that was opened wide, exposing sharp, needle-like teeth. Rosa grabbed my arm and buried her face in my shoulder, exclaiming that she was "grossed out." She held on to me for about a block without reservation, like it was no big deal, like I had known her for years. My body was relaxed as we strolled up to Mulberry. She had this great, comforting energy like a warm cup of milk on a wintry night.

Mulberry was busy that evening, swamped with people. We bumped shoulders with strangers and stopped at a few small stores. Rosa eyed a pasta maker and decided not to buy it. She told me she loved to cook. She was scoring major points with me already. There was a huge selection of Italian restaurants to choose from, and as we walked by each one, a maitre d' tried to entice us into his restaurant. Rosa politely shook her head and said, "No, grazie." She told me she had a special place to go where the food was excellent and cheap.

Down a tiny side street was a small, dark place called *Bella Luna*. The floor was uneven and the walls painted a bland, yellowish white. The tables were mismatched and the owner of the restaurant, a thin woman, sat at a table with a cigar box filled with money. A young, robust girl sat us down and gave us two worn menus. A candle sat on the table in a water glass and wax dripped into a plate underneath. It was charming. The smell of the place was almost too good to be true, as if it were embedded in the tables and walls and floors—this deep-roasted tomato, basil, Romano cheese, and olive oil smell.

"I adore this place. It's not fancy or anything, but the food is spectacular, all homemade, no pretense. I love it."

"It's great," I said.

"Can I order for us?"

"Sure."

"They have great gnocchi and their shrimp fra diavolo is fabulous; I have them put it over the gnocchi. It's spicy but delicious. Does that sound good?

"Perfect."

"And some grape juice?"

"Sounds great!" We laughed.

Although she looked exhausted, she still looked beautiful. Her hair was up in a twist and held in place by one of those large claw barrettes. She had both hands flat on the table and very softly patted the surface as if playing the bongos.

"Are you nervous?" I asked.

"I'm always nervous. I can never settle down after work; it

takes me forever. Before, I would have a drink. I can't do that now." She took her hands off the table and sat on them. The waitress came over, and Rosa ordered the food for us.

I started the conversation as we waited for our food, asking her questions about her life. I was fully intrigued by her childhood in Brooklyn.

Her father was a trumpet player and worked private parties around the city. Her mother was a singer and had actually cut a forty-five record in the mid 1970s that did fairly well. It was called "Kiss Me The French Way."

"Wow, I remember that song!" I sang a few of the lyrics and she joined in: open open open close close close those eyes, those eyes, those eyes and let let let let me kiss kiss kiss kiss you the French way the French way. We both cracked up.

"I have some copies if you want one, if you can find a record player," she laughed.

"What's a record player?" And we both laughed again.

The waitress came over and put down our grape juices. Rosa continued to tell me stories—how her mother once auditioned for Dick Clark. She was so amazed at how small he was in person that, in a slip of nervousness, she called him Mr. Tiny Dick. After that she knew she wasn't going to be on *American Bandstand* any time soon. In our throes of laughter, she knocked over our drinks, and we grabbed napkins in bunches and cleaned up the grape juice mess—despite the waitress, who wasn't happy over our silliness or the way we wasted the napkins. She told us she would get a cloth. It was the first time in ages that I had had a real hardcore belly laugh.

Our food came. And its fragrance was what I expect to smell in heaven. I looked down at my bowl of food: six jumbo shrimp and plum tomatoes and garlic over a bed of gnocchi.

"It smells great!" I said.

We started to eat. It was amazing, hot and spicy. And Rosa went on.

"My father used to make this for us every Friday night when I was a kid. My sister and I would wait all night for him to come home. We're talking the mid seventies. I was like maybe fourteen. That was a wild time in the City. He'd be home drunk from a gig in the Village, and my sister and I would watch him cook at three a.m. I don't think he knew any better, and he'd give us glasses of wine. We'd talk all night as we ate and laughed. Then he'd pass out on the sofa, and my mother would bitch from the bedroom that the smell was keeping her from sleeping.

"My mother, God love her, put up with a lot from my father. I think she felt kind of left out. My sister and I adored him. They both had big aspirations. They did okay, not great. But my dad still plays the horn at Seventy-Three, and Mom will sing if you ask her, although she likes to pretend she's all washed up. But I know my mother—she's still waiting for her big contract from Columbia Records." Rosa rubbed her eyes and sighed.

"They sound like a couple of characters," I said.

"They're musicians. They're nutty. Dad still parties. They can be fun. But they're drunks."

"My father was, too," and I told her about my childhood and all the gory details. Then I told her about Beth. She listened attentively while she ate, always keeping her eyes on me. I absolutely loved the delicate way she picked up the shrimp with her fingers and bit into it.

"You'd be great with the class I want you to work with. I wish you would give it a chance. They're adorable little kids. You'd be a perfect fit. Lots of adults who come from rough childhoods do magic with children. Do you feel you're too messed up to work with young kids? Is that it?"

I didn't answer her and went on eating. There was silence as she kept her eyes on me. She leaned over and dabbed sauce off my chin with a napkin. Our eyes locked for a moment.

"Don't be afraid, Oliver. They're kids who really need to be loved," she said.

"How come you don't have a boyfriend?" I asked.

"We're changing the subject, I see. Who said I don't have a boyfriend?"

"I'm sorry I assumed that you didn't." Ralph already told me, but I wanted the scoop from her.

"Don't assume anything, Oliver." She winked at me. She told me she did have a boyfriend, but they were taking time off. She told me that she was fairly new to the AA program. Her boyfriend's name was Charlie, and he was having second thoughts about their relationship. She wanted to marry him, but he hesitated because of her drinking, and that was one of the reasons she was in the program. She also said her family drove Charlie crazy because they depended on her so much. She would get calls from them at all hours of the day and night.

"They're musicians, they're wild people, what can I tell you?" She confessed she had a bad temper and that she once threw a book at Charlie. It had clobbered him on the head. She laughed.

"It sounds funny now, but his expression of total dismay when the book hit him in the face was awful. Looking back, it was rather funny!" She had a fit of uncontrollable laughter as she imitated Charlie's face after being hit with the book. I thought of my mother and how she threw things at my father when she was angry. I tried to smile as best I could.

"You love him still, don't you?" I asked. She became serious.

"Yes, I love Charlie more than I thought I did. It was devastating for a while, but I'll get over it. I have to move forward. I want him back, and maybe he'll have me back, maybe he won't, but I need this time to figure stuff out, so it's good and not necessarily bad."

"Oh, come on," I blurted out. I couldn't believe I'd said that, and I cast my eyes downward.

"I'm serious. I know it sounds phony, but I have no

choice. I have to keep positive about it. If I don't I'll lose it. I really love him, but if it doesn't work out, maybe someone or something else will come my way. Don't you miss your wife?"

"Sure I do. But I'm angry at the same time. A lot of why she left me was my fault."

"How so?"

"I'm messed up. I guess," I said. How could I tell her I was an asshole to my former wife and drove her to nymphomania?

We ate the rest of the meal in silence as the place started to fill up with locals who spoke Italian to the lady at the table with the cigar box. I found myself staring at the people drinking dark red wine out of water glasses. I wanted to leave, for I swear I could smell the wine on my fingers, on my clothes and taste it on my lips.

After we finished eating, Rosa suggested a walk through Mulberry and into Soho. It was getting cold out, and she grabbed onto my arm. As we walked, her head was down and she looked at our feet. She told me I had big beastly feet, and I told her that her feet were tiny like a mouse's. Then she stepped on my foot.

"Ouch! Mighty Mouse!"

"That's right, and don't forget it, buster!"

She giggled a deep, raspy giggle that I was becoming accustomed to and extremely turned on by.

As we entered Soho, she told me that when she was a kid, Soho was nothing but streets of abandoned buildings and how as teenagers, she, her sister and their friends would party inside the abandoned buildings for entire weekends. She said she wanted to break out of her world of Brooklyn and work and live in Manhattan. Being in the buildings brought her closer to her dream. It was all she ever wanted when she was a young girl.

"Now this neighborhood is the most expensive place to

live in the city, go figure."

Rosa stopped walking. We were in front of a posh clothing shop with enormous windows. Inside was a chaise lounge covered in sumptuous blue upholstery and draped with elegant scarves and hats with labels written in French. A headless mannequin wore a little black dress.

"This is where I live," she said.

"You're kidding! This is a great building."

"This building is the very building I would party in. In the wee hours of the night, when the sunlight started falling over the city, I would stare out the window, right up there." She pointed to the second floor above the clothing shop.

"I'd be all hung over, and I would dream of living in the City when I grew up. I bought this place for an absolute steal when it was only a shell of a place. Everyone said I was crazy. I used some of my student loans, and I borrowed money. I rented out the ground floor to these two guys who wanted to open a clothing shop, and they renovated the downstairs. I gave them a life-long lease, and they basically helped me pay for the building. But I did it. Who is crazy now?" She teasingly punched my arm.

"Ouch! You're violent!" I joked.

"Remember that, Pepper!" Again, she giggled.

Yum!

She moved in close to me and went on her tiptoes. She kissed me on my nose. I wanted to grab her in my arms, lay a big kiss on her, and make love to her right there and then on the sidewalk.

"Goodnight, Oliver"

"Goodnight, Rosa."

"Tomorrow is Saturday."

"I know."

"I make soup on Saturdays. Can you come over?"

"I'd love to."

" 'Night, Oliver."

I watched as she entered her home. I looked up until the second floor lights went on. I jumped up and clenched my fist. I had had a date with Rosa and I was going to see her tomorrow, too!

THIRTY

Rosa opened the door to her apartment, handed me a vegetable peeler, and told me to follow her into the kitchen. She was wearing a silky-looking, beige and black paisley printed pair of pants and an oversized black sweatshirt that was cut wide around the neck to expose a sexy white camisole underneath. On her feet she wore fluffy orange slippers that made me smile. Her place was rustic European—like walking into a Tuscan villa with its deep yellows, oranges, and reds. Her kitchen was from a different world. Modern Italian, very chic with stainless steel appliances. She handed me a butternut squash.

"Don't stand there. Peel!" she giggled.

Oh, that giggle.

We both stood by the sink. I peeled the squash. It took me forever, and she shook her head in dismay. She quickly peeled the onions, celery, and carrots and put cooked white cannelloni beans in a ceramic bowl. A bottle of dark green olive oil sat by the stove, while a massive, cobalt blue Le Creuset pot filled with vegetable stock steamed over a jumping flame. She was quiet and focused. She showed me how to cut the squash into small perfect cubes that were the size of orange gum drops. Meanwhile she added all the chopped vegetables to the steaming stock, mashed the garlic, opened a can of diced tomatoes, and added the beans, three cloves, and salt and pepper. The final touch was fresh sage and a swirl of olive oil. When she was done, she looked at me, waiting for my reaction.

"Tuscan Bean and Yellow Butternut Soup. It was my grandmother's specialty."

"It looks and smells great."

"Is it very cold out?"

"No, it's not that bad."

"Great! I want to take you up on the roof. There is a fantastic view of the city."

New York City sprawled before us. It was cloudy that day, but the view was still magnificent. Across the way, another couple waved to us from their rooftop, and we waved back. It made me feel officially coupled, even though it was only a second date. We looked north and watched as low clouds floated by and played hide-and-seek with the top of the Empire State Building. The wind blew a chill breeze our way, and Rosa leaned into me and turned her body south.

"Right after 9/11 it would freak me out to come up here. Charlie and I had planned on building a deck that weekend. We were planning a garden in the spring. That was when I was really drinking.

"This city is everything to me, and when that happened, it was like my world was totally crushed. It was hard for everyone, I know. But I feel like 9/11 was done to me and me alone. It's funny, though. Even though New York City has millions of people, I think it has an intimate relationship with every individual who lives here. Charlie was really patient with me."

Her face became blank; she looked on the verge tears. I asked if she was okay.

"Sometimes I feel really strong, and other days I feel awful. I miss him. I'm moving on, and that's scary." The wind was blowing steadier now, and she started to shiver. She put her arms around me.

"You don't mind, do you?"

"Ah, that would be a no," I said. She laughed.

"I'm cold," she said. "I guess being with you is making me think about things, and it's good; it's good to move on. I can't wait and put my life on hold for him, right?"

"Yes, right. I understand," I said.

"Obviously we like each other, and a part of me is sad that I'm moving on. Charlie is never going to call. I know Charlie; he'd rather avoid things than hurt someone. He has no intention of getting back with me."

"You like me? Like, *like* me? Like in *dating* like?" I asked.

"Get real, will you? Hello? I don't make soup for people I don't like."

"I made the soup, too."

"Kiss me," she said.

I held her close, and I kissed her. I pulled away, and she smiled sadly at me.

"Why did you stop?"

"I wanted to make sure you were okay."

"I'm fine." She buried her head into my chest. "You feel nice," she said.

I must admit I did feel anxious holding Rosa at first, and I wanted to run from her because I felt nervous. My chest became tight. Panic was starting to overwhelm me. I didn't understand it. But I closed my eyes and I fought it. I told myself I was acting like child, a complete crazy person. For weeks I'd been waiting for this, and here I was scared shitless.

Relax. Relax. Relax.

I pulled Rosa closer, and it was as though I had embraced my fear. Within seconds, all panic and fear was gone. I was holding the woman I'd wanted to hold for the last month. I was still alive. Nothing was being taken from me. I actually felt good. No, I felt great! I was okay, and to my surprise, I didn't want to let Rosa go. We both stood there and shivered in each other's arms.

When we went back inside her apartment, the robust smell of the bean soup made her place overwhelmingly cozy and warm. She turned the soup on low, poured us a glass of ginger ale, and we sat on her sofa.

"Well, it's not *Pinot Noir*. But it will do."

"We're not supposed to talk like that," I said, putting on the best false authoritative voice I could muster.

"Don't laugh. We're not supposed to be dating during the first year of sobriety either," she said gravely.

"Who says we're dating now?" I smiled.

"You know what I mean."

I picked up my ginger ale and gulped it down.

"Here's to breaking the rules!" I said. She smirked.

"You know what they say in AA. 'Get 'em while they're still shaking,' " she said.

"What's that mean?" I asked.

"Giving up drinking brings on a flood of emotions, if you haven't noticed yet."

"Oh, really, I haven't noticed," I joked.

"We're not supposed to be caring for anyone but ourselves this first year of abstinence. That's what the unwritten thirteenth step is all about."

"Let's see where this takes us, okay?"

Our eyes locked. I knew she recognized the fear and sadness in mine, for she had the same look in hers. I made the excuse I was still cold in hopes that she would nestle closer to me, but instead, she brought an afghan her grandmother had made and put it around me. She must have read the disappointment on my face.

"What?" she said.

"I don't know; I was hoping for you and not an afghan."

She moved in close and told me to put my feet up on the sofa. I did. She snuggled into me, and soon we both fell asleep.

It was late afternoon when I woke. I was still holding Rosa

in my arms. An autumn afternoon glow came in through the giant windows and lit Rosa's place in flaxen and crimson hues. In the distance, I could hear a plane flying overhead, and the buildings that I could see from my position were turning into brownish silhouettes against the sky. I could see other people in the yellow lighting of their apartments going about their business, and for the first time in a very long while, I felt as if I was truly alive.

Rosa was still sleeping, and I gingerly touched her nose, eyelids, ears, and chin with the tip of my fingers; she reminded me of a small buttercup still thriving after summer's end. She breathed evenly and softly, and I kissed the top of her head. As she started to wake up, she moved closer to me. I became excited. Without opening her eyes, she felt me through my pants. I kissed her neck and put my hand under her shirt and caressed her firm breasts. Our lips locked. We kissed heavily for a few moments. She unbuttoned my shirt and slipped it over my shoulders. I took off my pants, and I laid on top of her kissing her neck and feeling her slender but rounded hips. While she removed her clothes, my mouth never left her body, and we moved and jolted together, making love in a slow, perfect rhythm.

We spent that weekend together in bed. By Sunday night, we were tired and worn out from love-making, but still we wanted more. The heartache that I'd carried within me for months seemed gone, and for those two days I felt free from all problems.

Early evening on Sunday, Rosa and I sat in her bed nude and ate the last of the soup while watching re-runs of *I Love Lucy* on some obscure cable station.

"I should go home. I have to start looking for another job."

"Can't you at least give this class a try?" Rosa asked. She jumped on me and pleaded with me to come to the school the next day.

"I really, really need a teacher tomorrow. Please give this other class a chance. Pretty please?" She whined like a small girl and pouted her lips.

We laughed.

"Oh, so that is what this weekend was about? Seducing me and making me soup—all so I would teach for you?"

"Okay, you found me out. I'm a player. I'll do anything to get a teacher into my school."

"Well, it worked. I'll do it. I'll do it!" I pulled her toward me and kissed her forehead.

Rosa jumped up and did a little dance on the bed around me. Her naked body was divine—firm, but dainty.

"Oliver, I know you'll love these kids. I know it! You'll be great with them!"

"What are they like?"

"They're about six and seven, and they've got Down Syndrome or are autistic. They will love you!"

My eyes widened. "I don't have the proper training," I said.

"It doesn't matter; we don't have a teacher for them. There is a shortage, and many special ed teachers don't want to go that far uptown. It's a bad neighborhood, or they're racist, who knows? I know it's not easy teaching at my school, but it's challenging."

"Boy was I ever challenged. I did the best I could, I hope," I said. I put my hands behind my head. I closed my eyes. She was putting me on the spot. I wanted to change the subject, but I let her talk.

"Look, Oliver, these children mostly need special attention and patience and someone they can count on, and especially they need a man in their lives. Most of the children come from single homes and neglect. It's not like teaching the older boys."

I felt cornered. I looked over at her.

"I think I am going to pass. I know I said I would, but I

can't. I mean Rosa, the classes are mixed with Down Syndrome and autistic kids? I can't do that! That's kind of much, isn't it?" I scratched my head. I was grasping for anything that might allow me to back out of this, but Rosa's pleading eyes were melting my heart. She had so much passion and really cared for these children. I looked away from her.

"I have to mix all the kids, because well, I'll say only this—money, space, minorities. Need I say more? I'm trying to change things. I'm really trying and no one wants to give and sometimes I feel like I'm doing it alone."

"I don't know if I can do it," I said. She let out a small sigh. She looked at the ceiling, closed her eyes, and then turned on her side and faced me, resting her head in her hand.

She ran her hands down my chest and my thighs.

"Try it for one week, okay?" she said.

She rubbed her feet against my feet. It was so sexy. I knew I couldn't let Rosa down.

"Look at you! You're something else, seducing me so I will teach," I said. We laughed.

"Whatever it takes," she said and pulled on my ear.

I told her I would cover the class until she found another teacher to take over.

We made love again before I left for home.

When I entered my apartment I was greeted by June and Ralph, who were playing cards at the kitchen table. They looked over at me with huge, knowing grins on their faces.

"How was your weekend?" June asked coyly. She raised an eyebrow to Ralph but didn't look up from her cards.

Naturally, Ralph had to throw his two cents in.

"I think it's great you and Rosa are getting along. But you do know that during your first year in the program, you shouldn't be ..."

"I know, Ralph! Will you please let me have the one thing

that is making me happy through this entire disgusting mess called my life? Will you?"

"You're right, sorry pal!" he said.

"And don't call me pal," I barked.

"Well, you are a grumpy Gus," June said.

"You both drive me nuts. Goodnight!"

As I walked to my bedroom, June shouted at me, offering a piece of banana cream pie. I refused. They giggled again after Ralph made some silly comment to June about me and sex. I could hear them snickering. I was a bit embarrassed but felt good all the same.

I remember thinking that I was falling in love with Rosa.

I sat on my bed, leaned back, and stretched out. I could smell her all around me.

THIRTY-ONE

Franco came running when I entered the school. He was excited to see me. His eyes widened, but he tried not to hide his surprise at first. As he followed me into the school, he talked nonstop.

"Thought you weren't coming back?"

"I changed my mind," I said.

"What changed your mind?"

"None of your business."

"Shit. That cool. Ain't my business if you and Miss Rosa doing the nasty," he said.

"Franco, behave," I said. He started to point and laugh at me. I climbed the stairs.

"Ohhhhh. You done it with Miss Rosa!" He kept right by my side.

"Shhh! Franco. Control yourself."

"It's good you're back anyway. It's good. Shit. I downloaded some new music on my iPod. Mr. Clark let me use his computer. I have all kinds of music on this. You wanna hear some music, Pepper? I got some real good stuff. Here listen." He held the earphone up to me.

"I'd like to, Franco, but I have to go see Miss Rosa."

"I bet you do. She's hot. She real hot." He started to laugh.

"Not funny!"

"You coming back to my class? I'll be good. I'll be good for you in class. I'm going to get my ass out of here. No one goin' hold my ass down. Not even these fucked up kids. I'm not bad like them. You think I'm bad like them. But I'm not. I'm going to do real good. You'll see. Are you sure you don't want to hear my music, Pepper? It real good. I've been thinking; I can learn to write real good, and maybe I can write rap music! You know I could do that. Shit. I could do that. I got all kinds of rap on my iPod. You could help me write. Like when we write that letter to my father. What do you think of that? We could do that? Shoot, we could be a team. You gotta get new clothes, though. Cool clothes. I want no one looking like you writing with me. Shit."

"Franco, I'm teaching in another class. Not yours. But I'll be around if—if you need me. I'll be here still. We can write music together. We can do that one day."

"You promise me. You ain't just saying that shit?"

"Ahh, I'm not just saying that … shit." I found myself smiling. *What kind of songs could I write with Franco?*

"You crazy, Pepper!" He laughed.

Rosa met me at the top of the stairs. She looked at Franco sternly.

"Franco get to class!"

"I'm going. I'm going. You two got your business." Franco started to laugh as he strolled to his classroom. Rosa crossed her arms and looked at me suspiciously. I whispered to her.

"He knows. How he knows I have no idea."

"He's too smart for his own good," Rosa whispered back at me.

Franco looked back at Rosa and me.

"Shit Pepper, I knew you'd be back. I knew it. I knew you were different."

"You said I was like every teacher that came here."

"Shit. What the hell do I know? Shit. Pepper is back!"

"Watch the mouth, Franco!" Rosa shouted after him.

He ran down the hall.

Rosa took me down a hallway in the opposite direction behind closed doors. "We separate them. The other kids can be mean," she said.

I followed Rosa into a large classroom. My hands felt numb and my eyes started blinking like crazy. I could not believe how nervous I had suddenly become. I heard the children's small voices: shouts, babbles, laughter, but I couldn't look at them. I was fearful of what I might see. Instead, I glanced over to one corner where there was a colorful rug with blue and yellow plastic bins filled with toys, books, and building blocks. My eyes lifted to the big windows of the classroom, and I looked out. There was a wide, open view of Bolton. The shades were closed. Bolton was cut-off from my new world. I could feel the blood rush back to my hands. I looked at the children. I half-smiled.

In the center of the classroom was a long table that they all sat around—two boys and three girls.

"Hello, boys and girls! How is my favorite class?" Rosa said.

She happily marched toward the kids and sang,

Twinkle, twinkle, little star!
How I wonder what you are!

The children all laughed. She held her arms open, and three of them gleefully ran over and hugged her. The other two children sat, smiled, moaned, and tilted their heads. One girl stuck her tongue out at me.

Then I was greeted by Tatty, the paraprofessional. She was a woman in her late thirties, tallish, doll-faced, with smooth skin. Her brown hair circled her face and her brown eyes twinkled. She wore jeans and a shirt with a huge *Mickey Mouse* on its front.

"I'm Tatty. You must be the new teacher." Her voice was chirpy and gregarious. She put her long hand out for me to shake.

As I was about to shake Tatty's hand, I felt a tug on the

edge of my shirt. I looked down to see a small girl insisting that I go with her. I was bewildered for a moment, then Rosa motioned for me to comply.

"That's Kat. She wants to show you something."

The little girl guided me to the teacher's desk, which was a few feet away from Rosa and Tatty. I never had a child approach me before in such a forceful way, and I was a bit overwhelmed and embarrassed.

"She likes you. She knows a kind face. Right, Kat?" Rosa went over to the girl, bent down and hugged her. Kat slapped her in the face.

"Go away," Kat whispered angrily to Rosa and pushed her.

"I have competition," Rosa said lightheartedly; she looked up at me and rolled her eyes.

"Go away, go away!" Kat said to her and continued to pull on my shirt.

"Hey! Be nice. Be nice," Rosa said, and she stroked Kat's face softly. Kat repeated "nice" back to Rosa and then hugged her.

I'd never seen an African-American person with Down Syndrome before. Kat had multiple braided pig tails all over her head. She was extremely thin and wore a pink shirt with polka-dot pants. She was quick in her movements and smiled constantly. Her voice was low and twittery.

"Sit. Sit. Sit," Kat said to me as she took my hand and brought me to the teacher's desk. I sat. She looked up at me, tilted her head, put her hands behind her back, rocked in place, stared at me, and smiled blankly.

"You my Pappi?" she asked.

Rosa and Tatty sniggered. I felt the corners of my mouth lift and my eyes blink uncontrollably.

"I love it!" Rosa said. She covered her mouth to control her laughter, and her eyes widened. Kat then opened the teacher's drawers, took out pencils and scissors, and went about her business. Soon the other students came to the desk and watched. Cody and Cherri still sat at the table, resting their heads on their curled arms.

"Kat, stop opening the drawers! She likes to take things," Tatty said to me, scooping Kat up in her arms.

"Okay, class, all eyes up here!" Rosa said. The kids looked up at Rosa. They really paid attention to her when she spoke, and I loved the way she could take charge.

For obvious reasons I tried not to look too much at Rosa. No matter how much I believed in my breakthrough with 'letting love in,' I had my neurotic moments of doubt. I still wanted to please, help, and impress her.

In short, I was a big car wreck.

"This is your new teacher. His name is Mr. Pepper. Can you say his name?" The kids tried the best they could, and we decided Mr. Pip would suffice.

Kat, still held by Tatty, made grunting noises and stretched her arms out to me. She wanted me to hold her. I had no choice but to obey. She started to gently stroke my face, but within seconds she was using more and more force. Finally I got the same slap Rosa received minutes prior.

I repeated what Rosa had said, "Nice, be nice."

And Kat repeated back to me, "Nice, be nice." Then she laughed and slapped me again. "My Pappi!" She twisted to show she wanted me to put her down.

When I did, Tatty picked her up.

"You need to watch Kit Kat; she'll run out on you."

"Okay class, have a very good day. Bye-bye!" Rosa said. All the kids waved to her, and Rosa winked at me and mumbled, "Good luck Pappi. Have a good day. You'll be fine. Tatty is great." She jokingly nudged me in my rib cage and then left the classroom.

I said another prayer. I whispered to myself, *Please Dad, God, Mom, anyone, help me out here! I can't fail, I can't fail anymore.* I swallowed a lump in my throat the size of Jupiter.

Rosa had given me a folder with coloring exercises and letters to cut out, and she told me she had tons of books in her office. Their lesson plans were very simple because most of the kids had low cognitive skills. The trick, she said, was to keep them busy.

Keep them busy; make them work; don't let them sit there; give them structure; be patient; you never know what they can learn—what they absorb in their minds.

"Miss Rosa told me that you all like to draw the alphabet, and I have some special worksheets for us to work on together," I said as I walked toward the class. Tatty had seated them all.

"I hate you!"

This was my introduction to Cherri. She started to whine—not a full-fledged whine, but a noise that was high-pitched and nerve-wracking. She hit the table. Cherri was difficult; there is no other way to say it. However, we did have our good moments. Like when she wanted a snack or an apple juice. But, on the whole, she hated my guts for no apparent reason. Cherri was a seven-year old with a full head of wiry, black hair. She was overweight, had wide-set eyes and skin as white as porcelain; these features, sadly, gave her a severe, unwelcoming look, kind of like a little banshee.

"I hate you! Don't come near this table!" she screamed at me again.

"Stop it, Cherri." Tatty pulled up a chair and held Cherri's hands.

"Hate. Hate. Hate you. I want Miss Starky. I hate you. I want Miss Starky. I hate you. Hate. Hate. I hate you."

"Cherri, if you don't stop, you'll go in time-out," Tatty said. Cherri buried her head in her arms and whined.

Tatty explained to me that Miss Starky was their last teacher.

"Mr. Pip. I gotta go. I gotta go," said a deep and throaty voice. This was Maurice. He had dark skin and he wore a turtleneck. His eyes were a bit crossed behind his glasses. His hand twitched. I would quickly learn that Maurice spent more time in the bathroom than most senior citizens. "Maurice always has to go to the toilet," Tatty said to me.

Maurice jumped up and down and ran for the door. Tatty went after him and pulled him back into the classroom. The other kids clapped, with the exception of Cody. Kat had her head on the table and stared up at me, whispering "Pappi," over and over.

Tatty gently put her hands on Maurice's chin and bent down to him.

"Maurice, look at me. You must stay in the classroom. Look at me."

Maurice let out a series of deep, unintelligible groans. Tatty noticed my look of horror as she held his face sternly.

"Mr. Pepper, holding their faces and looking directly at them helps them listen better."

"Okay."

"You look stunned."

"I understand. I'm okay," I said. Truthfully, I was freaked out.

"I gotta go! I gotta go! I gotta go!" Maurice yelled and pounded his desk. Tatty held his hands down.

I was failing, I told myself. Failing. These children were out of my control. My stomach was in knots, and surely Tatty thought I wasn't going to be *any* good at this. But I could not fail, I told myself. I could do this.

I can do this!

I looked over at Cody, who simply sat and smiled tenderly. I bent down to him and said, "Hello." Without acknowledging my presence, the boy got up and went over to the rug area, where there was an assortment of toys and building blocks which he started to stack—humming all the while. Cody was tiny, with very light brown skin. His eyes were small slits, and his mouth was full and thick. He was autistic as well and had an angelic quality to him, but he seemed fragile, as if the slightest disturbance in his life would break him.

I felt a tug on my pants. I looked down, and there was Ruthie.

"Fuck you!" she said to me, sticking her fingers in her mouth and her tongue out at me at the same time. It wasn't a pretty sight. Ruthie had Down Syndrome and was much heavier than Kat. Her hair was gathered in one large ponytail and tied with a red ribbon. Her belly stuck out of her shirt, and her bum stuck out like a round ball, heavy from thick diapers. Ruthie then hugged my right leg and would not let go, no matter how hard I tried to peel her off me. Kat ran toward me and latched onto my left leg.

"Ladies, excuse me ladies," I said. They would not budge. They looked at each other and cracked up laughing.

Tatty came over to me and whispered, "Ruthie is no lady. She got a mouth on her. She does things you're not going to believe. She doesn't come from a good home."

"I gotta go!" Maurice said and ran to Tatty. He put his arms around Kat. Cherri kept repeating how much she hated me, and Cody remained on the rug, absorbed in his own world of stacking blocks.

Tatty was smiling as she tried to get the kids off me. "They like you," she said.

Like me? I thought. *This* is "like"? I felt like a complete loser; everything was out of my control. These kids were all over the place.

Kat looked up at me, grinned widely, and said in a soft voice, "You can't catch me." She put her small foot in front of her body and rocked as if preparing to run a marathon. She then darted out of the classroom so quickly, I swear I saw smoke rise from the heels of her shoes. She headed down the long hallway, and Tatty called to me, "You gotta get her! Quick!"

I ran after her, and when she saw me she stopped. When I got close to her she started to run and laugh. I stopped. She ran. When I didn't move, she stayed still. Finally she sat on the floor and spread her body out, and I went to her.

"Come on, Kat, come back into the classroom. Be a good girl."

She moved her head from side to side, clapped, said a sharp, "No!" and beamed with joy.

"Come on Kat, come with me," I said again. She shook her head again.

Tatty shouted from the classroom doorway, "Mr. Pepper, Maurice went to the bathroom in his pants, and I have to clean him up!"

I scratched my head and looked down at Kat. She was now making snow angels on the floor. I pulled on her hands, "Come on, come with me," I said. She stood, put her hand out, and without any reservations, took my hand and walked back to the classroom as if nothing had happened, singing softly to herself.

The classroom smelled horrible. Tatty took Maurice by his hand to the boy's room. She had diapers in her hand. I sprayed the room with air freshener, which made it smell like a giant peach sitting in human doo doo.

This wasn't going to work out. I would simply have to humble myself again and admit to Rosa that I was a complete failure, only capable of teaching art to rich girls.

"Shit! Shit! Shit!" Ruthie screamed.

"Stop that, Ruthie," I said. She stuck out her tongue and gave me the finger.

I would finish out the day, disappoint Rosa—more likely lose her—and continue with my lousy existence alone, but first I would lie to June and tell her I was working and happy and that everything was hunky-dory. Then I would encourage her to get married. I would get a job as a cashier at CVS, find a room in some flea-ridden joint, and live in squalor. Maybe I would be a drunk again, too.

I picked up a children's book about some underwater school bus and, my voice full of defeat, I called the kids.

"Okay everyone, come over to the rug; I'm going to read a story."

Kat came to me and swung around and whacked me in the thigh.

"Ouch! Stop that!" I said.

But she continued to slug me. She was having a great time for herself. Unlike me. Visions of sharp razor blades and nooses were dancing in my head. Ruthie followed her lead and hit me even harder.

"Both of you, stop hitting me!" I said.

I had a fantasy of slugging them. Was that bad?

"Fuck, fuck, fuck you, fuck you, fuck you!" Ruthie stuck out her tongue, went to the rug, and knocked over Cody's blocks.

Cody didn't react; he only moved closer to me. Finally the class sat Indian style on the rug, looking up at me. I felt a bit in control, although Cherri continued to mumble how much she hated me as she rested her chin in her hands. Her eyes shifted from side to side.

I sat down in front of the kids, opened the book and started to read. Maurice and Tatty returned to the room, and he took his place on the rug. Tatty sat across from me.

"I hate that book," Cherri said.

"That wasn't very nice, Cherri," I said.

I really wanted to tell her to "shut the hell up."

"That wasn't very nice," Maurice mumbled into his hand.

"Pay attention, everyone!" Tatty said, raising her voice.

"Sorry," Ruthie said. She patted Maurice's head and then slapped his face.

"I think someone hit me," Maurice said. He held his face.

"Someone did hit you," I said.

"Fuck you!" Ruthie said.

"Stop that! Be nice to Maurice," I said.

"Okay, I'll be nice, nice, nice," Ruthie said. And she patted Maurice, who only swayed in place with a stunned expression.

"I don't like you," Cherri said.

"I know. I know. I know, Cherri," I said.

"Maybe I like you," Cherri said.

She came to me and sat below my feet, where she touched my shoes and softly played on them as if they we bongo drums. Everyone moved in closer and started to laugh. Only Cody sat in place and smiled.

"Like. Like. Like. Like. Like," Cherri sang.

They all started to sing, and Tatty laughed.

"Okay, boys and girls, all eyes up on me. I'm going to read."

They all ignored me. Cherri cried. Kat and Ruthie did flips on the rug. Maurice farted and giggled. The only student looking at me was Cody. I bowed my head, befuddled, weary, and conquered. I ran my hand over my face.

"Are you okay?" Tatty asked.

When I looked up at Tatty, I glanced over at the clock to see how much time was left of this outrageous day. Then I saw under the clock a print of one of Van Gogh's *Sunflowers*. Underneath the print were the words: Van Gogh Exhibit 1986, Boston. Tears welled up in my eyes.

Please don't bawl, please don't bawl!

I wanted to be at Bolton teaching my girls. I missed being able to have students who would listen to me. I was good at teaching art.

Then a miracle happened.

Cody was pointing to where a moment ago my eyes had been fixed, on the Van Gogh print.

"What?" I said to him. He made two fists and brought them to his mouth. He snickered to himself.

"He likes that picture," Tatty said.

I stood.

"Do you like Van Gogh, Cody?" Cody didn't answer. He only sat very still.

"Look at me, class. Look at me, Cody."

I took the Van Gogh print down and held it up for all of them to see. I returned to the rug, and this time, I sat down on the rug with them and placed the print down. They formed a circled around it.

"Sunflowers!" I said and they all repeated. "Sunflowers!" They clapped again. I said, "Sunflowers!" They repeated and clapped!

Oh thank you, Vincent Van Gogh!

"This was painted by a man named Vincent Van Gogh. Say it: *Vincent Van Gogh*."

They tried to repeat his name; they didn't do so well, but they patted the painting with massive enthusiasm. Cody rocked in his seat and whispered, "Van Gogh." He didn't look at me or the print; he had his finger in his mouth and groaned slightly. I reached over and held his chin in my hand.

"Cody, look at me, Vincent Van Gogh was an artist," I said. He looked at the print and then looked away. He continued to rock in place.

"I'm an artist," Maurice said.

"I am, too!" Cheri shouted.

"Me, too," Kat said in a soft whisper.

"Fuck off! I am, too!" Ruthie said.

I then gave an abbreviated lecture on Van Gogh. It came out of me naturally, and although it seemed ridiculous, who am I to say they didn't understand me? Besides, I had caught their attention, and I had nothing else to really give them but what I knew. As I spoke, I kept my hands on the painting, swirling them around the flowers. They all swirled their hands along with mine; the kids pig-piled their hands on mine, all except Cody.

"Vincent Van Gogh was born in 1853. He was once a child like all of you. He grew up in a place called the Netherlands. He decided to become an artist in 1881. He went to art schools in Paris, but he primarily taught himself. He loved the country and moved to the south of France, and he drew scenes from nature—flowers, and trees. He painted pictures of many people he met in France. His paintings express his emotions, how he responded to the world. He used thick brushstrokes and thick paint that make his paintings almost seem like they were drawn with crayons. Do you all like to draw with crayons?"

"Crayons!" Ruthie and Kat shouted.

I looked over at Tatty, who was smiling. I then told her to get orange and yellow and red construction paper and put it on the children's desk. I stood and wrote on the board, SUNFLOWERS. I told the children to repeat each letter after me.

I clapped, and they clapped along with me the best they could. "Sunflowers!"

The class went back to the long table where they worked. Cody sat in his space on the rug and whispered over and over, "Van Gogh." I picked him up and sat him in his seat, and he laughed and tried to put his entire hand in his mouth.

"Hi Hi Hi Hi Hi Hi Hi Hi," he repeated. He then got up and went to a table by himself. I looked at Tatty. "Hi Hi Hi Hi Hi Hi Hi," Cody kept saying.

"We let him sit alone when he wants to. He likes it. He'll join us in his own time," Tatty said.

The kids watched me closely. I cut out large flower petals of red, yellow, and orange. I gave each child a stack of petals, and Tatty put glue on the end of them. I then pointed to the chalk board where I drew a round flower stem covered in yellow pollen on a large piece of construction paper. Each student took turns pinning a petal to the board. These eventually formed huge sunflowers. The kids were busy gluing, and some had started to cut. Feeling a slight tug on the back of my shirt, I turned.

Cody was standing by my side. I felt awful, for I had forgotten about him, but then my body went still. I looked at his hands, and he was holding a small piece of paper. On it was an almost perfect replica of Van Gogh's *Sunflowers*, which he had drawn in orange and yellow crayon.

"Van Gogh," he whispered.

THIRTY-TWO

June and Rosa became fast friends. It was good to see June with another woman. They gossiped and shopped together, and one day, they went downtown to see a play and talked about it perspicaciously for hours. It was some male-bashing play, and Ralph and I sat there, at a loss for words, while they prattled on about how women are the strongest of the species. Whatever.

The four of us had a few leisurely Sundays together at Rosa's place in Soho. One Sunday in particular, the girls went out shopping for a few hours. I was watching an old movie, *The Wild One*, with Brando. Ralph decided to put Rosa's books in alphabetical order. He was driving me crazy, because he talked through the entire process, repeating each title of the book and reading the jacket cover to me. Irritated, I jerked to my feet, took the books and mixed them up. He hung back and stared, and I sneered.

"You can be such an asshole, Oliver," he said.

"Thanks, Ralph."

"No, really. You need to grow up. I hope you don't act this way with your new students."

"Leave me alone."

Rosa and June came home shortly after our squabble. June had bought a new dress, sexy and alluring, low-cut and silky. She tried it on for Ralph, and when he saw June standing there all sexed-up in that dress, he dove on her, and they both fell on Rosa's sofa in laughter. It was creepy for me to see my conservative sister like that, but she was happy. And Rosa got a real kick out of my awkwardness. I couldn't take much more of them, so I decided to go for a walk. Rosa joined me. It was early November, and I had been teaching the new class now for two weeks.

"I think it's great, the way you and Ralph bicker. He really cares for you."

"He drives me nuts."

"It's his way of getting through to you"

"Getting through to me?" I asked.

"Why don't you like him?"

"I do like him. He drives me nuts; that's all."

"You have this hostility toward him, and he takes it from you. He's like this angel. He's a funny guy. So humble. And you can be harsh to him. I think you resent him because—you know he's going to take your sister away."

"That's not true. I'm an adult. I don't need my sister." Rosa saw right through me; she knew me. I liked it, but it was scary. I took a deep breath and let her talk.

"You and June are close, and I admire that. It should always be that way. But you need to let go a little, to allow for a little growth. Be nice to Ralph. It's not his fault he fell in love with June. You had Beth. Let June have her turn."

"I am. You're right," I proclaimed.

"When she was buying that dress, she was more worried over what you would think than Ralph. She wants to break out and change, too. I know you had that promise with your mother. But let her grow so you can grow, too."

"I'm not holding her back. I want her to be happy. Jesus! You'd think I were some primitive beast who keeps his sister down. June is strong-minded. She does what she pleases."

"She needs to know you're happy."

"I know. Tell Ralph to stop interfering."

"Hey, this is me talking, not Ralph. I'm only saying, lighten up."

"I've been doing everything to show her how much I like Ralph. So we argued today, big deal. And I really do kind of like him; he's grown on me."

"You seem like you're in a bad mood," she said.

"I'm fine," I said. But the truth was that the dread was back. That scared feeling that consumes me. I was grossly conflicted. On one hand, I was afraid of losing Rosa, especially when she would occasionally talk about Charlie. On the other hand, we'd only been seeing each other a few weeks; maybe we were moving too fast. I was worried we were using each other as crutches.

We ended up on the corner of Chamber and West Broadway. It was a cold day, so we ducked down the steps of the Chamber street subway and huddled in a corner, where I kissed her. She felt warm and sexy. She looked at me, her eyes filling up.

"Rosa, what's up? Did we do the right thing? Maybe we should have waited. Everything is going so fast. Is it me?"

"The holidays bum me out. My family is so fucked up. Look, I want our relationship to be based on raw honesty. Of course, I think of Charlie, and on occasion I miss him."

What I had suspected. Charlie, Charlie, Charlie!

"I see," I said.

"You look sad. Look, I adore you, but sometimes I do miss Charlie. I'm sorry."

"Should I be concerned? Should we end this?" I asked.

"No. I love my time with you, and I hope you do, too. I think maybe we're both scared. Let's get through these damn holidays."

"I agree. I feel the same way," I said.

She moved close to me, slipped her arms around my waist, and squeezed me tightly. A subway roared below us, and I held her tightly as people exited the station. When the station was clear again, I started to let her go and she whispered to me.

"Don't let me go, not yet."

Ralph and June made a repulsive Chinese Thanksgiving dinner for Rosa, Hank, and me. Hank was looking good; he was slowly losing weight. He requested his turkey slices without gravy. He'd warned June and Ralph in advance that he was not going to eat any carbohydrates.

"I can't eat anything exotic or fatty, no bread. I don't want to be rude. I'm being truthful," Hank said.

For the last few weeks, whenever Hank and I met for coffee at Starbucks on York, he was pretty quiet, preoccupied; he was very calm, told me he had stopped drinking as much as he could, but he wasn't ready to commit to quitting entirely. But there was a strangeness to him, an aura of contentment I had never seen. He looked like how I felt inside on some of the recent good days. I think Hank was slowly coming together. I figured it was all the changing we were both doing. He liked Rosa, and on one Saturday, we took the train downtown and went thrift store shopping. Hank and Rosa got along well, and Hank seemed genuinely happy that I had found someone nice.

Hank was lucky he had specified his diet restrictions on Thanksgiving, because June and Ralph made an odd, almost disturbing dinner. Fresh cranberry sauce with dried fish sauce. I thought I was going to puke.

"What happened to the good old days of cracking open a can of jellied cranberry sauce?" I bitched.

"Wake up, Oliver, it's the Twenty-First Century. Americans are sophisticated about food now. Everyone brings their culture to the Thanksgiving table," Ralph said.

"But we're not Chinese," I said.

"It all looks great. But I'm watching the waistline," Hank said. He flashed me a smile. I quickly, swiftly, slipped Hank the middle finger.

"We could have been Chinese in a past life," June said.

"I was brought up Italian, and we'd have pasta before our turkey," Rosa said. She nudged me to be quiet.

"I think that you should be a bit more sophisticated about food, Oliver," Ralph said.

"Yeah, Oliver, be more sophisticated."

"Be quiet, Hank. Really."

"I think everything looks great. I think everyone is right. Oliver, be more sophisticated," Rosa said.

"All I'm saying is, I didn't know cranberry and fish sauce were the pinnacle of sophistication," I said. I could feel Rosa softly kicking me under the table. I glanced over at Ralph, who looked sullen. He was looking at this giant spread of food he had worked so hard on over the last two days. June glared at me.

"But all the same Ralph, it's delicious. You both did a fantastic job. In fact I will never eat turkey again without cranberry and fish sauce." I smiled. Ralph perked up.

"Thanks Oliver. I used fresh cranberries and I made my own fish sauce from anchovies and herring bits," Ralph said. He proudly took June's hand.

"Oliver. Would you like more dressing?" June asked.

"I couldn't. I am so stuffed. But I love the idea of putting Chinese pickled eel in the dressing. Way to go Ralph; it was fantastic! Rosa, why don't you have more?" I said. I gave her a toothy smile. I could tell by her fixed stare she was going to kill me.

"Are you kidding? I couldn't eat another thing!" she said. She looked at June and Ralph.

"How about more of the acorn squash and pig's snout soufflé?" I said. I picked up the bowl and put it in front of Rosa. That's when I received a harsh kick in my shin under the table.

Hank was eating his plain turkey gleefully, smirking at me, hiding his laughter.

"No, thank you." She glared at me. "June and Ralph, everything was so well thought out," Rosa said.

The lecture Rosa and I got on Chinese culture was almost

enough to make me wish I had in fact leapt out my bedroom window the day Beth dumped me. Rosa looked at him and smiled as pleasantly as possible.

For the next two days I pretended to eat leftovers from our Chinese Thanksgiving, but really was helping myself to a pizza that I hid under my bed.

On Saturday, Rosa and June went to a reading by one of June's novelist friends. Ralph and I decided to skip a meeting and dine at a new—hold on to your shorts—Chinese place on York, after which we went to see a Chinese movie at the Angelica downtown. I couldn't say no to Ralph. I was trying to behave and be nice to him; after all, he hadn't given up on me, and I had been such an asshole those past months. Heading toward the restaurant, we walked along York Ave, and the wind blew off the East river and down the cross-streets, which acted like a massive wind tunnel for roaring wintry air. The last remnants of the sunny day were fading, and we walked rapidly. We jabbered for a few minutes about my teaching and his job at the library. Then he said he was ready to leave and make a change in his life. I got a bit tense.

"I'm going to ask June to marry me on Christmas. I want you to be the first to know."

"Congratulations, Ralph."

"I think she'll say yes," he said. He made two fists and punched the air. I laughed.

"She'd better, tough guy."

"Really. You mean it?"

"Yes, really. I want June to move on with her life."

"She's proud of you."

"Thanks, Ralph, for everything," I said.

"I knew everything would work out for you."

"I feel good. I'm glad you'll be my brother-in-law," my voice squeaked.

"You like me, finally. Wow!" He waved his hand grandiloquently.

"You're okay," I laughed. He slapped me on my back.

"Would you be my best man?"

"Me?"

"Why the hell not?"

"Because I've given you a lot of shit these last months."

"You were in such complete denial, but I understood your pain and the fear of sensitivity and all that machismo stuff."

"Oh brother."

He stopped walking and stood there with a big smile on his face, arms open. Tears sprung from his crinkly eyes.

"What now? Ralph. You're acting weird."

"I love you, Oliver." He walked toward me, arms open, and gave me a big, vigorous hug.

I froze in place, hands by my side, his face hanging off my shoulder; he sniffled. I could smell that familiar garlic smell from the Chinese food he ate every day. It wafted from his body in small, repellent waves. I was privately surprised that June would tolerate such a strong odor of garlic coming off a human being, because June, at one time, had been very particular about smells. I then hoped that my sister wasn't so completely desperate that she would settle for a man who reeked so badly of garlic, but with age, her sense of smell must have become less keen. I wanted Ralph to stop hugging me, so I put my arms around him and gently pushed him off of me.

"Okay, Ralph you can let me go now." He did, but first he kissed my cheek, and I wiped my face with the sleeve of my jacket. His ingenuous smile made me even more nuts.

"Jesus, Ralph, must you be so zealous?"

"Yes, I must. Haven't you been reading the book? I think you're having a delayed reaction. Many men do, but when the fear leaves you, your life will begin. The book creeps up on you. No delayed reactions from me, though. I've always been open. You'll change."

"I am changing. I told you that I liked you." I smiled at

him, and he grabbed my hand.

"Let go of my hand, Ralph."

"Let's hold hands like they do in Europe."

"No, people will think we're gay!" I said.

"I don't care. I'm not gay. I am a sensitive, loving human being."

"Can we go eat, okay?" I put on my best smile.

While poking around my poached flounder in red chili sauce, I told Ralph about school and the replica of artworks that Cody did, about how I felt challenged each day and was surprising myself with the feelings of attachment I was having for the kids.

"They're giving you a gift. Children are God's way of telling us that there is hope in the world," he said.

"Sadly, there is not much hope for these kids," I said.

"Then maybe you should gather them all together and shoot them dead," he said, looking up from his sautéed beef tongue in orange sauce.

"That's an awful thing to say, Ralph."

"It's as awful as saying there is no hope for them. Hope is life. Oliver, who are you to sit there and say there is no hope for them? It's your job to give them hope."

"Me? How?"

"You're doing it now. You're inspiring them. You're merely returning the favor. Hope works both ways," he said.

THIRTY-THREE

One night Hank called me at three am.

"You been drinking? I asked.

"No. I wanted to tell you that. I'm happy, fucking outrageously happy."

"What's going on Hank."

"I think I'm in love. And it's real. It's no obsessive stupid illusion, something real."

"That's great news, Hank, but couldn't you wait to tell me?"

"When I feel the truth I have to express it."

"Well, when you find yourself having to speak the truth at three am, call the Samaritans or something. Shit, Hank. I'm happy for you, but it's early. Can we hook up tomorrow for coffee?"

"Sure. Sure. I wanted to share."

"When do we get to meet her?"

"Well, uh, soon. Soon. They're shy."

"*They're* shy, how many are there? Come on, shy? Shy is nice. But Beth said she was shy, too. Shy my ass. Damn slut."

"Hey, Rosa is great. Beth's the past. How's school going?"

"Hank, every school day, I enter another world that most white people don't know exists. A world I never dreamed existed, either. Don't take me the wrong way. I am not saying, 'Look at me! I'm a hero.' I only arrived here by default. And I do not have any answers. But I love it. I'm starting to feel whole again."

"I'm happy for you Oliver. Have a good night. *I love you.*"

"Yeah, okay Hank." I hung up the phone.

His words, "I love you," rang in my ear.

THIRTY-FOUR

With help from Rosa, I received my certification for substitute teaching (no certification had been required in a private school). Then came my certification for a full-time teaching position; it was done rather quickly, but Rosa was a master at pulling strings at the New York City Department of Education. For a few days I called her *my little puppeteer*. She also suggested I study up on autism. Perhaps, she said, one day I would want to go back to school and work on a Master's degree in Special Ed.

In the meantime, after school and late into the evenings, I would go to June's library and read about autism. She would present me with piles of books. Ralph would look out from his office, adjust his glasses, smile, and nod approvingly. June would look at me proudly, but I sensed she was feeling something else. I couldn't decipher whether it was concern or happiness for me, but there was something changing about June; it was in her look or maybe her aura. At that time I decided that if it was important, she would tell me; she always had before.

As I studied, I understood my students more. I admittedly favored Cody's case. Sometimes, when Cody drew his pictures, I would marvel at the thought that his brain, although different in areas of social interaction and communication skills, was programmed with the awesome ability to draw magnificent pictures. Fascinating.

Since there was no set way that a child with autism was

supposed to behave, I found hope in that. I felt that Cody and the others had endless potential. It would take time and patience, but maybe, through my knowledge of art, I could make some sort of difference.

In the days that followed, I took most of the prints from the walls of my study and brought them to class. Franco helped me hang them. He would come by once and a while, and Rosa would allow him to sit in the corner of the class and do his school work. He wanted to prove to me how good he was.

Each day I would tell the class a story about the artist who created the work. I would allow the children to run their tiny fingers along the colors of the print. I would have them try and name the colors or repeat the name of the artist. Sometimes Cody would sit and look, and other times, he would only follow me around the classroom and hum.

I would sit with him and hold his face or his hand and go through the alphabet: *A B C D*.

"Repeat after me Cody. *A B C D*." He would pull away quickly. Sometimes he'd slap my face and walk away.

Other times I would sit with him, smile and ask him to smile back at me. I would point to my mouth. I would touch his mouth, and he would touch mine.

"Smile. Happy. Smile," I would say.

Sometimes he would give me a wide, gleeful smile, and other times he would shake his head and flap his hands.

One day, I sat with him in front of a small chalkboard. I put chalk in his hand and cupped it in mine. On the chalkboard I swirled his hands around and wrote.

I AM CODY.

"*I am Cody*," I would say. He would whisper back to me in his soft, simple way, "*I am Cody*," push my hand away, scribble over the chalkboard wildly, and then sit and stare at his scribbles.

I am Cody. I am Cody. I am Cody. I am Cody. I am Cody. I am Cody.

There were so many methods and therapies in treating children with autism that it was downright confusing. Some methods involved having autistic children walk on elevated blocks, or using color filters over a book page to help reading, or dosing them with vitamin B6. Some experts said typing helped autistic children express themselves. However, how could I have them type when most of these kids didn't know the alphabet?

After Ralph learned about the typing method, he gave me five old IBM electric typewriters that were stored away in the library. The kids had fun typing away. I would write a letter on the chalk board and they would type any old letter. Rosa thought it was great and said it was the exposure to letters that would help them, eventually.

I then tried my own method. I let the kids use paints. I brought in some of my old shirts for them to use as smocks. Tatty and I supervised them carefully, but still they made an enormous mess.

Maurice would cover an entire paper with one color and smash his hands all over it.

Ruthie, when she wasn't trying to drink the paint, made splattered images all over her paper. I called her Miss Jackson Pollock. She called me an asshole.

Kat liked to paint her hands, pressing them all over her paper, and everyone else's, too. I left a few of her handprints on the floor, and she was thrilled. Kat insisted that red was green, orange was blue, and green was yellow.

I do think that at times Tatty got exhausted with the children and my free-wheeling methods. But I knew it was better than having the children run wild. It was a thrill for me to watch them create their art. With each brush stroke or hand print they made, I searched for an occasional glimmer of genius.

Cody didn't like to paint. He only wanted to draw with crayons.

He wouldn't respond to the lessons, and on the days I

taught them, he would stand back and look at the other children, performing the gamut of typical gestures. He would either try to put his fist in his mouth, hum, flap his hands, or rock in place. But days later, sure enough, Cody would be working on a replica of a print I had shown the class days prior. His talent and eye for detail blew me away.

On one Monday, I showed the class Degas' work, mostly the ballerinas. And on that Tuesday, I taught them about Picasso's blue period. On Friday Cody used a blue crayon to make a replica of Degas' dancers, all in shades of blue. There was no predicting Cody when it came to his artwork. It was totally on his terms, and this spontaneity inspired me to return to school each day.

One day, I told the class they were Impressionists. Another day I exclaimed they were the finest abstract artists I'd ever seen. When we worked with clay, I called them little Rodins. I did everything I could think of to encourage them. They didn't have a clue what I was saying, nor did they care. I continued with my art lessons, and in the afternoons, I managed to incorporate the letters and numbers they really needed to learn.

Tatty read to them; we counted and sang. I grew to love those kids more than I'd ever dreamed possible.

After a few weeks, the classroom was covered from floor to ceiling with my collection of prints and their art work. My study was empty of all my prints by mid-December. I had stayed at the school much longer than I ever expected.

I began to notice certain things about Cody that I imagine were always there. Because he didn't talk much, they took me longer to decipher. Most of the time, I had to guess what he was needing or feeling.

There were moments when Cody would get up from his seat and walk over to me, and simply stand by me, resting his hand on my leg for twenty minutes. Then he would walk away. "Hi Hi Hi Hi Hi Hi Hi," he would repeat over and over.

He'd then go to the pencil sharpener and crank the handle around and around. Sometimes he'd weep quietly or look around blankly. After I'd been there for a time, I began to notice that, as the day went on, he would become more and more apprehensive, and that when it was time to leave school for the day, he would sometimes cry terribly and hang on to me.

One day in early December, the kids were particularly rambunctious and I shouted at them to calm down. It took Tatty and me forever to get them back into their seats. No sooner did we get one seated when another would run for the door. Ruthie, of course, kept telling us to "Fuck off!" And everything was a big game to Kat, who spun in her spot like a top, then stopped and put her fingers down her throat. Maurice had crapped his pants about three times that day already, and Cherri sat and stewed and mumbled how much she hated me.

Once we had everyone sitting, Tatty and I looked around and couldn't find Cody anywhere. Kat found him curled in ball weeping behind a bookcase.

He murmured to me, "Mad. Me mad. Mad. Mad me."

"No one is mad at you, sunshine," Tatty said.

"I wouldn't never be mad at you, pal. Never," I said.

He covered his head as if he were expecting me to beat him. This frightened me, and I tried to lift him gently up. He fussed. Then I tried again, and when I touched his back, he let out a howling scream. I quickly put him down, and he put his hand on his back. I lifted his shirt, and there I saw a round mark on his back the size of a dime. It was scabbed over, but apparently I had knocked off the scab while lifting him.

I told Tatty that I'd be right back, and I took Cody by the hand to the school nurse. She cleaned and dressed his wound, and I brought him back to class. The nurse told me that it was almost undoubtedly a cigarette burn. But to make accusations without proof would bring on the possibilities of lawsuits and endless trouble, especially for the children, who often suffered even more from enraged parents they'd promised never to tattle on. She advised me that the school needed to be absolutely certain abuse was taking place in the child's home before reporting it. I took her advice, but I sent a note home to his mother explaining how the nurse bandaged the sore on his back.

The next three days, Cody was absent. Now I was worried. I called his home each day. The phone would be picked up, and on it, I would hear his breathy voice.

"Hi. Hi. Hi. Hi. Hi. Hi. Hi. Hi."

"Cody it's me, Mr. Pepper, come back to school."

"Hi. Hi. Hi. Hi. Hi. Hi. Hi. Hi."

And then I'd hear the phone hang up.

I decided to go to Cody's house and find out where he was and talk to his mother. It was crazy of me. I knew it. I would ask Franco to come with me.

Franco had the daily routine of running by my classroom and screaming out, "Hey, Doctor Pepper!" and continue to run down the hallway.

The day I went to get Cody, I heard Franco coming, and when he came by the room, I jumped out at him and grabbed him. He cracked up laughing. I then asked him to take me to Cody's home.

"Why you want to go there for? His mother is whack," he said.

"Never mind why. Meet me after school and come along."

He agreed. We both made the trip uptown to Cody's neighborhood, which was not far from Franco's building. Cody lived in one of those big brick buildings.

My stomach was in knots as Franco and I stood in front of Cody's building.

A group of people stood out front; they were talking and looked harmless. I figured if I went with Franco, it would be safe for me. I don't know what I was expecting; however, I'd seen my share of *NYPD Blue,* and I wanted to be safe.

It was late afternoon. The sun was strong that day, and clouds shifted over the autumn sun making shadows of our figures on the sidewalk.

"He live in there. I have to go."

"Can you come in with me?" I asked.

"Why? You scared, Pepper?" Franco said.

"I need your help," I said. I glared at him.

"You gonna pay me?"

"Can't you do something out of the goodness of your heart?" I asked.

"Shit, you a damn fool. You buy me Burger King at least?"

"Yes, yes, it's a deal."

"You scared! You scared of the black people!"

"Be quiet, Franco. Let's go."

"Okay but you scared. Scared white ass honky! Scared of the black people!" He laughed and held his stomach.

I opened the large metal door and went in the lobby. People inside the lobby looked at Franco and me. *What the fuck are you doing here?* There was graffiti on the walls, people coming and going, elderly people pulling shopping carts filled with bags, mothers with kids, nothing really unusual to report. Only people getting on with their lives. The divisions of class and race spoke loudly to me. I couldn't express enough how awful it made me feel inside, how unfair and wrong that the only people who lived here in an obviously poverty stricken area were people of color. I knew not all people of color lived here, but the majority of the city's minorities did. I hated that I felt scared inside. I hated that I didn't have my flask with me to ease my nerves. It had been a few months now; I was happy about that, but I missed the crutch.

In the lobby, I pushed the buzzer for Cody's apartment. There was no answer. I pushed again. Still no answer.

"No one home. Let's go to Burger King," Franco said.

As a woman came in with her three small children in tow, I grabbed the door and went inside. I pulled Franco with me.

"Get your damn hands off me. I'm coming, shit, nigga!" Franco said. He pulled away from me.

Once in front of Cody's apartment, I knocked on the door. Music came from inside.

The door opened. A young twenty-something man stood before me. I could smell something strong and pungent, like a fruity, ammonia smell, or like a new plastic shower curtain. Undoubtedly it was some kind of drug. The young man slammed the door in my face. The music went silent. I heard people shuffling. I knocked again.

"It's Mr. Pepper. Cody's teacher. I was wondering where Cody is. He hasn't been in school and I was hoping I could see him."

"Cody not here right now," the man's voice said from behind the door.

"Could I please talk to his mother?"

"She ain't home, either," the male voice said. Franco nudged me.

"We gotta get out of here!" Franco whispered with a quick hush.

"Why?"

"'Cause that's Chris, and everybody know Chris. Shit!" His eyes widened. "I want to see Cody," I said close to the door. My hands shook. I could feel my heart pounding.

"You on your own, nigga. I'll be downstairs waiting for Burger King. If your ass still alive." Then Franco was gone. I timidly knocked again. My throat was starting to close up. My voice was a squeak.

"Please bring Cody back to school, okay? I don't care what you do or what you're doing, but bring him back to school. Please." As I walked away, I heard the door open. Cody's mother stuck her head out.

She was pretty and looked very young, bewildered and preoccupied. She had a towel wrapped around her body. Behind her, I could see a few men in their twenties; they all glared at me with expressions of warning.

I was petrified.

"Cody is okay. He'll be in school tomorrow. He been acting up, that's all. Scared like. I'll bring him tomorrow." She spoke in a monotone and kept rolling her tongue in her mouth.

"Miss Lotress, do you have any idea how talented Cody is? He's amazing. I only want to talk to you about him. I've been working real—"

A male voice cut over mine. "Get rid of that cracker before I do. Shut the fucking door!"

"I'll bring Cody tomorrow. Go." She slammed the door shut.

I went downstairs, and Franco was waiting for me.

Over a Whopper, Franco told me little about Chris, but what he did say alarmed me.

"He's a scary motherfucker, no one mess with him. He cut your eyes out of your head you cross that crazy fool."

"You need to tell more. I'm concerned for Cody."

"I don't need to tell you shit, Pepper. I don't want my ass dead. My father coming home one day. He wants me alive." Franco then got up and left me alone.

That night, Rosa had bought tickets to a new opera. It was long and boring. All I did was think of Cody.

The following morning, I ran into Cody's mother as she was dropping him off at the school door.

"Miss Lotress! I'm so glad you brought Cody back to school!"

"Yup," she said.

Cody looked up at me, and his eyes shifted. His hand extended for mine, and I took it as he let go of his mother's hand. I noticed a small pink nick on his face.

"What's that, pal, you hurt yourself?" I patted Cody's head.

"Hi. Hi. Hi. Hi. Hi. Hi. Hi. Hi."

"It's nothing. He runs into doors and stuff. He don't pay attention."

"He's a very talented artist, right Cody?"

"Hi. Hi. Hi. Hi. Hi. Hi. Hi. Hi."

Cody tilted his head back and forth and moved in close. His mother didn't smile or acknowledge me. She only pulled on the ends of her long brown hair and twisted it. She seemed intimidated and afraid of me as she shuffled in place. She lit a cigarette.

I was overwhelmed with pity.

"Does he draw at home?" I asked.

"Yup. He real good at it. Look, I have to go."

She looked down and pulled him on his shoulder; he quickly turned to her, eyes wide.

"I'll pick you up here. Okay? Don't you be goin' nowhere, you hear? I love you, baby. I got to go now."

Cody coiled his fist and put it in his mouth. She grabbed his hand to pull it out. "Hi. Hi. Hi. Hi. Hi. Hi. Hi. Hi."

"Don't put your hands in your mouth. You want Chris to think you stupid? He lookin' at you now." Cody's eyes blinked quickly as he looked toward the black Audi where Chris sat, cigarette hanging out of his mouth.

"I was thinking about taking Cody's class to the art museum next week before Christmas break. Would you allow that? It would be during school hours."

Chris honked the horn. Loud invasive rap music blared from the car radio:

> Sex'in with him, I watch ya, I see ya, I watch ya, I jam knocking in my Benz, I do it, I do it, in your hole deeper and deeper, I see you lick it, you do it, you

cost ya, it cost ya, bent over for me I'll do ya.

"I don't care. Bring 'im. He don't get no things like that though," she said.

"No, he does, more than anyone in the class he does," I said. I wanted to tell her how wonderfully talented her son was, and I wanted her to feel the same way. But Chris started to honk wildly.

"Is that Cody's father?" I asked.

"No, Cody got no father. I gotta run. Cody like you. Take him where you want."

She walked quickly to the car. From where we stood, I could hear Chris's "What the fuck?"

Cody and I watched as the car sped down the street and out of sight, the music still audible.

"Well, it was nice meeting your mother," I said.

Cody and I went inside the school.

"Hi. Hi. Hi. Hi. Hi. Hi. Hi. Hi," he said all the way up to the classroom.

As the time to go home neared, Cody would retreat to another space in the room and curl himself in a ball as if in despair. It was tough to decipher if the reaction was caused by his being abused at home or his autism. Maybe it was both, maybe there were other reasons, but I sadly and regrettably waited before I told Rosa about my concerns. I was frightened of the possibilities. It's not easy to imagine a child you love being abused and neglected.

I didn't want to believe it. And now it terrifies me to think how my denial and naïveté put this wonderful child in danger.

THIRTY-FIVE

Hank's waist was down three inches and he had started running with a professional trainer. The limp in his leg was disappearing, and he was looking better each time I saw him. His face didn't look like a watermelon anymore, more like a cantaloupe. And he was getting facials.

We met at a vegetarian restaurant on Third and Eighty-Sixth one night.

"So they put hot towels on your face and they squeeze all this disgusting shit out of your pores."

"Hank, I'm eating tofu. Too much information!"

"It's crazy, though. I feel like a new man. Kathy has changed my life. She knows everything about staying fit and eating well. Did you notice I hardly limp anymore, and she thinks my scar on my leg is hot! Can you imagine? Hot! 'Sexy' is what she said."

"When we going to meet this girl? Huh? When?"

"In time. When I'm ready."

"Ready for what? I'm your best friend, and I haven't met the love of your life? Are you ashamed of her? Is she fat? I don't care if she's fat. I like fat girls."

"No, she's not fat. I told you she knows all about fitness. At Christmas. I'm bringing Kathy to Christmas dinner. June said it was okay."

"June said it was okay? You come every year, Hank!"

"Can you hurry up and finish? I'm meeting Kathy downtown. I don't like to keep her waiting."

"I gotta go, too. I've been planning a big trip to the museum with the kids."

The next day at school, I went through all the permission slips for the field trip to the Metropolitan Museum of Art. All were in except for Cody's. I called his mother. On the phone, we made small talk, and she responded with "yups" and "nopes." Then I asked her again about taking Cody to the museum. I told her I need a signed permission slip.

"I'll get it to you. Cody, he like to draw. I gotta go."

In the background I could hear that guy Chris, "Get off the phone woman! Damn you always on that phone!"

"Have you seen his drawings?" I asked. I ignored the fact that I could hear him.

"I gotta go. Please. Cody is good. He like you. I have to hang up. I'll bring the slip in tomorrow. I been busy."

And that was the last time I spoke with Cody's mother. Her name was Tracy. The next day I got the permission slip.

Rosa said it would be much easier if I brought the kids their lunches on the field trip since all of them were on the school lunch program. It would guarantee there would be no forgotten lunches and save mass commotion.

The night before the trip, June and Rosa made a sack full of peanut butter and jelly sandwiches. Ralph and I took a walk to D'Agostino to pick up juice boxes and chips.

He jabbered in the way he always did about egg rolls versus spring rolls, and then he started in about love and the cosmos. I told him that if he tried to hug me or do anything to embarrass me, I would tell June he had Herpes. We laughed.

Rosa reserved a small school bus for us. Tatty looked apprehensive that morning and kept looking at me with irritation. She was not thrilled about this trip. Not one iota. I told her the children would be fine and that we only needed to make sure they were with us at all times. For two days we'd been making the kids practice holding hands. We walked all around the school's hallways making sure all hands were always connected. They did well; even when Kat vomited in front of Miss Lenny's classroom, they held on. Maurice marched right through it.

On our big day, we all walked up the great layered steps of the Metropolitan Museum of Art. We were a large chain of human flesh held together by our hands: two adults and five children with runny noses, each of whom sang their own songs, lost in their own worlds. Kat started to twist, breaking the chain and taking a seat on the steps. I tried to get her to stand up, but she rested her face in her hands, unaware that she was holding us all up.

Ruthie shouted "Fuck you!" to unsuspecting passersby, whose expressions reflected their disdain and horror. I smiled back at them, trying to ease their shock. But that only made them climb the stairs more quickly. God only knows what they were thinking. The good news was that Cherri was smiling for a change, and she didn't do much except sing while looking at her feet.

Once we got all the children back in place, we moved onward and upward. Maurice held Cody's hand and counted the steps as we climbed them; he could only count to four, but happily started from one over and over again. When we reached the top, he proudly announced, "five steps!" I was astonished that he'd learned a new number and praised him profusely. Cody whispered to me, "Twenty-six," in a deadpan voice. I smiled at Cody, patted his head, and gave him a wink.

Maurice was jumping for joy because he'd done such an outstanding job climbing the steps. Tatty hugged him, looked at me like I was a lunatic, and kept shaking her head.

"Lord, watch over us, watch over us, watch over us."

"Please, Tatty, it's not going to be that bad," I said as we entered the museum.

"These kids are going to tear this place apart. Don't you say I didn't warn you."

When we entered the Met, the kids became silent. Their eyes widened with incredulity. Their reactions gave me a quick instant of happiness and merriment, and I smiled at Tatty broadly, my fist clenched in victory. I was going to change these kids! I followed all their small, bright eyes as they looked at the Roman columns and the grand staircase. To a small child, these objects must appear massive. As that thought passed through my mind, all the kids began to cry hysterically.

Tatty shouted, "Stop it!"

The kids stopped on command.

I must admit even I was a bit frightened of Tatty. She wasn't going to take any grief from anyone on that day, not even me. When I first told her I wanted to take the kids to the Met, she had said, "All due respect, Oliver, but have you gone crazy? These kids can't handle stuff like that."

"I brought my other students, and these kids have the same right, don't they?"

"You mean those rich girls you told me about? Come on, Oliver, give me a break. These kids aren't no spoiled rich kids. These kids are from the ghetto. Do you know what that means? It means even if they were normal, the chances of them making it in this world are pretty slim. You can't be comparing these kids to rich white kids."

"Every person, rich or poor, is entitled to art and hope. Come on, Tatty, this is going to be fun. Trust me."

"You are one crazy man. That's all I can say."

"You're telling me!"

I did a little *ba de ba ba,* and she rolled her eyes and chuckled.

"Okay, but I'm warning you," she said.

I led them through the Impressionist Wing first, because I felt the children would respond best to the vibrant colors of those paintings.

When we were among the paintings of Renoir, Monet, Van Gogh, and Bonnard, I gave the same lecture I gave my students at Bolton. I pointed out to my little students the activity of the artist's brush, the color used, and as usual, I became overwhelmed and enthralled by Bonnard's use of color. I was almost lost in one of his paintings, when I heard Tatty yelling. She was chasing Ruthie and Kat as they ran around the statue of Degas' fourteen-year-old dancer. I brought Cherri, Maurice, and Cody into the room where most of the Van Goghs hung. I held Cody's hand, and Maurice held his other hand, while Cherri held Maurice's other hand.

I began my lecture on Van Gogh. Tatty came in the room, goading her charges. She was holding Kat's hand and practically dragging Ruthie, who was refusing to stand up and walk. The tops of Ruthie's rubber tennis shoes screeched on the floor as Tatty pulled her along. I continued with my lecture. We received a series of looks as people walked past. Some reacted with wide-eyed disbelief, as if I were insane. Some smiled; some oohed and aahed. Others didn't look at us. Their refusal to see us was the most upsetting.

I upheld my philosophy that every person has the right to know about art and beauty. Even if these kids seemed not to care what I was saying and even if they didn't know the difference between red, green, yellow, or blue or how to count or read, they could still experience art, couldn't they? That day, I felt such immense satisfaction and was so thrilled to be teaching art again that nothing could have dispirited me.

I began another lecture in front of Van Gogh's *Irises*. They all sat down and looked up at me, clapping as I spoke.

"Van Gogh's contribution to the history of modern art was his utilization of color. He was one of the first artists to use color on items in his paintings without reproducing their natural colors. Van Gogh had specific and well thought out ideas about painting, which he clearly explained in hundreds of letters to his brother and friends. He wanted to represent emotions through the use of color, line, texture, and light, and express how he felt about a particular scene or subject. Most of these paintings represent his joy in the colors, beauty, light, and warmth of the south of France."

Maurice raised his hand. "When are we going to eat?"

"Hungry!" Ruthie shouted.

"Stand up, everyone. Follow me, and be quiet!"

They obeyed. We all stood in front of Degas' *The Singer in Green*. Cody looked at the painting of the little girl and giggled quietly. The children ran toward one of Van Gogh's *Sunflowers*, and Tatty went after them. So much for obeying me! I stayed with Cody. He sat on the floor and stared at the young girl in the painting. I bent down and pointed with him.

"Cody, remember when we talked about Edgar Degas? He painted this. Look at the painting. Look at my fingers and where I am pointing."

I lifted Cody's chin with my other hand, and he looked at the painting.

"Cody, see how the harsh lights highlight the lines of her face and collarbone, and how the entire area around her body is covered with light and vibrant color? Do you like the bright colors of her dress and the picture's background?"

Cody only stared at the painting, nodded, and tried to put his fist in his mouth. This meant he was enjoying the painting.

"Cody, what colors do you see? Yellow, orange, and turquoise? See how they contrast sharply with the young girl's pale skin? The girl's face, arms, and upper chest seem carefully modeled. Look at the background, which is composed of freely applied colors. Do you like it? Do you like the painting, Cody?"

"Degas. Yellow. Yellow. Hi. Hi. Hi. Hi. Hi. Hi. Hi. Hi," he whispered.

"Yes, I know you enjoy art. I know you do!"

"Hi. Hi. Hi. Hi. Hi. Hi. Hi. Hi," he said as he continued to stare at the painting.

I took Cody's hand, and we joined the other children who were playing ring around the rosie in front of Jean Courbet's nudes. They were weak with laughter and fell on top of one another. Ruthie was shouting and repeating the word, "Tits!" and pointing to the painting. I knew I had to move the kids swiftly into another room, but they would not budge. Tatty sighed and crossed her arms, and small beads of perspiration lined her forehead.

"Come on everyone, hold hands!" I said. We walked onward in a human chain. Maurice howled that his belly hurt, which meant he was soon going to take one of his famous craps.

"You must contain the children," a security guard said as he tapped me on my shoulder.

I promptly gathered my crew, and we went downstairs and ate our lunches in the cafeteria. The kids ravaged the sandwiches but were quite orderly.

"Are we going back to the school now?" Tatty asked. Her look was still skeptical.

"We have more to see. Please, Tatty, hang on a bit longer, okay?" I pleaded.

Next we were off to the *Arts of Africa, Oceania, and the Americas*. Cody was frightened of the statues and the masks and held onto my legs, making it difficult for me to walk. The girls seemed captivated by this room and pressed their tiny faces against a glass case full of African wooden masks. Enchanted, they gazed around the room. I was practically hopping with excitement. I told them they were among wooden sculptures from Sub-Saharan Africa and the Pacific Islands, that some of the things were made of gold, silver, copper, ivory, and that everything was very, very old.

Maurice clapped his hands and jumped up and down; he

had a glint in his eyes. He jerked his small head back, "I'm African! I'm African!"

"Halloween!" Cherri said as she skipped toward me. She took me by my jacket and pulled me to a large wooden mask.

"Look. Look. Mask. Mask," she said. I patted her head. I told her it was indeed a mask. I looked at the masks and thought of my life. I wanted to stay in the museum forever.

"I like you," Cherri said.

"I like you, too, Cherri," I said.

The kids loved the Wrightsman Galleries.

At this point, Tatty was strutting along, arms folded. She was pissed; the kids had really given her a run for her money, and she was the type who needed everything in order. I should talk, though. I was the same way.

"Okay, kids, this room displays splendid examples of French furniture and many salons from grand Eighteenth Century French houses," I said pompously.

They waved their heads around, stuck their tongues out, farted, coughed, hit one another, and onward we went to the next rooms.

"This room is from the early Renaissance *studiolo*, or what we call a small, private study. This is from the palace of Federico da Montefeltro, Duke of Urbino, in Gubbio, Italy. Let's all take a look, shall we?"

"They don't know what the hell you're saying," Tatty mumbled to me. Her eyes narrowed in disapproval.

"You never know," I said. I shrugged my shoulders, trying to get Tatty to smile, and she gave me a silly smirk and started to giggle.

"You're nuts! Nuts!" she said.

"I have to poop!" Maurice said. He was standing beside Tatty and me, and we really lost it.

"Don't laugh at me!" Maurice said.

"We're not, baby doll. You have to wait. Can you wait? Remember we don't go in our pants anymore," Tatty said.

"I don't go in my pants anymore. I promise," he said.

"Hold it for a few minutes," I said.

It was impossible to keep the kids back from the bedroom displays; Kat managed to run into one of the bedrooms and climb on one of the priceless beds; apparently she thought it was naptime. The alarms went off, and a security guard with a cadaverous face reminded us that we must watch the kids more closely or we would have to leave.

I apologized. Ruthie told him to "Fuck off!"

Tatty grabbed Ruthie's face, "Stop it now!"

The security guard left.

"It's coming out!" Maurice screamed.

"What's coming out?" I asked. I was horror-struck.

"My poop! My poop!" He held on to his bum, jumped up and down, and then ran from us. I tried to chase him, but Cody was gripping onto me, and Ruthie was kicking Tatty.

Maurice ran into the most elegant of rooms, lifted a large red drape that hung ceiling to floor, and ran behind it. I freed myself from Cody's grip. I dashed into the room, but it was too late. Maurice appeared from behind the curtain and looked up at me proudly. His pants around his ankles, he looked like an actor who had given a grand performance to an adoring audience.

"I didn't go in my pants!" he beamed, a proud smile on his little face.

I smiled, too. "I'm very proud of you, Maurice."

I held Maurice by his sleeve, and we took the kids by the hands and left the museum. On the bus ride back, I used my cell phone to call the Met about Maurice's indiscretion behind the red curtain.

When I turned off the phone, I smiled. After all, as far as anyone knew, it might have been one of those lovely little Bolton School girls who had defecated behind the red curtain.

THIRTY-SIX

Back at the school, the kids were all met by their parents—except Cody and Kat, whose parents were notoriously late.

Tatty and I sat down on a bench with the two kids in the school's lobby and waited. It had been a long day, and I was fatigued but satisfied. I felt it had been relatively beneficial for the kids.

Soon Kat's mother showed up, full of apologies as always. She wore spandex pants, frosted lipstick, and had breasts out to Milwaukee. After she left, Tatty looked at me and smiled weakly; she was exhausted. Cody sat next to me on the bench, his head buried in my rib cage; he was fast asleep.

"Tatty, go home. You've done enough."

"You sure?"

"Yes, go. I'll wait a bit more, or I'll just take him home." Tatty rustled Cody's hair, and he woke. He looked up at her with one of his gleaming smiles.

"Mr. Pepper will wait for your Mama with you, okay? I'll see you tomorrow."

After Tatty left, I called Rosa on my cell. She had left school early for a meeting in Brooklyn at the Department of Education. Our plan for the evening was to meet downtown at four o'clock. One of her friends, Katherine—a spurious vegetarian—was having a showing of her art at a Gallery in Soho. It was a display of sculptures made from bars of soap. I wasn't looking forward to standing there while Katherine, an eager smile on her face, waited for me to verbalize my thoughts on her work.

"It's me. Cody's mother is not here and there is no way I can make it downtown on time," I said.

"I really wanted you there tonight," Rosa said, her voice pleading.

"Come up to my place after the show. We'll have dinner at that German place you like."

"I don't want to do this night alone," Rosa said. Her voice was becoming increasingly stressed.

"Tell her you think her work is fabulous and has given you an entirely new perspective on soap. Tell her you feel soap isn't *only* for washing anymore."

"Very funny. Look, Katherine told me Charlie was going to be at the show tonight, and I don't know how I feel about that."

"Skip the show and tell Katharine you came down with typhoid."

"You're full of jokes today, aren't you? How was the museum?"

"It was wild. I think the kids really enjoyed it, though," I said.

"Good, glad to hear it. Look, this is what I'm going to do. I'm going to see the show, pop in and out, and head up to your place. Is June home?"

"She should be. Wait for me, and take it easy. And if you see Charlie, say 'hello'; tell him you're happy to see him, and leave."

After I was done talking to Rosa, I felt a pain in the pit of my stomach. Every time Rosa mentioned Charlie's name, it made me weary. She told me about her woes with Charlie as if I were supposed to help her 'get over him,' as if I were her friend and not her lover. I guess I wanted to be both, but talking about her old boyfriend seemed off limits to me. I didn't get it. I wondered whether Rosa took our relationship seriously. But then again, here I was giving her advice on how to react when she saw him. It was twisted, and it confused me.

Cody held my hand tightly. He hummed and carelessly swung his legs as they hung off the bench. I felt my eyelids getting heavy, and the knot in my stomach more twisted.

I must have dozed off for a minute or two.

The dismissal bell for the higher grades startled me. Teachers and students walked past as they left for the day. The wise-ass boys I'd had back in October made their usual callous annotations.

It was odd, though. Some of those boys acted like they were happy to see me, as if I were some long lost buddy from years ago. I didn't understand their logic, my logic, anyone's logic.

"Mr. Pepper! Mr. Pepper!" Franco was standing in front of me.

"Franco, what's up, dawg?" I said.

Franco laughed at me. "Don't be black. You white. You make a fool out of your white ass."

"How are you, Franco?" I laughed, too, at my attempt to be "cool."

"Guess what?"

"What?"

"My father got my letter, and he wrote me back! He said he love me!"

"I'm glad Franco," I said.

He beamed a meaningful, satisfied smile at me, and he stretched his hand toward the sky. I leapt up and we clapped our hands together in a traditional high five.

"You waiting for Tracy?" he said.

"Who?"

"Cody's mother."

"Yeah."

"That ho is always late."

"Franco, that's not very nice."

"It cool dawg, she knows what she is. Later, homie!" He ran out, and the large doors of the school slammed shut and echoed up the stairwell.

Cody moved closer to me. His mother was now half an hour late. I went through my briefcase, found Cody's phone number on the permission slip for the museum trip. I called his house. No answer. After an hour, with no sign of Cody's mother, I took him by the hand and went outside. The winter sky was dimming, and the air was changing.

I decided to take Cody home myself. We took the long subway ride all the way uptown to his house. All Cody said was, "Hi. Hi. Hi. Hi. Hi. Hi. Hi. Hi."

At Cody's apartment, I received the same unsavory stares as before, but a few people said "hello" to Cody. We managed to follow someone in. We took the heavy metal elevator up, and I held Cody's hand as we walked down the hallway. He squeezed my hand repeatedly as I knocked on the apartment door. There was no answer, but I could hear music coming from inside. I knocked a bit harder, and the door came loose. It was slightly ajar, so I pushed it open and stuck my head in.

"Anyone home?" I said. Cody pushed the door open and pulled me inside. Again, the place reeked of chemicals.

On the coffee table lay a glass pipe and a small torch.

The apartment was dim, orderly, and scattered with worn furnishings. I was expecting much worse. Cody pulled me down the hallway toward the source of the music. I passed the kitchen and saw a box of Captain Crunch and a half-bowl of the soggy cereal, probably Cody's from that morning.

"Wait, Cody! Miss Lotress? Miss Lotress?" I called out.

But Cody pulled on my jacket and insisted I go with him into his bedroom. As I entered, I could feel Cody's small hand slip from my grip. I stood in the darkness of his bedroom.

"Cody? Cody?"

He turned on the light. He stood before me, eyes glowing with pride as if he wanted to please me. He extended his arms, pointing to the walls. There were hundreds of his own renditions of Van Gogh, Monet, Degas. I gasped, overwhelmed by the sight. It was almost like my study when I had prints on the walls.

"Me. Artist," he whispered.

"Yes. Yes you are, Cody. An amazing, an amazing artist. Look at all you did. Look what you can do!"

Then, out from under his bed, he pulled stacks of papers with sketches on them. I sat on his bed and looked at the drawings of his classmates, Tatty, and me. All of us from different moments in class. I fumbled through them, astounded, bowled over, while Cody stood with his fist in his mouth, rocking in place. He made groaning noises that sounded like slight attempts at laughter.

"Good work, Cody, good work! I am so proud of you. I am *so* proud of you."

I held his face and spoke directly to him. He leaned into me and hugged me.

Outside the bedroom I heard someone running down the hallway.

It startled me. Then I heard the front door slam abruptly. The sketches fell from my lap. I stood and told Cody to wait for me. I left his room.

"Miss Lotress? Miss Lotress? You there?" I went to the front door and opened it to see the elevator was going down. I walked back into the apartment. The music was still coming from the other bedroom. I walked farther down the hallway with trepidation.

"Miss Lotress? Are you there? Are you okay? Hello? Anyone home?"

I pushed the bedroom door open slightly. I walked in. The room was dark, lit only by the outside lights of the building. My eyes were glued on Cody's mother. She was spread out on the floor, her head resting in a pool of dark blood. Her throat was sliced from one side to the other; her body was badly bruised. Her eyes, glassy and wide-open, were staring upward, glazed over in death.

I heard groans coming from behind me. Cody stood behind me, rocking in place.

THIRTY-SEVEN

I picked Cody up and ran down the stairs. I only remember repeating over and over, *Oh God, oh God, Oh God!* When I arrived at the ground floor, I called 9-1-1 on my cell phone. Cody gripped me so tightly around my neck, I could hardly speak. The police came and curious crowds gathered as they took Cody's mother's body out on a stretcher.

Cody would not let go of me as the police brought us to a police car. We sat in the backseat, blue lights swirling around us. They all looked at me as if I were the murderer.

"Mr. Pepper!"

Franco was coming toward the police car, on a bike.

"Mr. Pepper, what's going on, dawg?"

"Franco!" I was happy to see someone I knew.

He whispered to me. "People say that was Cody's mother they took out. That Chris dude got her. He's one creepy motherfucker. He pimp Cody's mother out when she was only thirteen. She give skullys while he deals. He got the goods."

"Goods? Skullys?" I asked. I pulled Cody closer to me.

"He deal crack. She give head. Skullys. He deal the hard shit, Pepper. Now don't you rat on me. He bad. He come looking for me."

"I won't. I won't. What about Tracy's mother? Is she around?" My voice was cracking.

"She die. She a rock star, too." Franco said.

"Rock star?"

"Crack. She like the crack!" he said.

"Franco, go home; be safe."

"I am home."

The policeman came to the car, and Franco rode off.

Cody and I were both brought to the police station. I called Rosa, and she came immediately with June and Ralph. Cody would not let go of my hand, and every time a policeman or the emergency social worker came to speak to him, he would bury his face into my leg or motion for me to pick him up. When I did, he would rest his head on my shoulder.

Hank showed up, and I was grateful for his presence.

After being questioned for an hour and filling out forms, I waited for the emergency social worker to get in touch with an emergency foster parent. There was no one available. Cody had no relatives in New York. Rosa and I talked the social worker into letting us take him for the night. June and Ralph were in agreement. We dropped Hank home and headed for our apartment.

After putting Cody to bed on the pull-out sofa in my study, June made coffee for us, and we all sat in the living room. I was pretty shaken up, and there wasn't anything they could say or do to calm my nerves. My mind wandered as they discussed the night's ghastly events. Their questions about what I'd seen and what I'd done went unanswered. Rosa tenderly rubbed my arm. My body was trembling with waves of dread. My childhood and the death of my father appeared before me. I tried to sit very still, holding onto the arms of my chair, resisting the panic that threatened to break through. I told myself I could not let my childhood and all my bullshit from the past devour me. I remember thinking that I had to find some inner strength for Cody and, although I was scared out of my mind, I knew it was my destiny to be his father. It was that simple. The idea of letting him go from foster home to foster home troubled me. It was one of the truest feelings I'd ever had. I stood up.

"I want to adopt Cody," I said.

"What?" Rosa crinkled her lips and squinted. June put her hand on her chin and gave me one of her patronizing glares.

"It's only logical. I want to adopt Cody."

"Oliver, I think that you're upset. Sit down. You need to get some sleep." June's voice was soft, but I detected a note of doubt. "Give it some thought; relax; you look pale," she continued.

I paced the room. My mind raced with thoughts about what I had to do and whom I had to talk to, what steps I needed to take.

"There is no time; he'll go in some foster home and then another one and then he'll be put in some state institution when he is eighteen," I said.

"You don't know that for sure," Rosa said.

"Cody is bright. He could be brilliant, and he's an amazing artist. He desperately needs to be loved and understood, and I can't—No, I *won't* let him go to some foster home to be raised by strangers who won't nurture his talent or give him the love he needs."

"But you don't know if he has family members. You can't jump the gun on this," Rosa said.

"Rosa's right," June said. "It's been a long night. Let's all get some sleep. We'll talk further in the morning."

"No, we have to talk about this now," I said.

"Oliver, you know as well as I that you can't take care of a child," June said.

"What the hell does that mean?" I said.

"It means you'll adopt Cody and, well, I'll end up taking care of him. I'm tired of being a caretaker. I have plans of my own. It's not always about you, Oliver."

"God, June, where is your heart?" I said.

"My heart has always been in the right place, always, but right now my heart is thinking of me. You have too much going on in your own life to take care of a child."

"I resent that. I know I can do it. I've grown," I said.

"Okay, come on you two. Tonight was pretty traumatic," Rosa said.

"I agree with Oliver," Ralph said. "June, every person knows what they're capable of. Personally, I think it's a marvelous idea." He came over and hugged me without reservation. I hugged him back.

"It feels right. Ralph, you understand don't you?" I said.

"I do, pal. I do."

June stood up; she glared at Ralph, then me. She crossed her arms. "Look Ralph, this is one situation you need to stay out of," she said.

"That's not fair, June."

"You can't control everything, Ralph. I know what's best for my brother."

"Who's controlling? I think your brother knows what's best for him. Maybe that's why he's never grown up; no one has giving him a chance."

"Go home, Ralph. I'm in no mood for your *tough talk* tonight," June said.

"Fine, I will," he barked at June. "And I'm sick of being used when it suits you!"

"Oh, be quiet and go home!" June screeched.

"Please, you guys. Don't fight because of me," I said.

"Look, everyone. Let's not do this," Rosa said.

"I'm only saying that it is a bad idea for Oliver to adopt a child, and just because Ralph says it's okay, we're all supposed to agree," June said.

"You're getting on my last nerve!" Ralph said.

"Both of you, stop it. It's my life, and I'll do what I think is right for me."

"But ultimately it will come down on me. I'm going to bed!" June said. She marched out of the room.

Ralph shook his head dejectedly and left, slamming the door behind him. Rosa looked at me, ran her hands through her hair, and sighed.

"I know you love Cody. I know you care. But you need to think long and hard about this. It's a major commitment," she said.

"You doubt I can do it, too? Don't you? You're like June."

"Women intuitively know what's right."

"That's such bullshit!"

"Okay maybe, but I'll be honest with you, Oliver. I'm not sure I want kids. I'm unsure about a lot of things in my life right now. I'm taking everything real slow. But either way, your decision can't be based on what I want or what anyone thinks; it can only depend on what you feel you need to do. I'm going to go home tonight. We'll talk in the morning. Think about this, and whatever you decide, I'll support you."

Rosa stood, kissed me on my face, gave me a sad but warm smile, and left.

Screw everyone. I was going to do everything in my power to adopt Cody. Sometimes you know something fits perfectly. It is destiny—cut out for you by God, like that last piece of a puzzle that fits perfectly and completes a picture. You can't argue about where that last piece goes, because it belongs there. That's how I felt about Cody. I didn't care who agreed or disagreed about what I was going to do. Cody was my missing piece. I knew that with all my heart and soul.

THIRTY-EIGHT

Although June and Ralph didn't see eye to eye on my decision, I knew, in the end, that June would support me.

I lucked out, in a way, because it was difficult for the social worker to find foster parents for Cody that week.

June allowed Cody to stay with us, and since Rosa worked for the New York City School Department and I was Cody's teacher, they made allowances with the stipulation that, when a foster parent became available, Cody would have to leave us and go with foster parents who had a stamp of approval from the state. I would have to wait to be Cody's official foster parent until I was approved.

I filled out all the forms the next day, and to make sure June and I weren't a pair of axe-owning, psychotic, child-molesting, kiddy-porn lovers, the Social Worker came to our apartment for a quick cup of java and some Oreos. Her name was Miss Curtis. She came and approved the house and the sanity of June and myself.

The week that Cody was with us was magic. Each day Cody and I walked the streets to school. I felt such pride having Cody by my side. We'd stopped to look at the Christmas trees and the wreaths with big red ribbons that lined the sidewalks of Eighty-Sixth Street.

On our way home from school one afternoon I bought a few poinsettias, and June placed them all around the house. Cody sat for an hour staring at one. I could fantasize that

Cody was my son and I was a good father.

It wasn't perfect having Cody; it was challenging as well. At night he would wake up screaming with night terrors, he would pant and whisper "Mama, Mama, Mama, Mama," cry, and hold me. Then he would bite or hit me until I calmed him down. At times I would feel useless; all I could do was reassure him. I was there by his side to tell him that I would protect him and that I knew how he felt, but it was frustrating because I didn't know if he understood me or not.

The next morning, Cody always seemed to have forgotten all about the night before. "Hi. Hi. Hi. Hi. Hi. Hi. Hi. Hi," he would say while examining his spoon and drizzling his oatmeal on the table.

"Good Morning, Cody," I would say, pouring myself a cup of java.

Gilbert, the guy who owned the clothing shop, loved Cody and came out of his apartment every morning to give him a lollipop and, one day, a string of colorful love beads to wear around his neck. Cody loved the beads and didn't want to take them off. He held onto them and ran his hands through them for hours on end. I told Gilbert that Cody might be my son one day. Gilbert gave me two thumbs up and said, "Well, it looks like this Christmas is going to be full of surprises!" I told him that I hoped so.

The week before Christmas break, Cody, Hank, and I picked out a small Christmas tree and brought it to school. Our hands where heavy with sap, and Cody smelled his hands repeatedly. He liked the pine smell. Hank put Cody on his shoulder; this was surprising because the boy was reluctant to let new people touch him. It all seemed natural to Hank. He sang songs to Cody, and Cody slapped his bald head with sticky hands. He stuck his fingers in Hank's ears. It was nice to see this new side of Hank. As a kid Hank had always been intense, and to see him skipping around Second Avenue acting like a goofy kid was pretty nice. It did get a bit embarrassing when Hank changed gears from small kid to raving queen. He wrapped his scarf around his head and started dancing around, swinging his hips like he was Carmen Miranda.

Hank was down twenty pounds. There wasn't a doubt in my mind that he was gay, and that his "girlfriend" was really a "boyfriend." But I knew Hank; no matter how truthful he said he was, he had to be "truthful" on his own terms. So I let the queen reign as he pleased.

The kids made small ornaments out of construction paper. Ruthie ate most of the candy canes that I had brought in to decorate the tree with, and Kat put two candy canes down her pants and then tried to give them to me.

No thanks, Kat.

Cherri made a beautiful, ornate star for the top of the tree that looked more like a *Star of David*. After I picked her up and let her put the star on top, she told me I was "creepy." She told me she hated my guts.

Maurice bawled and told me that he celebrated Kwanzaa. Tatty told me she did, too.

So on Friday, before winter break—consistent with the overly sensitive, politically correct man I was becoming—I invited Maurice's mother to come in our class and help us celebrate Kwanzaa.

I picked up a Kinara and candles and placed fresh fruits around it. I was supposed to put fresh corn there as well, but I couldn't find any, so I bought frozen Jolly Green Giant Corn, a touch I thought was clever and amusing.

Apparently I was the only one, because Maurice's mother, who was a dedicated, serious African-American woman found it insulting.

Anyway, the kids and I decorated the classroom with the traditional colors of Kwanzaa: green, red, and black. We sat on straw mats, and the kids played bongo drums.

Maurice's mother was tall, with striking good looks. She wore a traditional African costume. Her expression was stoic, but it registered pride as she recited the African Pledge in her deep, robust voice. The kids all gave her their full attention.

> We are an African People!
> We will remember the humanity, glory and suffering of our ancestors.
> We will honor the struggles of our elders.
> We will strive to bring new values and new life to our people ....

When she was done, the kids went nuts banging on the drums. They ate June's cupcakes and then we sang Christmas songs.

Franco was allowed to come to the party, too. He devoured two cupcakes then sat and laughed as the kids tormented me.

"You are one crazy white guy, Pepper. You funny. Funny!"

"I'm glad I amuse you, Franco."

"You a fool. These kids are crazy like you, crazy!" He howled with laughter.

Christmas was on a Monday. On the Saturday before, Rosa and I took Cody to the Christmas show at Radio City Music Hall. Even though Cody sat there like a sack of potatoes fixated on the love beads Gilbert had given him rather than the show, we had a good time. Afterward we walked around Rockefeller Center, peeked in the NBC windows like all the other people from Iowa or wherever, then decided to take Cody to Wollman's Rink in Central Park. The rink at Rockefeller was too crowded.

"Hi. Hi. Hi. Hi. Hi. Hi. Hi. Hi," Cody said as we walked through the crowds up Fifth Avenue to the Park while the sound of small bells rang in the hands of the Salvation Army workers roaming the sidewalks.

We tried to put double-bladed skates on Cody, but he went bananas, so we put skates on our own feet and let him examine them. He touched them carefully and sat for a while running his fingers along the leather and metal.

"Hi. Hi. Hi. Hi. Hi. Hi. Hi. Hi," he said.

We tried to put the skates on him again, but he kept flailing around.

"Screw it," I said, and we each took one of his hands and slid him around the rink with his shoes on.

He loved it.

"Hi. Hi. Hi. Hi. Hi. Hi. Hi. Hi."

"Winter Wonderland" was playing on the speakers, and Cody's eyes blinked gleefully as we circled the rink.

Later that afternoon, we took Cody to Serendipity, a restaurant on East Sixtieth that serves foot-long hot dogs and incredible hot fudge sundaes. He made an enormous mess, chocolate fudge sauce all over the place—in his hair and on his clothes. We laughed. What could we do?

On the way home, he saw a McDonald's, and he wanted more food. He insisted on touching the window, so I picked him up and his hands traced the famed yellow arches.

He pointed to the small photo of French-Fries and patted it.

"Hi. Hi. Hi. Hi. Hi. Hi. Hi. Hi."

I had to run in and get Cody his fries. As we walked home, I stopped in a toy store and bought him a ream of thick white paper and a one-hundred-piece crayon set; Rosa bought him a truck with monster wheels. We decided that in addition to the abundance of gifts he would receive on Christmas, we would make this indulgence. We overdid it a bit, but it was fun and it made us all feel good. Cody sat all night spinning the wheels of the truck.

"Hi. Hi. Hi. Hi. Hi. Hi. Hi. Hi."

On Sunday, Christmas Eve day, we took Cody on a horse and buggy ride through Central Park. He was obsessed with the driver's top hat, and the driver let him wear it, even though it fell over his face. It was a trial trying to get Cody to give it back. He screamed so violently that we had to buy the damn top hat from the driver to calm him down. Then we stuffed a scarf in it so that it would fit on Cody's head.

Happy again, we headed home through Central Park. Cody walked ahead of us, his new top hat on, and flapped his hands, stopping to touch each tree he passed, murmuring some secret message to each one.

On Christmas Eve, June and Ralph were preparing a special dinner. They had spent hours in Chinatown getting all these "special ingredients." I was not looking forward to it, but I kept my mouth shut and did my best not to be an asshole.

Thank God Rosa was preparing Christmas dinner. A simple roasted turkey dinner with chestnut dressing.

When we arrived home, Ralph was cooking up a storm. The place smelled like Ralph's breath—garlic and Hoisin Sauce. The good news was that Ralph had brought home a lush Scotch Pine to decorate after dinner. June had bought expensive zoo themed ornaments at *Gracious Home*. They were uniquely painted and embellished with a variety of sparkling beads and metallic paint—gold and blue horses, silver and black zebras, orange and purple lions and brown and white shiny monkeys. Before putting them on the tree, a delighted June dangled them from her fingers by a bright red ribbon in front of Cody, who was in complete wonderment.

Hank had told me how excited he was about coming. I don't think I remember him ever sounding so happy. When he arrived, Cody was napping. June and Ralph were setting the table and Rosa was wrapping gifts when the buzzer rang. I leaped to buzz Hank in. I was so thrilled that we both had stopped drinking and found people that we loved.

However, this was a bigger deal, because Hank had never been involved with anyone. I had suffered years of his obsessions over women who never looked his way; they were twisted delusionary love affairs that only existed in his head. It was sad, because he was trying to hide who he was. I was still waiting for him to come out. I was hoping he wasn't going to hire an escort and pretend that she was his girlfriend.

Hank was the last to arrive. I was only imagining what he was going to do. I hadn't seen him in a few weeks.

I opened the door.

"Hank! Hank? Oh my god, Hanky, you look terrific! That shirt looks great on you. June! Ralph! Rosa! Come see Hank!"

"Can I come in?" Hank laughed. His arms were full of gifts, and behind him was Gilbert.

"Hi, Oliver!" Gilbert said. June and Ralph stood in shock; they couldn't believe Hank's metamorphosis. I introduced Rosa to Hank and Gilbert.

"I hope you don't mind me coming, but Hank said it was okay," Gilbert said.

"Of course it's okay!" Ralph said. "We have millions of egg rolls, enough to feed all the soldiers in Tiananmen Square. I just hope they're okay."

"The eggs rolls are fine!" June said. Ralph looked like he was going to cry.

"Where's the new girlfriend?" I asked, pretending not to know what was soon to unfold. Hank looked at me and frowned, then smiled at Gilbert. It wasn't the kind of smile you give a friend; it was the smile you give another guy if you're having wild, nonstop, I'm finally having sex with him.

Bingo. It was official. Hank was out.

"I'm gay. Merry Christmas! I'm queer, I'm here, and *don't* give me a beer!" Everyone laughed.

"I know you're all shocked," Hank said.

"I am so shocked. *So* completely shocked!" I said. I was about as shocked as though I'd gone into an Italian restaurant and learned they served Italian food.

"Well, I'm happy for you Hank, finally!" June said.

"Gilbert, I just love your pants!" Rosa said.

"Thanks. Love yours, too. Purple is great with your coloring," Gilbert said.

"Got them on sale. Love pinstripe pants on guys."

"Thanks. Where was the sale?"

"That place on Lex and Eighty-Sixth. It just opened. I can't remember the name."

"Oh, you mean Girls Just Want To Have Fun?" Gilbert said.

"Yes!" Rosa said.

Hank smiled at me; I could tell he liked that our partners were chatting a bit.

"Come on in. Sit down everyone. Ralph, honey, get the egg rolls," June said. Ralph looked nervous. "Ralph, it's okay. We said we weren't going to talk about the egg rolls, remember?" June patted Ralph's shoulder, and he nodded and went into the kitchen.

June whispered to us. "Please, will you all do me a favor? Say the eggs rolls are wonderful. I'm afraid they may be a disaster. Ralph has been crying all day. He said he was in his manly monthly cycle and couldn't concentrate. I think he forgot to season the filling for the eggs rolls."

"What do you mean? Ralph gets a period?" I said with a laugh. No one else did.

"All men have their 'periods' but it's without the bleeding, just the PMS part. Didn't you read that part of the book?" Gilbert said. Rosa and June looked at each and nodded in approval.

Hank leaned forward and looked at everyone.

"Speaking of manly feelings, it was hard for me to hide this gay stuff from you all. You know how I like to be truthful," he said.

"I know that about you, Hank," I said.

"The day I walked into Gilbert's store, I knew I had found someone to love."

And to think of all those times Hank grabbed my ass and balls, all those free feels he copped! Damn that horny Hank.

"Well this calls for a celebration! I'll make us a big pot of Qi Hong Tea!" June said.

We all sat on the sofa and drank Qi Hong tea. We ate Ralph's greasy, cabbage-filled egg rolls, which tasted like cabbage filled doughnuts. We told him they were wonderful. Hank told us how Gilbert and he had reconnected at a reading for *The Castration of the 20th Century Man.* One thing had led to another, Hank said, and well … "It happened." Hank placed his hand lovingly on Gilbert's thigh.

"That book!" I said.

"Delayed reaction," Ralph said. Hank and Gilbert looked at each other and nodded in unison. I didn't care what they thought. They were nuts.

"But he's getting there," Ralph said. He smiled at me. Hank and Gilbert nodded and smiled.

Cody woke up and made his way to my side. Once again Hank was great with Cody; he did his Samantha *Bewitched* thing by wiggling his nose and making objects appear in his hand, like quarters and marbles, the sort of thing an uncle does.

Cody looked at Hank like he was insane, and I can't say I blamed him.

Every time Hank put an egg roll in his mouth, all I could think of was a penis. Hank was officially gay; I was thrilled for him and for me. No more free feels, though.

After a delightful dinner of Shanghaied Duck Ddeok, Gilbert and Hank wanted to give their gift to Cody.

It was a Malibu Barbie. Hank said it was to ensure that Cody grew up liking women and their accessories.

"Women are allowed to relish all the pretty things that life offers and men aren't allowed to like pretty things."

"I like pretty things," Gilbert said. "Don't you like pretty things?" he asked me.

"Yes, I do," I said, and I held Rosa's hand.

"That's very insightful, Hank," Rosa said.

She was trying hard to be amenable.

Ralph, of course, couldn't agree more, and they talked about him coming to a new group forming on the Upper East Side for gay and straight men.

To change the subject, I suggested we decorate the tree. Rosa and I placed lights on the branches while Cody sat with a Christmas ornament in his hand; it was a small reindeer, and he turned it around and around. June and Hank sat on the sofa with Cody in between them and watched. Hank and Gilbert put small hooks on silver balls to hang. Rosa and I would periodically run over to Cody and hug or tickle him, and he would flap his hand for us to go away. I hoped he felt warm and safe with us, and to ensure he did, I put on Bing Crosby singing "White Christmas." I wanted Cody's Christmas to be perfect. As far as I was concerned, I couldn't ask for anything more than what I was blessed with that Christmas.

Before Hank and Gilbert left, I managed to get Hank alone in the study while the others washed dishes and cleaned up. Cody was playing on the floor with a paper clip, and we both watched him with expressions of merriment on our faces. Hank told me he couldn't meet me in the morning.

"What do you mean? We meet every Christmas morning. Since we were kids!"

"I can't," he said.

"But we do every year," I said chuckling, still thinking he was joking.

"I'm going up to Westchester tonight to meet Gilbert's parents, and in the morning we're flying to Florida to see my parents."

"Oh," I said impassively. "What do they say about all this?" I asked.

"They say it was about time I came out of the closet."

I picked Cody up and held him on my lap. He was still fixated on the paper clip. My cheeks felt hot.

"I'm sorry I can't meet you, but you did this for me. You evoked change. We'll always be friends, Ollie. I'm going to be forever grateful to you for having the balls to change, 'cause it changed me."

"Tell me something. What about Elizabeth Montgomery? What was that? A big lie?" I asked.

"I was in love with Darren."

"I knew it! And what about all those crushes on women at the bar—those endless proclamations of love?"

"Drunken talk and covering up how I really felt. When I stopped drinking, a flood of emotions came my way. I wanted to be loved by a man, and I wanted to have sex with a man in the worst way, but not necessarily in that order."

"But what about having sex with that girl, you know, Judy, what was her name? When you were twenty?"

"That was like having sex with a piece of liver."

"God, Hank!"

"Come on Oliver, you always knew I was gay. I was eating and drinking myself into denial. For the first time in my life I feel like a complete man." He stood up and started to take off his shirt.

"What the hell are you doing?" Hank laughed and slipped off his shirt. He was completely smooth.

"I'm not hairy anymore. It was lasered off. My body hair was like this dark, inscrutable forest I was walking around with, and now everything is crystal clear to me."

"Well, I am happy for you Hank. But please put your shirt on. I think you're scaring Cody."

"It's going to be a great year for us. A great year. I know it." He buttoned up his shirt.

"You look ten years younger," I said.

"Don't tell anyone. I had Botox. It's a miracle."

"You're out of control," I said. I laughed.

"So tell me, do you love Rosa?"

"I think so, but not as much as I loved Beth," I said. His eyes locked with mine.

"Did you really love Beth?"

"What do you mean? Of course I did," I put Cody down, and he started to unfold the paper clip, twisting it and examining it closely. Hank's and my eyes locked again.

"What's up, Hank?" I cracked my knuckles.

"You know what? I believe that true love is so powerful that it can change people's lives; it doesn't let you grow apart like you guys did. It doesn't grow so comfortable that you neglect one another."

"Hank, I appreciate the insight but this is the first time you've been in love."

"No, it's not." He bowed his head. "Jesus, Oliver, I was a latent homosexual who drank his blues away in a bar with you. Those women I talked about, those feelings of longing and love and sorrow and pain, they were about you. I was in love with you."

"What?" I said.

"I was in love with you all those years. Merry Christmas."

"Jesus, Hank," I said.

This was one Christmas gift I did not want to unwrap! I mean, I loved Hank, but I did not love him in that I-love-you way. Why did he have to tell me this?

"Hank, really, let's not go there, shall we? Some things are meant to be private. That's why the word 'private' was invented."

"Why? Why? Because it makes you feel uncomfortable that I was in love with you? So what? Is that shameful? The truth is, if you were gay and you proclaimed your love for me, I would have gone running because I wasn't emotionally ready for love. Many people aren't. I don't feel that way about you anymore. I was lonely. I had no one. I was afraid. But loving you like I did, I learned a great deal. There was nothing you did that I couldn't understand or find compassion for, and I always wanted to be with you. You just wanted a friend and a drinking partner. It was perfect for both of us. All Beth wanted to do was change you, and you weren't ready for change. She didn't love you enough to let you naturally evolve. Beth wasn't nice to you. She was impatient and stubborn, and you were a hurt drunk. I knew all that about you, and I still loved you, and that's why you spent all your time with me and not Beth. The minute she left, you started to evolve."

"I don't know what to say Hank," I said.

"One night, right after you told me that Beth had lost the baby, we went out drinking. We both got plastered. I walked you up to your place. When Beth saw us stumble in, she was disgusted with both of us. I put you to bed. Beth went to sleep in the study."

"Please don't tell me we got it on. Please, Hank."

"No, no! But I sat on the edge of the bed, and you called me 'Daddy.' Now, in the gay community, that would be considered pretty sexy and hot."

"Oh great." I ran my hands through my hair. I kept my eyes on my feet. But nevertheless, I listened to Hank speak.

"I leaned over and I hugged you. I told you I was your Dad and everything was going to be okay. You smiled, and you slept. For the rest of the night, I watched you sleep, and I cried. I cried because I loved you. I cried because I was gay. And I cried because I knew I could never have you. I had such fear inside of me. I knew I couldn't make you love me. In my despair, my frustration, and my anger, I started exploring my sexuality in some seedy places. I had to do it. I had to somehow figure out who I was. My fear grew in me like wildfire."

"Don't say 'fire' too loudly. June may hear you."

"After you punched me out and we didn't talk for a while, I met Gilbert at the Toolbox, that gay bar on East Ninetieth and Second. He told me he would see you and me in the neighborhood strolling up and down the streets, joking, laughing, drunk. Gilbert said he thought we were lovers. The gay duet of the Upper East Side. Gilbert told me we were an example of real love between two men. He loved that we could laugh and drink together. Gilbert even saw us the time you grabbed that hot dog out of my hand and ran off with it laughing. Remember how pissed I got at you?

"Gilbert said he saw you most mornings. He said you always looked lost without me by your side. I told Gilbert we weren't lovers, only good friends, best friends, and that you were married and miserable, and I was single and miserable. I told him you and I couldn't commit to anything; we were scared of being hurt—two lost souls on a journey to nowhere.

"But Gilbert disagreed. He said we were committed to each other. And it occurred to me that he was right. It was the truth. I could commit. Gilbert also said that today's world is full of fancy buzz words: *needy, co-dependent, commitment-shy, obsessive*, all labels bestowed on us to emotionally cripple and put fear in us. Gilbert told me to stop the fear and to stop over-analyzing. He said to simply look at the surface of what things were. For so long, I feared that I would not have you as my lover. And if I told you how I felt I would not have you as my friend anymore. I feared being who I was. Damn, Oliver, I wanted to ruin our friendship by sleeping with Beth so I wouldn't have to deal with my fears of feeling something for you. It was nuts! But the second I stopped fearing how I felt and went with my gut and trusted myself, you came back to me. No matter what, I have you forever; you have me. You're my best and dearest friend, and I will always love you, Oliver. I'm so proud of you and our friendship. It's been one hell of a year!"

He then pointed at Cody. "This is amazing! Look at you, taking care of a child. It's beyond amazing. I'm so proud."

"Thanks Hank," I said sheepishly.

"Now, here's the hard part," Hank said, standing and pacing in front of me.

"I'm glad you're trying to adopt Cody, and I'm happy you found Rosa. My only advice, Ollie, is not to use this kid to resolve any guilt you have over Beth aborting the baby."

"I love Cody." There was an echoing silence. I looked over at Hank, and he was grinning at me. It was the first time I had said I love Cody out loud, and I said it again.

"Hank, I love Cody. I love him and I want to be his father." I looked at Cody, and he was still playing with his paperclip.

"I want to be his father. And that brings me to June," I said. "She has always taken care of me, Hank, and I've been so selfish I haven't let myself be needed by anyone. Now it's June's turn."

"Hey, I needed you."

"And I needed you. I'm grateful for our friendship. Beth and I were not meant to be."

"It's okay; love doesn't always turn out the way we want it to. But right now I love Gilbert, and I'm bringing all I've learnt from your life failures to this relationship. I definitely know what not to do." He started to laugh.

"You're still an asshole, Hank. A truthful one." And I joined him in his laughter.

"Merry Christmas, Ollie!"

"Same to you, Hanky!" He came over to me and gave me a hug. I felt myself trying to suppress a well of melancholy because nothing would be the same between us; we had become new people these past months, and our friendship had grown deeper that night because of it. I would always fear that Hank would try to bugger me, but regardless, I would love him forever.

Gilbert came into the study wearing a big smile. "We should head out soon, Hank," he said. He had such an animated, pleasing way about him that you couldn't help but like him.

"Okay, right. I'll go say 'bye to everyone," Hank said. He picked Cody up and kissed his forehead. Cody flapped his arms. Hank giggled and put him down.

Gilbert winked and whispered to me after Hank walked out the door. "Thanks, Oliver. You made him happy tonight. I can see it all over his face."

"Hanky is the best. Thanks, Gilbert," I said.

Gilbert left me alone with Cody. He came over, climbed on the chair and sat next to me, paperclip in hand, whispering softly, "Hi. Hi. Hi. Hi. Hi. Hi. Hi. Hi."

THIRTY-NINE

Christmas morning came with an over-abundance of gifts for Cody. In a bizarre way, the scene was sort of heartbreaking: Rosa, June, Ralph and me, all bug-eyed and eager as we helped Cody open his gifts. We all had a look on our faces that said we wished we were kids again on Christmas morning—happy and still believing that the world was full of fairies and magic.

And even though my world was once again full of fairies, Cody had seen his mother with her throat sliced, and I doubted he thought the world was so magical. I didn't know what he thought or felt inside, and it was frustrating as all hell. Sure, there was a part of me that wanted Cody to verbally express how much he loved me, loved my sister and Rosa and Ralph, loved his new life with us. But he only sat and did cunning, sweet things, like look my way after I opened his gifts and hum the same tuneless song he always sang or murmur the ten or so words that he knew: Hi, Mama, Van Gogh, Me, Artist, Hit, Mad, Sunflower … and I think I heard him say "asshole" to Ralph once.

It was a relief and a nice change to sit down to a traditional Christmas dinner. Nothing Chinese. Not that I don't adore Chinese people and the culture, but I'm not one for things soaking in fish sauce or dried seaweed. It was a plain old turkey dinner with plain old cranberry sauce and plain old mashed spuds and plain old carrots and plain old Christmas pudding.

I ate my Christmas dinner with gusto. Rosa had done an outstanding job.

Then Ralph did it: he had to stop the silence, the devouring of good food. He started by hitting his apple juice glass with his fork. Everyone looked his way except Cody, who was twirling a turkey drumstick in his plate.

"Hi Hi Hi Hi Hi Hi Hi Hi Hi Hi Hi Hi Hi."

"I have an announcement to make," Ralph said.

"Can it wait till after we eat, Ralph?" I said.

"No, it certainly cannot! You see, the Chinese believe that good news during dinner means good digestion."

"But we're not Chinese, and we're eating our Christmas dinner," I said.

"Go on, Ralph," Rosa said. She kicked me under the table, a habit of hers I was becoming accustomed to.

"We're getting married," June said. She held out her hand and, on her finger, was my mother's jade ring, the one my father had given her: Dac Kein's light!

"I know Daddy would have wanted me to have this as my engagement ring, and Ralph agreed," June said.

"Well, this is great news, sis!" I said. I knew it was coming; I only didn't know when, and I was hoping not during my turkey dinner.

"We decided on a New Year's Eve wedding," June said.

"But we have another surprise," Ralph said.

"What is it? Let's see, you're both moving to China!" I laughed.

"How did you know?" Ralph said.

"I didn't tell him," June said.

"What, are you serious?" I said.

"February first," she said.

"When I was at the China–U.S. Conference on Libraries last year in Boston, I was approached to work in Beijing. I refused at first, and, well, they asked me again, and I've accepted."

"China? Libraries? Wow, that's far. Hey, I'm happy for you guys," I said. I tried to sound happy.

"Did you know that libraries in China can be traced back to the time of Confucius?" Ralph said.

"I have something else to tell everyone," June said. She reached over for Ralph's hand, and he took it lovingly. "We're pregnant." June smiled.

"But you're forty-three years old," I said. What did this mean? Why had I said that? She was going to get married and leave me. What was I thinking? This was how it was supposed to be. You get married, you move on, you live. I smiled the best I could. June was happy. *Stop*, I told myself. What kind of man was I?

"The doctor said it was fine. Plus the doctors in China are more advanced in obstetric medicine then they are in the States."

"They use a lot of herbs. Fascinating stuff," Ralph said.

"I'm sorry I've been so grumpy lately. Hormones," June said.

"She's been a monster!" Ralph said. He laughed.

"Stop it, Ralph," June said. "God, don't irritate me today. Oops, sorry. See?"

"Well this is wonderful news, congratulations!" Rosa said. June started to bawl. I was nudged by Rosa to go to her, and I did.

June stood, and I told her how happy I was for her. I kissed her and held her, and she felt bony but strong. It had been a long time since I was that close to her; her grip on me was unyielding, but I slipped away from her. When I shook Ralph's thick hand, he stood, pulled me toward him and hugged me so hard I almost landed in his plate. I didn't yell at him. I went back to my seat, and we all continued eating our Christmas dinner. I was so consumed by the news, my inside organs twisted in a perplexing combination of happiness for June and dire fright that I would have to listen to Ralph's sermon on *Beijing* and the *Yanshan Mountains* and how he couldn't wait to see the *Temple of Heaven*.

Late that night, as Rosa slept in my bed, her hands folded under her quiescent face, I found myself unable to sleep. I couldn't stop thinking about my mother and how we promised her that June and I would stay together forever. I always thought it would be me who broke my mother's promise. But there it was … June was the one leaving, carrying on with her life. I went into the study and checked on Cody. He was sleeping serenely, and I noted with amusement the pile of gifts we had proudly stacked by his sofa bed. I went into the living room and turned on the Christmas tree lights, which illuminated the room in a white, luminous glow. There was such peace and silence around me, and as I sat on the sofa, June appeared in her bathrobe. At first I jumped. I thought she was some kind of Dickensian Christmas ghost coming to drag me through the drudges of my past.

"Christ, June! You scared me," I whispered.

"Sorry, Ollie." She sat next to me and rested her head on the back of the sofa. Simultaneously, we kicked our feet up on the coffee table.

"Thanks for the Chanel No. 5," she whispered.

"Sure. Thanks for the Faith Hill CD and the nose hair clippers."

"You're welcome."

"China is pretty damn far."

"I know, but I'm excited," June said.

"It's going to be the first time we've been apart, except for college."

"I know. Mother wouldn't approve," June said. She yawned.

"Our mother was crazy."

"Bonkers," June laughed sadly.

"Her mind was fried, excuse the pun." We laughed.

"Can you believe we actually had to sleep with fire extinguishers by our sides? That was twisted, and it was wrong."

"God love her. But we are nothing like her. Or Daddy. They were good in their own way, you know?"

"I know June," I whispered.

A reflective silence wrapped itself around us, and for a moment, I felt my mother's presence.

When June and I had been a little older, Mother had had a critical breakdown and set the lobby of our building on fire with a small culinary torch.

Mother was home again after a month.

After only one month at home, she broke down again. Our mother had traded in all of our father's stock and bonds. And, on a cold icy day, she left the house dressed in her bathrobe, slipping away from June, and stood on the corner of East Fifty-Ninth Street and Lexington Avenue, handing out wads of cash to total strangers, most of whom greedily grabbed at what she offered them. Hank called us from a phone booth and told us what he'd seen our mother doing. He had tried to get her into a cab, but she'd refused. In fact, she had slugged him in the face.

My sister and I called an ambulance and rushed down to meet our mother. But we were too late. Mother had completely depleted our life savings, and we were left in financial ruin. She had gotten it all in cash over a series of weeks; she planned the entire thing. We were forced to sell our house to pay off our debts and to pay for the medical care my mother received.

June, my mother, and I moved into the small apartment on York Avenue where we still live today. Even then, we refused to institutionalize mother, despite the fact she still had fits of confusion and anger, still lit small fires, and became incredibly hostile to the Vietnamese man who owned the Laundromat next door. It was painfully embarrassing to watch my mother stand in front of this poor man's store and hear her scream at him, "You fucking faggot! You fucked my husband!" The poor man didn't know what to do. It was finally clear to us that we had no choice but to find a home with professional care for her.

My mother spent her last years in a nursing home in Queens, three blocks from her childhood home. She became old and senile long before her time. She had refused to eat properly all those years, so lack of proper nutrition had made her bones as brittle as winter branches. A cheap copy of Monet's *Ice Floes* hung on the wall by her bed, and she stared at it endlessly.

When she was not contemplating the Monet, her brain was jumbled with scattered images of the privileged life she had once led. Some days she would remember us and call to make sure we were still together. Then she'd remind us that we were bound together forever; we should never forget that.

My mother left the jade ring my father had given her to June. We were both surprised that she still had it with her, because she hadn't worn it on her finger since the day she'd read about Dac Kein.

Dac Kein's light has not shined for a good many years. I once doubted that it would ever shine ever again. But it was now on June's finger!

I reached over and held June's hand. Her expression was solemn, her eyes cast downward. I felt the Jade ring.

"Oliver, I had to move on so you could. You understand, right? You seem like you're doing quite well without my help. You'll be fine."

"I know. I know," I said.

"Keeping Mother's promise was like holding onto her. We have a right to live our own lives."

"It feels nice to move on," I said. I voided my voice of all hesitation and smiled happily.

"I know you're faking happiness for me. I know you're scared. But it will be for the best."

"I know," I muttered. There was no fooling her; June knew me too well.

"You've done some good living these last few months. I'm proud of you," she said.

"Thanks, June. And I haven't seen you playing with the knobs on the stove lately."

June folded her arms across her chest; she became pensive. "Oliver, there has been no need to." She hit my shoulder.

"I'm sorry I was such a pain in the ass all these years."

"You were only a boy who wanted to be with his father." Her voice was soft, and it suddenly sounded heartbreaking.

"What does that mean?" I asked. I turned to her.

"It means you were not responsible for our father dying. Try not to blame yourself. I know that somewhere inside you, you blame yourself."

Two large tears ran down her face. "I'm sorry for crying. I know how you hate that but, like I said, my hormones are making me so crazy, and these Chinese herbs I'm taking are giving me horrible gas."

"I don't think that feeling will ever go away," I said.

"I hope so; this gas is a killer."

"No, my feeling that I'm responsible for Dad's death."

"Probably not, and I also think you know intuitively it's not true," June said. "But it's like anything we carry around with us. We look for any excuse to confirm that we're bad. I think human beings do that sort of thing."

"Maybe you're right," I said.

"Maybe I'm wrong, too, but I am certain of one thing. Those feelings of love you had for Daddy will never go away. I think that's why you're so good with Cody." She blew her nose.

"Am I good? Do you think I'll be a good father?"

"Are you kidding? You've amazed me. I was wrong. I feel so good about moving on with my life now. I feel like you're safe and good and heading toward all these great things." She grabbed my head and kissed my ear and lovingly pushed me away.

"You're a little creep," she tittered.

"I'm happy for you, June. You've been a great big sister."

"Don't make it sound like it's over; I'm only going to China, not across the other side of the world for crying out loud."

"China is across the other side of the world."

"Well, there's always e-mail. I should go back to bed. Ralph says the Chinese believe that a pregnant woman walking around late at night stirs up evil spirits." She looked at me with a silly grin and shrugged her shoulders. "He's odd, but I love him."

I watched as June walked back to her bedroom.

And now all I wanted was to be Cody's father and to give him a secure place to live, a place to call home, and a voice or skills to articulate his fears, hopes, and dreams.

FORTY

It has been months now, and much has happened since the days of Cody.

I recently received a call from Miss Curtis. But before I tell you about it, let me go back to a time when I waited and waited for the news on whether I would be Cody's father or not.

I had made my bedroom into a boy's room and June's old bedroom into my bedroom. I'd decided to switch bedrooms because June's room always gets the morning sun, and well, the sun can wake a kid up. A young boy needs rest. I also figured that if, one day, my little niece Olivia came for a visit, she'd want to stay in the bedroom her mother once lived in.

Olivia was born this past August in Beijing.

June sends me thousands of photos of Olivia via e-mail, and I print each one out and pin them up on my study's walls. Sometimes at night, when the day is done and I long for June and her chicken pies and stews, I wander into my study and look at those photos taken in various parts of Beijing. I know happiness and love exist in the world when I see June holding baby Olivia, whether in front of the Temple of Heaven or The Great Wall of China. I usually focus on June's bright, beautiful smile and the little pink face of Olivia, which peeks out from the little blanket she is bundled up in. I miss them terribly. Ralph e-mails me daily. He tells me they are enjoying their work in Beijing. They both work on a library collaboration that has been in existence for a good many years between China and the U.S.

Yes, I'd be lying if I didn't say I missed Ralph and his dark rimmed glasses, his bad breath, and the way he freely showed his feelings. I'd not only lost a sister to Beijing, I'd lost a brother.

In a few months they're coming to the States for the China–U.S. Conference on Libraries in St. Louis. I'm going to fly there and visit with them for a week. Rosa says she may come with me.

The day Ralph and June left, we all went to JFK. I hugged them both goodbye and watched as they walked down the jet way. (We had special permission to go into the terminal since their gig in Beijing was a government thing.)

When their plane took off, I had a horrible panic attack right there in JFK. Rosa knew I was flipping out, but she didn't say anything. She grabbed me by my hand, and we took a taxi home in a spooky stillness, the noises of New York City muffled by a voice inside my head. *June and Ralph are gone, gone half way around the world. You have no choice now but to grow up and be a man.*

Rosa and I broke up a few weeks after they left because I was a pain in the ass. I snapped at her a few times, and she told me to "Fuck off"—it was our first real argument. I was going through some heavy separation anxiety, I was worried about Cody, and in addition to that, Rosa was upset over Charlie marrying some woman he had met on a whim.

I told her point blank I didn't like feeling like a "stand-in" boyfriend. I knew she hadn't properly mourned the loss of Charlie, and I didn't want to be a shoulder to cry on about her old boyfriend anymore. I told her I thought it was inappropriate, and she told me I was wishy-washy and "fucking hesitant" about everything.

We both knew it was getting ugly between us, and so Rosa and I decided we needed time apart. When we'd see each other at school over the next few weeks, we would make the best of it. At night I isolated myself. I didn't want to speak to Hank or look at my e-mails from June and Ralph; the only thing I did was take Cody out for an ice cream a few times after school with permission from his foster parents.

During our separation, there were many nights I was tempted to go to a bar for a quick glass of whiskey or pick up a six pack. But I never did, no matter how much my feelings of dread mushroomed into a calamitous panic. I would lie in bed very still, determined not to drink, eyes wide open. I let the feelings I was frightened of run through my body. And on some nights, when the panic was worse than others, particularly the nights when I felt myself being pulled into a higher realm of dread, I prayed to my father for help.

If I had to do it all again, I would have waited the required AA year before Rosa and I started to date, but we didn't, and we're surviving. I think we're going to be okay.

Two days after that Christmas, foster parents were found, and Cody left us. I told everyone we couldn't be weak and we couldn't entertain negative thoughts; after all, I would see him in school. I smiled and acted bravely for everyone.

The foster parents were very nice and made arrangements for me to visit with Cody on the weekends if I wanted. I was confident that, in a few days, Cody would be with me again, and I told myself the separation was temporary.

When Cody left us, he didn't cry, he only took Miss Curtis' hand and walked off. He looked up at me with no expression. I snapped my knuckles and smiled a toothy grin at everyone. I felt like my heart was being ripped out of my chest and stomped on, but all the same I was thankful I could feel my heart being ripped out of my chest and stomped on, because for so long I hadn't felt anything. The good news was that Cody would still be in my class until everything was settled.

I waited and waited for my foster parent application forms to be processed. I had multiple home studies done, and I wrote a short autobiographical statement and sent it off to the Administration for Children's Services.

Those few weeks went by fast, and I continued to teach. I remained focused. I treated Cody just like all the other children, but at the end of the day, when Cody went home to his temporary foster family, my heart sank.

The kids continued to draw, cry, piss, poop, and tell me they loved me or hated me, and I felt myself growing each day into a person who had a huge capacity for giving love. Yes, it was true, I found myself caring for these little monsters more than I thought I would. I was thinking about them constantly. As I'd pass a store or a clothing shop, I would think: *Kat would like that, Ruthie would laugh at that, Maurice would be scared of that, Cherri needs a haircut.*

After Cody left us, I received the call. Miss Curtis was coming to discuss Cody's future. June and Ralph had left. We'd had a spectacular wedding for them down at Rosa's place in Soho; it was a fantastic time (even though the night before Ralph had made seaweed soup for his last hurrah Chinese dinner and it had given me diarrhea all the next day).

Rosa thought it best I meet Miss Curtis alone; I paced my apartment, making sure all was in its proper place—beds made, kitchen cleaned, no lead paint. Rosa and June—before she left—had helped me turn the study into a suitable room for Cody. June bought a kids' bedroom blanket set; the quilt was decorated with smiling cows. June had sewn curtains from the sheets that came with the bedspread.

There was snow on the ground that day; it was bitterly cold, and I was so nervous I almost wiped-out on my ass on icy Second Avenue. I stopped and bought some gourmet coffee on Eighty-Sixth; I had it brewing a half hour before Miss Curtis came. I waited by the front window looking down on the street and up at the New York City sky; it was lined with gray, smooth clouds that were blotting out the sun in thick parallel bands. When the buzzer rang, my hands started to shake so badly I thought they were going to jump off my arms and crawl into a hole.

We sat on the sofa. Miss Curtis pulled out my application. I winced.

She was blond, about fifty, and bags were forming under her piercing green eyes. She wore a brown suit jacket with earth-tone plaid pants. Her sonorous voice buzzed menacingly in my ears like the beating of a house fly's wings.

She placed my application on the coffee table and gave me a sullen look. She then put her hand on it, sighed deeply, and tapped her fingers on it.

"What? What? This is not good, is it?" I asked.

"I'm sorry it took me so long to get back to you. In fact, two days ago I approved your application to be a foster parent. It's official. You're a foster parent. Congratulations," she said.

My body melted into ease. I could breathe easier, and my hands became putty. In fact, I was a bit dizzy; I leaned back on the sofa. I let out a huge yelp of relief, and then one of complete joy.

"When do I get Cody?"

"Let me finish?" She took some papers out of her briefcase; her musky perfume seemed to puff off the documents and settle in my nostrils. She looked up from her folder and adjusted her glasses on her sharp nose.

"Tracy's half-sister has come forward. She wants Cody. She's from South Carolina. She left New York years ago. I've met her, and she's a good woman. She's married and has three of her own children. Two boys and a girl. Her husband and she own a bakery in Charleston. I saw it on the Food Channel. It's practically famous—a charming place."

"I don't understand. I love Cody, and I'm going to be his father."

"I'm sorry, Mr. Pepper, but the law states that a child goes with the closest relative. I know this is painful. I see it every day. There are so many other—"

"Cody is going to be leaving school, too? He's going. Right?"

"Yes. I'm sorry. But there are plenty of other children that need homes."

"I don't want another child."

"I'm sorry. He's leaving tomorrow. Mr. Pepper, a child isn't like a new car or home. I'm telling you that there are other children—"

"I heard you. And you're the one making it sound like Cody can be replaced like a car or a home, not me," I said.

"I know you're upset. I'm sorry. It was wrong of me to suggest another child right now."

"Will they let me see him before he goes?"

"Of course; they have no hostility. In fact, quite the contrary. Cody's aunt suggested they meet you. I told them how fond you are of him and about all the wonderful drawings and books and all about your wonderful family."

"Thanks," I said. As soon Miss Curtis left my apartment, I looked around my spotless space and screamed, *Fuck it! Fuck it!*

I wanted a drink. Rosa, Hank, and Gilbert came over, and I told them the devastating news. We all sat around, downcast, as though someone had died. They walked on tiptoes and fed me, and did all those things nice people do when a person gets heartbreaking news.

I did the right thing and kept telling myself that this was good for Cody; he had a blood relative who wanted him. He would be loved by people who were featured on the Food Channel. I was all peace, love and charity. But my mind would quickly switch gears. It was like: *Huh! I guess the fucking Food Channel is more glamorous than what I could offer.*

I was in the movie *Tootsie;* didn't that count for anything? It was with Hank, when we were twelve; it's the last scene and we're crossing the street on West Sixty-Fifth and you can see us for about four seconds. *Fuck the Food Channel.* Oh, hell, I finally realized, who was I trying to kid with this *be nice one minute, be pissed-off the next*? So I decided to stay pissed-off and disappointed for as long as I saw fit. I had a right to my anger.

Food Channel, bullshit.

The next day in school, I told Tatty the news, and she covered her mouth in disbelief and started to bawl for me. I found myself comforting her, which was good for me, considering that I tend to be self-centered.

I sat the kids down and explained that Cody was going away. Cherri cried and told me it was my fault, and even though Cody had not arrived yet to say goodbye to the class, Maurice rocked in place and repeated, " 'Bye Cody. 'Bye Cody. 'Bye Cody."

Ruthie and Kat tumbled and laughed; I don't think they comprehended that part of our squadron was going away for good.

When Cody's Aunt Isabella walked into the classroom, I looked over at her standing in the doorway. She had a big smile on her face and the same smooth skin as Cody. Our eyes locked, and her face became long and concerned. I'm sure she could see something in my eyes. I stood and motioned for her to enter the class, and she looked back at me with a polite, reciprocal curiosity. Cody held her hand.

"Class, this is Cody's Aunt Isabella. She's brought Cody in today to say goodbye. He's moving to South Carolina. Cody's Aunt Isabella has been on the Food Channel." I stressed Food Channel, and I looked at Tatty as her eyes grew concerned.

"I like food," Maurice said. Isabella laughed.

"Hi Hi Hi Hi Hi Hi Hi Hi Hi Hi Hi Hi Hi," Cody said. The rest of the kids all shouted *hi,* ran up and patted him. He flapped his arms and hid behind Isabella. I rubbed my forehead and asked Cody's aunt if he could stay for the story. She agreed. The kids all sat down.

"Who wants to pick the book? Cody?" I asked. Cody bowed his head, which I gathered meant no.

I then chose Kat. She went to the bookshelf and, without thinking, chose a picture book, which I had bought for the class weeks ago, on our old friend Mr. Van Gogh. I swear Kat knew what she was doing when she picked that book.

Cody sat in the center of the kids. Some were kneeling, fingers hanging out of their mouths. I began to read the story, turning each page, not looking at Cody or any of the kids. I kept my eyes on the book, suppressing the grief that was building within me.

"Vincent Van Gogh was a Dutch painter who used vivid colors and wild brush strokes in his paintings ... "

Please don't bawl, please don't bawl, I kept telling myself, Please don't do it, don't do it ...

And I didn't do it. I finished reading the book, dry eyed and ready to say goodbye. The children clapped and rolled on the floor. Tatty stood over them, trying to control them, and Cody sat very still, looking up at me through all the disorder to say, "Hi Hi Hi Hi Hi Hi Hi Hi Hi Hi Hi Hi Hi." I took his hand and led him to the front of the classroom, where we stood before my tumbling, laughing class.

"Okay, everyone say goodbye to Cody," my voice was stern. Isabella stepped back.

They all raced over to him. *'Bye 'bye 'bye* they all said. Kat went to him and hugged him, and Ruthie followed. Cody flapped his hands for them to go away. Tatty came over and fell to one knee. She gently took Cody by his chin, and their eyes locked.

"I'm going to miss you, little guy." Cody only tilted his head and groaned. I walked Isabella and Cody out to the hallway.

"Everyone has been telling us how wonderful you've been to Cody. We appreciate all that you've done, and you're welcome to come to Charleston any time. I think Cody would like that."

"I'd like that, too." I was trying my hardest to be polite, and although I knew this was the best for Cody, I was angry. It was selfish and wrong, and I knew it. I kept my bogus smile on my face and listened to her go on about how wonderful I was and what a difference I'd made in his life.

When no more niceties could be swapped and it was time to say goodbye, I knelt down to Cody.

"Cody." His eyes wandered. "Cody," I said again, and I held his chin. "Cody, I want you to have this book about Van Gogh. Remember him? We became friends because of him."

I looked up at Isabella. "He said 'Van Gogh' to me when I first met him." She nodded at me. I handed Cody the book, and he took it in his hand. He tilted his head and tucked it under his arm.

"Cody, I wish I knew if you understood me, because you made a big difference in my life. And—and I am thankful for all you did for me. Ah, hell I know you're only a kid, and I'm some pathetic guy who, what the hell do you care, right? Right, Cody?"

Isabella took a step forward. "I'm sure he cares. No one knows for certain what goes on in their minds. Somewhere inside he could be saying 'thank you.' "

She smiled down at me.

"Hi Hi Hi Hi Hi Hi Hi Hi Hi Hi Hi Hi Hi."

"Yeah, hi back at you kid."

"Hi Hi Hi Hi Hi Hi Hi Hi Hi Hi Hi Hi Hi."

"Cody, you take this book, and I'll hope you think of me. I'll be thinking of you and all that nice stuff people do when they go away. Best of luck Cody, and keep drawing."

I knew I was wasting my time, no matter what Isabella said to me. Cody continued to tilt his head and murmur. He rolled his fist into his mouth, and then it happened. Without me even having any control over it, tears started streaming down my face, not one or two tears, but a flood. Enough to embarrass the hell out of me and to make me feel weak and terrible. But Isabella put her hand on my shoulder. She smelled sweet like summer honeysuckle.

"I'm sorry, this isn't right," I said. I stood.

"Why, because you're crying?" she asked.

"Yeah, I guess."

"Don't ever feel ashamed about crying. I finished reading this great book on the plane. She pulled out of her pocketbook: *The Castration of the 20th Century Man*. Have you heard of it?" she asked.

"No," I said. "I have never heard of it." I took the book and cleared my eyes. How could I not think of Ralph, Hank, and Beth? My life?

"I want you to have my copy. Read it and don't ever feel ashamed to show your feelings. Look at all that you did for Cody. Most men don't do this sort of thing. You're a real man for the twenty-first century, Mr. Pepper."

"Yeah? Really?" I said. I took the book and smiled bitter-sweetly.

"Mr. Pepper, I mean it when I say you're welcome to come to Charleston. You're invited anytime," she said.

"Thanks. Thank you," I nodded. I shuffled my feet, hoping she would leave now. It was done, goodbyes were said, and there was no use in lingering.

"We'll be in touch," I said.

I watched as they started to walk down the long hallway. Cody quickly stopped and looked in my direction, then at the book I had given him. He was murmuring soft, almost inaudible phrases, repeating the word, "Sunflowers. Sunflowers." He tilted his head, and Isabella turned and looked at me, surprised and pleased. She nodded at me reassuringly, and they walked away.

And that brings me to the present. Miss Curtis called me days ago and said she was thinking of me, and that's how all this bedroom switching thing happened. You see, she told me she had a boy in need of a foster father. He was thirteen-years-old. His father had been killed in prison. He was angry, upset, and had had an emotional breakdown. He had been put in a state youth hospital, and his aunt didn't want him anymore. But that boy kept asking for one person. He asked for me. Can you imagine? Me.

It was Franco.

I knew he had to be completely distraught. I don't know how it's all going to work out, but Rosa said to me, "Listen to your heart."

And my heart said yes.

I'm going to try and do all I can for Franco. Sure I'm scared, but I figure as quickly as Cody came into my life, he was gone. At first it felt permanent, but as the days and months went on, I knew Cody was still around me, because a paternal part of me continued to bloom. Maybe it was all the bawling I did when he left; I mean, I can't believe how much I feel now, and because of it, I think I'll be a good foster parent to Franco. I can teach him about expressing his feelings, drawing on my own experiences.

A while ago I started going to Gilbert's discussion group on *The Castration of the 20th Century Male*: *How to Grow a New Set for the 21st Century*, and well, I am not only a member of the group, I'm the group's treasurer. I've read that book over and over.

Head Mistress Miss Macey phoned the other day.

"Oliver, I'm delighted to extend an invitation for you to return to Bolton for the fall term. Mr. Morgenstern bricked up that window, and all is good now."

Oddly enough, I was happy to hear Miss Macey's voice. I really missed that stuffy old headmistress.

"Miss Macey, there is nothing I would like more than to return to Bolton."

"Wonderful!"

"But I can't possibly accept."

There was a silence.

"I did what I thought best for the school and for you," she said.

"And I thank God for you, Miss Macey. But please try to understand that my heart is now awake. The Bolton school is too comfortable. Comfort makes the light within us die, and you have to keep that light burning brightly at all times in order to grow. Plus that window in my old classroom, well, it was my savior."

"I have heard that you're at that school next door."

"That's right, Miss Macey," I said.

"I'm happy for you, Oliver."

"Thanks. I've been very busy, and it's been good. I've been involved in a long and lengthy project. It's perplexing and difficult, and it can cause delayed reactions. But I'm making progress. You see, I'm growing a new set for the twenty-first century."

"Excuse me? I don't understand," she said.

"And you never will understand. I'm sorry about that. Goodbye, Miss Macey."

I hung up the phone and smiled.

Then I left to pick up Franco.

Courtesy of Becky McLeod

John C. Picardi is the author of the awarding winning play, The Sweepers, and Seven Rabbits on a Pole. His plays are published by Samuel French and have been produced off-Broadway and across the United States. He is a graduate of Johnson & Wales University, where he majored in Culinary Arts. He later graduated from the University of Massachusetts at Boston with a degree in English and Creative Writing and earned an MFA from Carnegie Mellon University. He lives in Massachusetts.

You can find John online at www.johncpicardi.com.

Made in the USA
Lexington, KY
14 March 2012